VESSEL OF DESTRUCTION

SUPERNATURALS OF DAIZLEI ACADEMY
BOOK FOUR

KEL CARPENTER

Vessel of Destruction
Kel Carpenter

Published by Kel Carpenter

Edited by Analisa Denny
Proofreader by Dominique Laura

Cover Art by Yocla

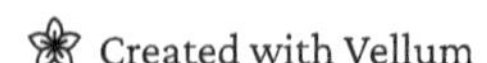

About the Author

Kel Carpenter is a master of werdz. When she's not reading or writing, she's traveling the world, lovingly pestering her co-author, and spending time with her family. She is always on the search for good tacos and the best pizza. She resides in Maryland and desperately tries to avoid the traffic.

To Analisa

You're a really good friend. Thank you for pushing me to finish. I'm sorry about the hippo.

"Every end is a new beginning."
V.E. Schwab, *Vengeful*

CHAPTER 1

THE SUN ROSE HIGHER WITH EVERY PASSING SECOND, BUT NOT even it could smother the chill of something colder than winter as it settled in my bones. I tugged my jacket tighter around myself, inhaling Ash's scent. Smoke. Fire. An inexplicable wildness that loosened this feeling in my chest.

I'd been standing at the lake for four hours, twenty-three minutes, and sixteen seconds. Before that, I'd been laying on the couch staring at the ceiling with my muscles locked for what felt like an eternity. Lily now had Cirian's soul. I'd failed her in every way, and there was nothing I could do to fix it. Leaving seemed like the best solution. Not for good; just for space. For fresh air and the bite of the wind. It gave me clarity. Stopped me from doing something a little . . . crazy.

Stopped me from taking the elevator two floors down and three lefts turns, straight to the room where Lucas was being kept. It was a makeshift prison guarded by four of the finest Shifters alive. They were usually in charge of guarding the Alpha, but instead were wasting their time with *him*.

I couldn't help wondering if I made a mistake not killing him when I had the chance. If the rage and fear and desperation within my chest would not be there if I had given it an outlet. Deep down, I knew that killing him wouldn't change this, and it wouldn't make me feel better.

But still . . . I wondered.

And I waited.

Thirteen minutes passed before I heard it. That slight rustle of leaves as a cloak dragged over the forest floor. The snapping of a single twig as an old lady made her way to me.

"Anastasia is dead," I whispered over the lake, but she didn't respond. The slight patter of Livina's heart made me angry inside. How was it that she was cursed with a thousand years—over ten lifetimes—and my sister didn't get to keep her one?

The unfairness of it cut deeper than anything.

"Cirian's soul now resides in Lily, but you probably know that already. Just like you knew that we were Fortescues, didn't you?" My tone was accusatory because I had no doubts that the old hag knew. After seeing those pictures, I had to wonder how much of my life had she played a hand in. Was it simply the deal she struck with the ancients, or was there more?

I laughed once to myself because that was a dumb question.

Of course, there was more.

There always was.

"And my parents—did you have something to do with their deaths as well?" The words were barely a sound, let alone a whisper as I turned my back on the lake. Four hours, thirty-seven minutes, and fifty-four seconds. That was the longest I'd been able to stand in front of a body of water so massive ever since the incident with the Hydra where I'd nearly drowned. I should be proud, but instead I was being forced to acknowledge that there are some pains in this world that are worse than the darkness or dying.

Watching my sister make the worst decision of her life was one of them, because I didn't know how I was going to save a girl corrupted by someone worse than the devil.

I looked at the Crone; at her multi-colored eyes and sagging skin. The weary frown of her lips and frizzy gray strands of hair. I wanted to hate her, and maybe I did.

But I also understood her, just a little bit.

She didn't die like she was supposed to, and because of it she endured a thousand years of watching Cirian reap what she sowed.

She watched the only people she cared about die.

I understood that, and I wished that I didn't.

"I am sorry." Her voice was aged. It cracked like an ancient statue, as if the lining of her throat had endured too much. She was forced to live, but that didn't mean her body took to it.

"For which part?"

"All of it."

She walked around me. Her joints popped as she bent her weathered knees and settled back onto a large rock by the water. Using her staff, she lifted it and tapped the rock across from her, motioning for me to sit.

"If I had the chance to do it over, I would, but—"

"And my sister? You not telling me that we were descended from Valda, but from Cirian as well—would you do that over?" My anger was rising like a tidal wave within me, but I would not let myself snap. Killing her would earn me nothing, and that's assuming she could die.

"I didn't have a choice in the matter," she replied with a rasp and tapped the rock again. I flicked my gaze between it and her.

Did I want to do this?

Did I really want to sit down with this woman and find out if the truth was as bad as I thought? To risk finding out that it may be even worse.

Did I want to put myself through this for the slim chance that something she had to say could save them?

I took a shallow breath through clenched teeth and sat on the edge of the flat stone. The Witch smiled sadly at me, her chapped lips curling into a grimace.

"There was a time when I had a choice, and I made the wrong one. The ancients took that from me. For the last thousand years I have existed to be their vessel and theirs alone, to ensure that the price demanded would be paid." As she spoke, she swung the staff toward the lake with more grace than I expected for a woman a thousand years my senior. The blue orb touched the surface of the water, glowing briefly. When she lifted it away, a picture spread, growing from the ripple she'd created.

In it was a woman with lovely brown skin and

exquisite curls, holding a swaddled baby with a shock of blonde hair that turned black.

"What is this?"

"The first of Valda's line," the Crone replied. She smiled at the image on the water, but it wasn't a happy thing. In my mind Valda brushed closer. *"Atlanta."*

That word held so much emotion. I swallowed, averting my eyes.

"You raised her? The baby?" I asked, ignoring the pounding in my heart. Livina nodded, and the picture changed. "I raised her, and her daughter, and her daughter's daughter—all the way down the line."

The beautiful blonde baby morphed and grew into a young woman. "Mom," I breathed. My hands trembled, and my breath shook, coming out in puffs of white.

"When your mother and Mariana were born, I had a vision of you." She pointed a crooked finger at me. "I knew that they would finally break the mold. That the ancients had decided they had punished the earth long enough." In the lake image, my mother and Mariana sat in a house I remembered all too well. Alexandra burned it down. "Every generation of Konigs I raised died in childbirth or were lost to the madness. They were the first that didn't. When they were young children, I picked a human home and planted them in it, taking the human's memories and making them think they adopted them." The picture changed again, and this time it was Daizlei where they stood. The crisp cut lawn and stained-glass tower was something that I would never forget.

"I moved the pieces to ensure that they were found at the right time, in the right place, by the right people—

and brought to Daizlei undetected." When that ripple across the lake changed this time, a heaviness started to settle inside of me. A suspicion I hoped was wrong. A sense of unshakable knowing that I could not deny.

My mother, a much younger version of herself, strolled hand-in-hand down those cobblestone walkways with my father.

"You set the scene for them to meet so that I would be born." The words barely left my lips when the scene changed again. I saw their lives together. Their wedding. Them finding out they were pregnant. Me and my sisters being born, and growing up, and—it stopped abruptly. The images vanished.

"You mother was a Konig and your father a Fortescue. You weren't born by chance. You were born because the gods deemed it so." My heart pounded so hard that I could barely hear her over the blood roaring in my ears. "Two families that caused the world more suffering than any other thing, finally came together. The result was three of the most powerful children that will ever walk the face of this planet. You may hate me, Selena, and I wouldn't blame you. But everything I have done was to protect your family. Everything your parents did was for you. All of you."

I sat, staring at the lake. After last night, watching Lily kill Anastasia and take in Cirian's soul. Listening to how our birth was written a thousand years ago. That we were destined for this. That my parents died for this . . . it killed me a little bit inside. I couldn't stop it. I knew that. But it didn't ease the guilt or the anger of it all.

I took one hand out of my pocked and partially

unzipped my coat. Reaching inside, I withdrew a small stack of pictures. Photographs of my life with handwriting scrawled across them. The top one was a picture of the Crone. They were the same photos that Elizabeth had given me in an envelope the last time she saw me. She said they'd change the world. She wasn't wrong. I don't think she realized how much they'd rock mine, though.

I thrust my hand out toward Livina, and her strong somewhat detached demeanor slipped as she let out a heavy sigh. She knew these pictures. Good.

Long, bony fingers reached out and curled around the crinkled edges. Delicately, she took the photos and started flipping through them.

"My mother used to sing me a lullaby almost exactly the same as what is written on those pictures, but still just different enough that I didn't get it until now." I swallowed and looked away. I could give myself that. A few seconds to gather my thoughts and steady myself. "They knew about this. About you. About Valda. And I would bet my life—the 'he' that is referenced in those pictures is Cirian. They knew he was coming. They knew he was in Anastasia." My chest seized as if someone had reached in and squeezed. The pressure was bearable, but the emotion wasn't my own in this case. Heat flooded my head from panic. In the distance, I felt him —Ash. I felt his shock and surprise at me being gone. It didn't take him long to figure out where I was, and the panic eased as a steady reassurance filtered through our bond, calming me. Even here, twenty miles from the residence and without him knowing a word we'd exchanged . . . he was my rock. My reminder to breathe, and let it go.

"They did know. Your mother was stubborn. I wiped her and Mariana's memories when they were children, but like you, she fought it—and even the greatest magic in the world isn't enough to hold up under the will of a Konig." She nodded her head, still flipping through the pictures like what she just said didn't undo everything I knew about myself and where I came from. "She knew something wasn't right. That the flashes she was seeing felt more real than reality at times. Like you, she came looking for answers, and then she gave up everything—her and your father both did—so that no one would find you or those same answers."

"My . . . memories? You took those." My voice shook with anger. Rage. Its bite was colder than an eternal winter. Sharper than any blade. Hotter than even hellfire.

"Your parents and I had a deal. Your mother was already dying, and your father wouldn't have been long after her. A signasti that loses their bondmate doesn't last long. A sickness sets in. It was a better end for them both. An easier one—"

"Don't," I said harshly. I stretched and curled my fingers within my coat pockets. It was the safest place for my hands. Far from her neck. "Don't justify what you've done or talk like you know what was best for them. You made a deal that killed them. How can I possibly trust that it happened that way? My parents were—"

"—pieced together from what they wanted you to remember. They weren't real." Her words were like a slap to the face, and I flinched.

"Because of you," I spat. If she was trying to convince me to be civil toward her, that was the last thing she should have said.

"It was the best way. The safest way, for you three. Your parents knew that." I watched her in stunned silence for a minute, and then two. I examined the slump of her shoulders and the grimness in her face. The way her eyes held sadness, even while being every color of the rainbow.

"They came looking. That doesn't mean they had to die!" I snapped, jumping up from the rock where I was sitting. Thick storm clouds rolled overhead, blotting out the sun. Lightning flashed, and the air thickened with power—but for once it wasn't me.

Blair.

Goddamnit—something had to have set her off. Which meant my chat with the Crone was coming to a close, regardless of the missing pieces I had yet to find.

"Your mother was the first to survive childbirth and the passing of Valda's soul. The only reason she survived was because Eric was her signasti—but even a signasti bond can't stop death." Her words whispered up my spine, prickling like a trail of knives across bare skin. "Analysa was losing her fight to the madness when she managed to find me. She only had months. They both did. When they learned the truth about her past and the role you would play in the coming years, they made a trade. I wipe your minds and buy you five years of the closest thing to a childhood you would get—in return they paid with their lives. Magic has a price, Selena. Nothing in this world comes for free."

The words came in. I understood what she was saying, but they didn't register. There was no *ah-ha* moment where my memories came to me. There was no door unlocking. I understood what she was saying, but I couldn't remember it for myself.

"Give them back," I demanded.

"You aren't listening. I can't just give and take because someone wills it, even me. Your parents knew the price so that no one would find you before you were ready. I can't just undo magic that cost two people their lives, child. I'm sorry, I really am, but your memories are gone." Thunder boomed in the distance as the incoming storm built faster. The winds blew with a ferocity that wasn't natural. My hood flew back, freeing my long dark locks of hair.

I could stand here and argue. I could hurt her. I could try to kill her.

But that wouldn't bring them back, and it wouldn't fix anything.

I had to face the fact that my memories were pieced together by magic. Some might be real. Many were not. And that dreamland was perhaps the only place I might find the truth. That hurt.

"You talk of the price of magic. This curse has been in play for a millennium . . ." I turned to the Crone. There was only one question left. It was the most important because her answer was not just life or death. It was everything. "What is it going to cost me to break it? What is the price, Livina?"

The Crone sighed. Her lips pressed together, and she shook her head. She didn't want to say it, and I knew.

Deep down, I knew that Jo wasn't wrong. That there was something more that the Crone had left out beyond the other part of my heritage. My legacy.

"Three lives broke the balance when I brought Valda and Cirian back . . . and didn't kill Atlanta. Three continued that day. It will take three deaths from Valda and Cirian's line by your hand to right it."

I closed my eyes over the roaring. Waves. Waves were coming. They were pushing and pulling and threatening to drag me under.

Three deaths.

Alexandra. Lily. Me.

Fate was a cruel, cruel thing.

But I could not let this ocean drag me under. I could not let fate define me.

I may be the Mother, but I refused be a monster.

I would find a way to save them. To save us.

Or I would die trying.

CHAPTER 2

I STUMBLED THROUGH THE TREES, MY MIND STILL TWENTY MILES away. The training field was crowded but there was no clash of steel or lion's roar. Only an unsettling hush that had fallen across the residence. A heavy tension was in the air that was more than just the shifting winds of a building storm. And there, at the center of it, I heard a voice.

"She took my will from me. I'm telling you—" The sound of it made the carefully crafted control I had over myself begin to unravel. Just a little.

I stepped forward, closing the space between myself and the crowd that still hadn't noticed me. They were too busy focusing on *him.*

"That Anastasia is dead." The second voice was cold like the kiss of death—and angry. So angry.

"Yes. I felt her influence leave. Look, you need to believe me—" The crack of lightning that cut him off was so large it filled the sky and thunder boomed. The ground itself shivered in response.

"You knocked out your guards and attempted to run." The voice of Blair's demon was unyielding. Uncompromising. And above all—unforgiving.

"Because *she's* gone and as soon as she returns my days are numbered." I had a good guess who the "she" in this equation was. "After what I did there is no way she would let me live. Not for all the information in the world. She is many things—but forgiving is not one of them."

"Is that so?" My voice carried across the training yard.

A pause so deliciously filled with fear. No one, not the Shifters—not Lucas—not even Blair commented. Then as one, the body of the crowd turned and parted for me like the red sea—not because I moved them—but because they chose to.

"Selena," he whispered.

And I stared—because it was all that I could do. A million thoughts ran through my mind, but I was completely sure that not a single one would slip through. My shields were impenetrable now—to all but Ash.

I stared at him with my chin high and my hair whipping in the wind. My posture was straight and stiff and the presence of power saturated my skin. It filled my blood and bones and even the very breaths I took as I watched him.

Yes, he was correct that I was not the forgiving type. But the man that kneeled at Blair's feet was not the Lucas I remembered. He was not the boy who had been my friend. Nor was he the sneering figure that tried to kill Ash.

He was a broken husk of the person he had been. A toy that Anastasia—Cirian—used then threw away.

I could not forgive what he'd done no matter the version of him that did it, cruel as that might make me. Lily was turned and now held Cirian's soul, largely because of the role he'd played. Ash would be dead if not for my gift. And me—I lost my best friend, who in many ways was my only friend—or so I thought.

In losing him, I gained so much more. I found love, happiness, and a measure of peace—and even if I lost it all in this war, I still held it. I tasted what it would be like were there not a prophecy that demanded my life.

No, despite the ocean of despair waiting to drag me under—despite the fury clawing at my chest, seeking some sort of reprieve from all the pain—despite the soul-crushing deed the ancients demanded of me—all I felt when I looked at him was pity.

He was right that I still wanted to kill him, but I also knew deep down that I couldn't do it. That Ash was right. Lucas may have broken something inside of me, but killing him wouldn't fix it. The first step in not being a monster was killing out of necessity—not anger.

"I wouldn't hold it against you if you did," Valda whispered.

"But I would."

His eyes were black last time I looked at him. Now they were green. Bright, brilliant green that cracked and splintered under my steady gaze. He slowly lowered his eyes and then his face to the ground, as if giving up entirely.

No, I couldn't kill him.

But he didn't know that.

"Hello, Lucas."

He flinched, backing away from Blair on his hands and knees. He hurried to get to his feet, and turned, running into Ash. It seemed that the less angry I acted, the more scared he was. Smart boy. He knew my tricks.

"I want to go back to my cell now," he hissed. Ash didn't even spare him a glance. He watched me come forward between the rows of Shifters, hands in my pockets to keep from showing how tense I really was. Lucas moved to get away, but with Blair to his right and me approaching from behind him that didn't leave much room to run. "I want to go back!" he yelled, stumbling and then falling. No one caught him.

Not as his expensive suit that Anastasia had no doubt dressed him in splattered with mud. His knees hit the grass, and he curled inward on himself, hanging his head.

Broken. He was truly broken.

"If you're so eager to go back, why were you trying to escape?" I mused the question aloud, even though I already knew the answer. "Where would you go?"

Silence. He lifted his head, but his mouth was set in a firm line. The edges of misery and despondency lined his face like wrinkles.

"I don't know," he said truthfully. I nodded.

"Nowhere to go and thousands of Shifters to get through, assuming you got past Blair. Color me surprised, but that doesn't sound like the choice of someone who wants to live." I lifted an eyebrow, and maybe it was cruel to kick a man while he was down. Perhaps it was petty of me, but I didn't care.

"Maybe I don't want to live." He said the words so quietly, so hopelessly, that I had to work to hide my grimace. I hoped that Tori wasn't somewhere in the crowd listening.

"But you don't want to die by my hand either?" He nodded once, almost imperceptibly—but I didn't believe it. "You're lying. You know how I know?" He looked at me again with very real terror.

Oh yes, I'd figured him out. I'd pieced together moments that were Ash and moments that were him from my days at Daizlei. Lucas wasn't nearly as good a liar.

"I had the chance to kill you twice last night, and I didn't. If I truly wanted you dead, you would be. We both know that, which leads me to think you waited to break out not because you'd rather they kill you—but because you knew I would stop them." He didn't dare let even a speck of hope shine through if he felt it. That's good. It would make this easier. I won't have to pretend. "You may not be able to live with the things you did, but you're the only person alive that has any leads to my sister. So whether you like it or not, you're going to live, and you're going to help me find her."

His mouth fell ajar, but it wasn't him that spoke.

"What do you mean he's the only one alive?" Blair's demon was an astute one. I'll give her that. I'd been hoping to have this conversation with them in private, but hoping for things didn't make them happen.

I took a deep breath because as soon as the words

came out there was no going back. The next Fortescue would have to move quickly to establish themselves before the paranormal world truly collapsed and all hell broke loose. Word of Anastasia's death would reach every corner of the globe in less than a week. The following months would be a scramble for power as every species came out of the woodworks to challenge the Court for their unethical means of ruling. With no Fortescue holding power, the Supernatural Council would inevitably crumble and fall—leaving the world open for the taking.

I couldn't let that happen. I wouldn't let her death bring about an even darker age, one the world might not recover from.

"I mean that for once in his life Lucas is telling the truth." I paused and took a breath. "Anastasia Fortescue is dead. Murdered by the Vampires she'd formed an alliance with."

Gasps. Whispering. Muttered words of anarchy. Just as I'd predicted.

People were simple that way. Paranormal or not, they all had the same motivations, triggers, and impulses.

"Settle down," Ash said, his voice projecting over the crowd. The Shifters brought themselves from a dull roar down to a true whispered hush, but they'd already flustered a demon that was sitting on the razor-thin edge of control and chaos.

The winds blew uneasily. I glanced at Blair whose eyes were flickering between gray and black. Her demon wasn't one to go quietly, but the shock of it threw her for a loop. I held my hand up for silence. Behind her Johanna slipped through the crowd, soundless as a wraith. She crept up on Blair from behind and raised her eyebrow. I shook my head slightly. Watching. Waiting. And then Blair's eyes rolled back in her head. She clenched her fists and fat droplets of water fell from the sky. When she opened them, hail descended on us.

I twisted my hand and mentally pulled her body to the ground, running at a breakneck speed to stop her. She thrashed, attempting to slash Lucas, only missing by a hairsbreadth as I crossed the remaining twenty feet and grabbed him by the jacket, throwing him behind me. Johanna was already moving to restrain her arms as I pulled the Kabar from my belt and brought the hilt down on the back of her head.

She fell into Jo's arms, limp and unmoving. I pinched the bridge of my nose and smoothed my hand down my face, letting out a heavy sigh. The sheer number of times I'd had to do that in the last week was disconcerting. If anything she was getting worse, not better.

I bent over, holding out my arms, and Jo silently passed me the unconscious girl. Blair looked like she was sleeping, if you could overlook the fact that she was one of the lightest sleepers I knew. I clasped one arm around her back and the other under her knees. We had roughly two hours from now before she woke up, at which point only three of us could be in the same room or her demon would begin to feel cornered. One of us, likely me, would sit near her and the others would nonchalantly hang by the door. We had it down to a science, and I hated it. I hated what her demon put her through—put them both through—but I couldn't change it.

We all had to adapt.

I leaned back with her in my arms, pointedly ignoring Lucas's wide-eyed stare as Ash approached me. I knew the drill. Get her out of here while he dealt with the Shifters. We'd regroup after dinner once everyone had time to think.

"Someone needs to deal with him. Do you have any shields on the property?" I asked in a hushed whisper. Half the people in a ten-meter radius would probably still hear it, but there was only so much you could do with Shifters. Their reflexes and hearing were better than anyone's, apart from Vampires and demons.

"No, we'll have to improvise until we get something more official set up. Johanna can watch him for the next few hours while you handle her." His eyes flicked downward toward Blair and back up to my face. I glanced over at Johanna.

"Will you be safe from his ability?"

She nodded. "I can handle the boy. Get Blair taken care of while Aaron handles the Shifters. We need to have a meeting this evening about what we're going to do with him," she jutted her chin toward Lucas. "And we need to discuss this business of Anastasia. I'm not surprised the Vampires killed her, but it is faster than we expected or planned for."

I nodded, only lingering for a moment as Ash leaned forward and brushed his lips across my cheek. Chaste, but I wasn't one for public displays of affection.

As I turned to leave and the crowd parted to let me pass, Lucas lurched to his feet.

"You saved me." He sounded lost, like a small child.

Confused. He was trying to sort through what didn't make sense even though he saw it with his own eyes.

"I didn't do it for you." The walls slammed down over his expression. There was the hate he wanted. That made him feel safe. He knew where we stood when I hated him. It's when I felt nothing that he panicked.

I brushed him off and continued walking, feeling the tension of his stare on my back as he played it over and over in his mind, trying to decipher whether or not I was lying.

I didn't know the answer to that myself.

CHAPTER 3

A DOOR SLAMMED BEHIND ME AS WOOD HIT WOOD WITH A hollow thud. I was surprised I got the better of a day before the Heir to House Graeme came to me. Fortunately, she wasn't the only one, and I'd only have to say it once.

"What's this I hear about Anastasia being dead?" Scarlett's uniquely British and German accent mixed in an odd way when she was angry. Beside her, Liam sighed.

"That's what we're here to find out, love."

Love? I cast a wary sideways glance, but common sense told me not to ask. What Liam and Scarlett did was not my business, certainly not when the latter wanted to rip me a new one. Yet another reason why the precarious place I'd found myself in wasn't ideal.

I waited for them to find a seat before dropping my hand away from the curtain where I was watching the training yard of the residence. Turning my back on the window, I faced the room with my hands clasped behind my back.

"I'll cut to the chase. As many of you have already heard, Anastasia is dead—"

"How do you know this?" Scarlett interrupted. I wanted to roll my eyes, but that wouldn't help the situation. It wasn't their fault they didn't possess the same means of getting information. Just like it wasn't mine that Valda's curse prevented me from telling the truth about what happened. About Cirian and who Lily would inevitably become.

I pushed those thoughts from my mind, focusing on what I could say.

"I watched my sister execute her."

Scarlett's lips parted in surprise. She blinked, regaining her wits, and her jaw slammed shut.

"The High Council doesn't throw away pieces on a chess board without good reason," Johanna said from her place on the end of the long couch. Her expression was troubled. "If Anastasia is truly dead, then there are much larger things at play here than I'd thought." She leaned forward, resting her elbows on her knees. Her eyebrows were drawn in concentration as if she were looking at a puzzle but realizing there was a missing piece.

"Do you know why they killed her?" Oliver asked. He had one arm thrown across the back of the couch behind Jo and one leg crossed over the other. Always the picture of utter perfection, no matter the circumstance. The Council had trained him well at never revealing his true intentions, but I noticed the way his eye strayed toward

Blair every few minutes. He kept it in check, knowing she had a signasti and her demon would eviscerate him if he ever acted on it.

"It should be obvious," Alexandra answered before I could respond. "Selena pretended to be her and attempted, then failed, to kill Kamarov. We'd set it up so that Anastasia would come after her, but I guess the Vampires were more pissed than we thought they'd be . . ." Her voice trailed off as Jo started shaking her head.

"They wouldn't kill the Head of the Supernatural Council for that. Even if she had killed Kamarov, there has to be another reason. For them to want to get rid of her, she'd need to be—"

"Without use," I supplied. Johanna's eyes slid sideways. Yes, she'd heard that phrase before.

"Yes."

I looked away. How much do I say? Do I tell them about the darkness I see growing inside Lily? That she goaded Victor toward it, and he's too blind to see? Would they want to save her if they knew that?

I bit the inside of my cheek because I had to say something to at least point us in the right direction—even if it wasn't the full truth. "Lily has noticed this growing fascination that Victor has with her," I started slowly. "He mentioned that she was gifted to him from Anastasia as a wedding present." I glanced at the ceiling, fighting the urge I had to vomit at the very idea of her being murdered and then enslaved as a *gift*. "But that his fiancé lied to him. They were getting married so that Anastasia had the numbers to secure her reign as a Queen instead of just the Head of Council. She wanted more power, and he wanted breeding stock that could give him babies."

"Anastasia was infertile," Alec cut in. Every head turned to face him, all but one. Blair kept her icy demeanor about her. She watched the fire behind me and nothing else. I wondered if that was because staring at anything else might trigger her demon, or if she really just didn't want to see the looks on their faces after her episode today.

"And you know this how?" I asked, turning my attention back to him.

"Because he was once her right-hand man," Jo answered. Alec nodded, pushing off the wall to come stand behind the long couch. His golden hair and tanned skin had seen better days. While his eyes still shined, the rest of him had lost its luster.

"Over a year ago she had me pick up and drop off some tests. I was bound to secrecy as long as she was alive, so it didn't matter much if I knew what they were for." He shrugged, but the tension in his jaw told me this was a harder conversation to have than he made it out to be.

"And the High Council?" Ash asked. "Do you know anything about her deal with them?"

Alec shook his head. "That was something she kept from even me. I knew she was meeting with them, but I was barred from being in the same room."

I nodded. Their group fell into a troubled kind of silence. The kind not born from awkwardness or stunned realizations, but because we were at a loss. What do you do when the endgame changes? When you're no longer fighting a battle against one person, but a war against thousands?

"What about Lucas?"

I had to work at keeping my face schooled in neutrality. Tori pushed away from the couch, and Alexandra moved aside from the spot on the floor where she rested against the girl's legs.

"What about him?" I asked carefully.

"If Anastasia really is gone and he wasn't just spoutin' off, shouldn't he be released?"

No one wanted to answer her. Least of all me because there was no way in Hell I was letting his ass walk free until I got what I wanted.

Johanna saved me from having to break that news.

"We still can't determine how much of his actions were his and how many were influenced for Anastasia," she said softly. She must have understood how difficult this situation was on all of us, and that no matter Tori's wishes, there was no way he could walk out of here until this was all over. If at all. "He'll need to remain guarded until I have the chance to properly question him."

Tori said nothing, but the purse of her lips made her thoughts abundantly clear. I couldn't blame her. I was in a dangerously similar situation with my own sister.

"I need to know what he did every minute of every day he was with her. I need to know where they went, when they were there, who they met with, and if he ever saw Lily at any point."

"Some of us also have people missing too, you know," Scarlett muttered under her breath. Resentment coated her tone.

"Yes, and if your brother was also turned and being led down the path my sister is you would do everything in your power to find him. Would you not?"

The set of her chin was stubborn, but there was a vulnerability in her eyes that said she would do exactly that. For her twin, she would do anything.

"I will help you get your sister back, but I want an oath that you will help me find out what happened to Sebastian and my parents." I nodded, swallowing the lump in my throat.

"We'll find out what happened to them, and if they're alive in some capacity . . . we'll fight for them too." Scarlett gave me a level-eyed stare, and I think it was one of the first times she regarded me without a hint of contempt.

"Then we have an agreement." Scarlett dipped her chin, and I did the same. An uneasy alliance. Wasn't that all we'd ever had, though? Alliances built on hope for a better future. Oaths traded for things that may never come to pass.

"I don't mean to sound like an ass here, but even if we find out where your sister is, we don't have the firepower to do anything about it," Alec pointed out. "There's ten of us and thousands of them. Not to mention that the Supernatural Council is wide open for someone to attempt to seize it. As soon as news spreads of Anastasia, there are going to be two groups of people. Those who want to use this to rise to power, and those who want the entire Council—as well as its laws—abolished. No matter what each of us individually thinks of that, we can't allow it while the Supernatural seats at

Court are vacated. The Court has been making the laws for the paranormal community for thousands of years, and if they don't exist then there is nothing to keep the Vampires in check from openly attacking people. Not to mention, more power hungry Supes from using their abilities on humans to get ahead." He was right. He was absolutely, one hundred percent correct. Anastasia was only a piece of what we were now going to face if the unseen government of the paranormal community started to collapse.

"What are you suggesting we do in the meantime?" I asked. "As you've pointed out, there's only ten of us. We lack the information to even know where or how to make our next move." I ran one hand through my hair, pacing back and forth as I thought aloud. "We're sitting ducks. Meanwhile, the High Council is finding a way to use this against us. They're going to have to do something once word gets out."

"Then we make the first move." My head whipped toward Blair who had silently moved farther from the group. She now stood in front of the window by the fireplace, looking to the sky. I wondered if she could feel the wind and the water around us, the same as I felt all matter.

"And what do you suggest that is?" Oliver asked.

"Swear her in." Blair nodded toward me. I froze on the spot. "Swear them both in," her gaze flicked between me to Alexandra. My sister froze, and it was only the stillness in her that clued me to her surprise. "It only takes three houses to do it, and we have four. The only reason the Council stopped swearing outsiders in was because the Fortescues responded by killing them and their Houses into extinction. There's only two Fortescues alive now, and both have enough power to hold their seats should it ever be contested. Establish them as representatives and find allies. Without Anastasia, there is no reason to solely focus on Selena when Alexandra is just as capable. This is all our fight, and we all have our parts to play." She paused, and there was a wintery chill to what she said next. Something that carried more weight than anything else said in this room tonight. "Something is coming, something big . . . and we're going to need all the help we can get if we want to survive it. We don't have to be friends. We don't have to agree on what happens after this." She looked away from the window, and I swear she saw straight into my soul. That she knew what burden was sitting on my shoulders. "But some of the most powerful people in the world are in this room right now. I can't help but feeling like some force brought us together. Call it fate. Call it the ancients. I don't really care, but I will die before I let those blood-sucking bastards take over the world."

There was a dangerous kind of light in her eyes. It was the sort of spark that started revolutions and fed rebellions. Goosebumps broke across my flesh as one by one the rest of the room nodded.

Scarlett, Liam, Oliver, and Johanna all got to their feet. Their faces set in hard resolve. I wondered if one day I would look back and ask myself how it was that children were having to become adults, because all the adults were dead or evil, and the world asked it of us. Demanded it from us. I wasn't sure if I would live to wonder when the price for a new future was so much more than they realized.

I locked eyes with Ash and didn't once look away as I was sworn in. If someone asked me even a day later I probably couldn't remember a single word spoken. Only the feeling in the pit of my stomach like this was it.

The beginning of the end.

CHAPTER 4

My lips twisted into a grimace at the footsteps coming down the hall. They were far too quick to be a guard or someone reporting to Ash, and too loud to be anyone that was staying in the en suite. Which left only one person.

The doorknob turned, and I braced myself as the wooden panels banged against the larger bookcases. A volume or two fell out, toppling to the feet of the girl responsible.

After a night of doing everything in my power to avoid sleeping, I didn't have the energy to engage with her beyond asking, "What can I do for you, Keyla?"

She narrowed her eyes at me and flicked her long braid over her shoulder, attempting to appear standoff-ish. She cocked her hip to the side and crossed her arms over her chest. "Where have you been the last three days?"

"Busy." The strain in my voice and dark circles under my eyes should have been evident of that. No one had ever accused her of being particularly observant.

"Busy avoiding me?" she shot back. Johanna and Oliver paused and looked up from the sofa across the room where they'd been talking.

"Let's take this to another—" Johanna started. I raised my hand, waving her down. Unhooking my ankles, I dragged my legs over the side of the armchair to the floor and moved to stand.

"You stay. Keyla and I will take a walk."

"What if I don't want to walk with you?" she piped off. I snorted because I didn't have the energy to laugh.

"Tough shit," I said, strolling past her. She followed. I knew she would. We made it as far as the railing on the second floor before her restraint snapped.

"Where have you been? Why couldn't I find you? I had to get my dad to tell me where you guys were—" I held up a hand as I pressed the button to summon the elevator. "Are you *silencing* me?"

"I do believe that is what the hand gesture means, yes," I replied. She opened her mouth, her brows furrowing in indignation as the elevator pinged. The doors slid open, and she let out a frustrated growl as we stepped in.

Ground floor, I projected to the sentient magic that powered this thing. The doors slid shut, and her evil eye ensued.

"I'm not avoiding you."

"Then what do you call moving your room so that I can't find you—"

"The room was trashed, Keyla." She blinked as the

elevator doors opened. I held out a hand, motioning for her to go first. She walked past me briskly and then turned to make sure I was following.

"Yeah. So? Who trashed it?" she asked loudly as we walked past a huddled group of Shifters. They also gave me the side-eye, but it was for very different reasons. I turned my attention back to the hallway before me and to the girl at my side.

"Not important. The point is we had to move rooms because it wasn't fit to sleep in." I wasn't lying . . . well, not completely. The room was trashed from Ash and I's claiming, and we had moved temporarily for it. But after everything that had happened, I was more comfortable staying closer to the others. Where I could keep an eye on Blair. Not that I would tell anyone else that. We all knew that she wasn't stable, and one wrong move could end with hundreds dead.

That was the power of Valda's line. Our legacy.

Keyla's tromping pulled me back to the topic at hand: convincing a thirteen-year-old that I wasn't avoiding her. Easier said than done when it was her own insecurities that fed that ideation.

"Well—why didn't you tell me?" she asked, using her body weight to lean against the metal bar. It popped in and the lock released, opening to the great outdoors of Carson, Nevada.

"I've been a bit preoccupied." I thought back on the last forty-eight hours. That was an understatement.

"Too preoccupied to let me know you moved?" She raised her voice, and I shot her a warning look. Keyla scowled, and continued stomping beside me as we walked around the edge of the training field toward one of the trails.

"Actually, yes, I was, and I'm not going to apologize for it. There are things going on right now, Keyla, and sometimes you won't get hours with me every day." Her bottom lip quivered. Her eyes shimmered. Goddamnit. Not the waterworks. I held in a groan as she looked away, trying to compose herself.

"Did I do something wrong?" She kicked at the leaves as we walked. Melancholy taking hold.

"No. You didn't do anything," I sighed. She stopped. Her golden eyes looked large and a little doll-like when they were glassy.

"Then what is so important that it's taking up all your time and you can't hang out with me anymore?"

"I never said we couldn't hang out anymore," I corrected.

"But you implied it!" she shouted. The birds scattered in a flapping of wings and rustled tree branches.

"No, I said we wouldn't be able to spend hours a day together. Not that we couldn't spend time together. Don't put words in my mouth, Keyla White." She pursed her lips and scrunched her eyebrows. If her death glare was meant to look scary, it failed miserably.

"Don't talk down to me, Selena Fortescue."

I froze, and she did the same. "What did you just say?" Leaves fell from the canopy, softly brushing against the wind on their way down. Keyla swallowed hard and looked away.

"I'm sorry—I overheard you guys talking last night —"

"So you were snooping," I interrupted. She clenched her jaw but didn't deny it.

"I was listening—"

"Clearly. For once I didn't hear you coming half a mile away," I scoffed. We continued walking deeper into the woods where even the mice scuttling was loud.

"Ohmygawd"—she groaned loudly—"you know what?"

"I know a lot of whats, you'll need to be more specific," I replied dryly despite the heavy press of exhaustion. A slow but steady pain was beginning to build in my right temple. It was the makings of a tension headache caused by too many hours awake, too much caffeine, and an all-consuming worry that despite my best efforts, we would fail.

I glanced away to hide my wince. A rustle of leaves caught my attention. I stilled.

"Keyla." She kept talking. "Keyla," I repeated. Harder this time, an undercurrent of urgency bleeding into my voice as I wrapped my fingers around her upper arm and pulled her close.

"What are you—" she broke off as her eyes went wide. A twig snapped right behind me, and I knew without looking that someone had moved into her vision. She shuffled closer, whether subconscious or not I couldn't tell, but the hammering of her heart and stench of fear was unmistakable.

My demon shifted anxiously. Whoever it was, she did not like them near Keyla. Especially when we could only hear two heartbeats.

Leaves rustled again, masking the sound of footsteps.

Without a beating heart or breathing lungs, it was easier to mistake the very slight brush of silent feet against the forest floor. The five bloodsuckers that stepped out from the trees in front of me were very real, though.

A twig snapped behind me and I pulled Keyla closer, wrapping an arm around her waist. Her breathing sped up as she stared stock-still at whoever was behind me.

"You're on Shifter territory without an invitation," I said, making no effort to subdue my demon or the hostility in my tone. She would shield Keyla and rip them apart in the same breath if I let her.

"We come on behalf of the High Council." Several more Vampires moved through the trees behind me, backing the one who spoke. We were up to eleven now, and that assumed no more chose to show up.

"Even stranger, considering that you and your buddies are jumping me in the woods and not setting up a proper meeting. Care to tell me why you've come?" I scaled back my hostility only a fraction. I wasn't worried for me, but another half dozen were making their way toward us. That brought the number of assailants up to seventeen, and I had Keyla in tow. Keyla, who I was ninety percent certain would not be much help in a fight with the undead.

"The Dark Prince wishes to speak with you." The paper-thin whisper of vocal cords that had been forced to endure too many years was telling. While those facing me were Made, I had suspicions about the one speaking and the way he blatantly ignored what I'd said.

I took my arm away from Keyla's shoulder, and she reached out, wrapping her shaking hands in my T-shirt.

Her eyes pleaded silently as they swiveled from the Vampire to me.

"Let go," I whispered. She shook her head slightly, like the Vampires wouldn't see. "Do you trust me?" My lips were no more than a hairsbreadth from the skin of her cheek. She stared at me for a full fifteen seconds before nodding.

I grabbed her hand and lowered it to my waist—to the cold, hard, metal that sat there. Her fingers wrapped around the handle, and she pulled the dagger from its sheath. Then she turned around, and the metal in her hand—while probably useless against this many—gave her confidence.

I turned around as well, pressing my back to hers.

Seven Vampires stared back and three of them had dark eyes.

The Born.

Bile rose in my throat as I looked at faces that felt too familiar. One of them had been subjected to enduring Lily's darkness the night she had almost killed Nikita. They weren't the highest ranking Born, but they were high enough to be in the Council chambers that day.

I remembered.

"The Dark Prince should have sent a letter; instead he sends a party of Vampires large enough to kidnap or kill." I swept my hand out and the tree limbs moved, revealing the others that had carefully positioned themselves out of sight. They forget that I don't need my eyes to see. To know. "If he meant for this to be a peaceful endeavor, he has failed, and unless you wish to start a war with the Shifters, I would leave now."

One of the Born stood directly in front of me, not three feet away. A single step and swipe of my hand was all it would take to behead him, but I would not start this war. I would not make that decision for the Shifters. Even if his dark eyes and crop of hair so light it shined unnaturally beneath the trees gave me nightmares.

"I'm afraid I can't do that. Much as you and I might wish. My liege has asked that I retrieve you, so that you both may speak freely. If you decline to come nicely . . ." He left the statement open-ended. Kidnapping it was.

Mentally I started calculating how far we'd gone from the residence and how fast Keyla was able to run. She could beat almost any Shifter, but a Vampire? No. Not even she was that fast unless she had a head start.

Would they leave her if I feigned coming with long enough to kill them? What if I went all the way . . . what if I could somehow find and save Lily myself . . . what if . . .

A presence brushed against my mind. I pulled away, trying to hide it from him. To keep it under control, but I'd already let Ash in, and there was no way for me to close him out if he chose to see.

"What's wrong?" he projected across the bond.

I felt it, the moment he realized the situation I was in. The very second he put together what and who I was staring at.

"You do not get to go with them. Do you understand me—"

I blocked his voice, focusing on the Vampire in front of me. It was my choice. Not his. "If I go with you, you let her go. Right now. I watch her leave and none of you follow her—"

"No," Keyla gasped. "No, Selena, you can't do that."

"Agreed," the Born said. His face made it clear it meant little to him either way. "The child is without use to us."

Without use. I froze, struggling against the pending inferno that was building. My demon was angry. So very angry at what these people had done to Lily. Ash's own animalistic fury was beating through me as he started to close the distance between us.

"Leave me," I told her. Ordered her. Maybe I shouldn't have demanded it. Maybe it was too much to ask.

Keyla's only response was to scream.

"Vampires! Help! Somebody help—"

One of them moved behind me, and I was only a fraction of a second faster in turning and grabbing Keyla's arm, pulling her behind me. She tripped, and her knees smacked the forest floor in the same instant a wicked crack filled the air.

My head spun far enough back I was staring at the Born now behind me. He sighed and began tugging at the cuffs on his dress shirt. I reached up, cupping the back of my head and holding my chin, forcibly turning my head back while my neck rapidly healed itself.

The Made blinked, realizing his mistake. He'd meant to strike Keyla, but hit me instead. In a way, they were unlucky that I couldn't die so easily. While the High Council wanted me, losing me would be less of a pain than what came next. A troubled expression was only beginning to grace his face when I back handed him hard enough that black blood sprayed my face. He toppled to the ground, a fourth of his head caved in. It wouldn't kill him, but for attempting to hurt Keyla I was saving his death for last.

"Are you the chosen messenger?" I asked the Born who had spoken.

"I am," he answered warily. He was worried where this was going after seeing his slave's brain splattered on the forest floor. He should be worried.

Power filled the air, thickening it with a deadly tension. I reached out, preparing to wipe them from existence all in one go when—

It vanished. Every speck that was oozing from my pours and seeping into the world around me simply . . . disappeared. I looked around, searching for the source, but Ash wasn't here and the Born had no powers. I examined the Made, all thirteen of them. I turned in circles, but not a single one of those thirteen stepped up. Their faces were blank, not mocking.

If not them then . . . slowly I looked down at the girl kneeling by my feet. Her eyes glistened with unshed tears, and her skin gave off the slightest hint of a glow . . .

"I'm—I'm sorry—I don't kn-know how t-to control it—" Her voice shook as the glow continued.

Somehow, a latent half-breed and a second child of a forfeit Supernatural had a power strong enough to subdue even mine. I stored that information away for later and turned back to the seventeen-person problem at hand.

I didn't have my powers to keep us safe.

No matter.

There was only one being on this planet that was both stronger and faster than a Vampire. One that was infinitely harder to kill.

I closed my eyes and inhaled the scent of blood, magic, and dirt. She came forward without me needing to think or ask. After what they'd done to Lily and what that Made would have done to Keyla . . . there would be no mercy.

She would show them that I didn't need to be a matter manipulator to make them pay. I opened my eyes and smiled cruelly, knowing that it was the face of a demon that stared out.

They didn't even have time to scream.

CHAPTER 5

I GRASPED TWO DAGGERS FROM MY BELT AND THREW THEM AT the two other Born. The metal blades hit hard enough to shatter the bone of their rib cages that protected their unbeating hearts. Wind whistled in my ears as my heart began to race.

Both bodies fell backwards from the impact of the throw and hit the ground with a hard thud.

I was already reaching for the last dagger in my belt and the other in my boot. Without my ability to summon them back, two daggers and my own bare hands were all that would keep us alive against the fifteen Vampires that were now baring their fangs.

Fourteen of them would die this day.

Their bodies would stain the forest floor a shade of obsidian, and I would revel in it. I may not want to be a senseless killer, but I could be a justified one. The difference between being a monster and being someone's savior, was not what you did. It was which side you were on. The motivation that made you do something so dark it would stain your soul.

My motivation was simple.

Justice.

Survival.

I held onto that—onto the picture of Lily's face as I ducked under the swinging arms of one of the Made. I turned and stabbed him through the back, ripping his head off for good measure. Just to be sure.

"Watch out!" Keyla screamed. Without my power telling me where they were, I was at a bit of a disadvantage. I'd denied that same ability for years though, and this was not all that different.

I ducked, twisting around in the same motion. The Made behind me faltered as I came back up with my dagger outstretched. It slid straight between his ribs, and into his dead, rot-infested heart.

His skin darkened, turning gray—ashen—as he dropped to his knees and slumped over.

I cut the next Vampire down, pushing my hand holding the dagger straight through his chest. My other hand wrapped around his neck to hold him still as I pulled back out. The gaping hole oozed a sickly-scented ichor. I was already turning before the body hit the floor.

Eleven Made swarmed me as I searched for Keyla. Their red eyes fixated on my arms, painted black with Vampire blood. I held them both up as I parried in a circle, distracting them with pretty moves.

"Keyla!" I called out.

The only answer I got in return was her scream. A tendril of fear ran through me.

I moved in the direction it came from, and the horde moved with me, changing position to continue our dance, even as my attention moved toward the trees. In the very back a girl with reddish-brown hair and ivory skin stared intently at the ground before her. Her hands were wrapped around something—no—they were wrapped around *someone*. Keyla's voice choked out and without waiting another moment, I struck.

Moving faster than any Vampire could, I flung out my hand, and the dagger in it began spinning. It whirled horizontally as it sped through a gap not eight inches wide. A splatter of black exploded where the Made woman's face was. I wheeled back, slashing a wide arc around me before throwing the second dagger.

It landed true.

Her head was nailed to a sycamore tree, right between her dull, dead eyes. Uneasy glances flitted between me and the corpse as Keyla let out a choked gasp, her tanned skin turning a tinge redder. I ran through the gap of Vampires between me and her, but I didn't dare get on my knees to help her just yet.

"Breathe," I whispered. Her eyes locked on mine. Gold flecked with black. She tilted her head forward a fraction and then back. A subtle nod as her nostrils flared and she inhaled slowly.

The golden tint of her skin winked out of existence and power swept into the forest and through the trees with a frightening headiness. My power. My strength. A slow smile crept up my face.

I may be down my daggers, but my true strength was something that could not be seen or stolen. Perhaps temporarily smothered by a girl far more remarkable than the world knew. But not taken.

Every single Vampire took a step back and turned to look at the Born who was shaking his head. One messenger. That's all I needed to send my sister and her keeper a note.

"Next time one of yours steps on Shifter land with the intention to use force, I will not be this merciful. Tell your liege if he wishes to talk, a letter will suffice." I waited for the Born to tip his head. Those dark eyes unfathomable as they were undammable.

Ten heads exploded in a shower of blood.

It stained my clothes and soaked my hair. It permeated the cracks of my skin and settled in the crevices of my nails. Every inch of me was coated in the metallic scent of the undead's vitals, tinted with a sweetness that wasn't natural. My demon blinked at the Born, and he seemed to understand that was his final warning.

"Allowing you to return is a kindness. You have ninety seconds before the Shifters will reach me and begin hunting. Tread lightly. You may have just started a war." With that send-off, the Born hightailed it out of there. He was over a mile away before I let down my guard enough to turn my back on his retreating form and help Keyla. Her breaths were thin and her face a molten red, tinged purple, but she was breathing. Her heart pounded in my ears as I knelt down before her. She inhaled sharply, her features fracturing as her face fell and the heaviness of what happened finally started to settle in.

"Shhh . . ." I whispered, pulling her to me. Her arms

wrapped tight around my neck and waist, vice-like as she clutched me and began to unravel. Broken gasps and silent sobs racked her body as I held her.

"You—they—you tried to leave me!" she stuttered, her voice rising. "You tried to—" She gulped in air, swallowing hard.

"Shhh . . ." I repeated, trying to calm her. Using the palm of my hand, I started to rub rhythmic circles between her shoulder blades. The black blood that stuck to my skin like tar smeared over the back of her jacket. I grimaced as the Shifters' footsteps became known. Just a crinkle of leaves in an otherwise quiet forest. A whisper on the wind.

They spread out around us, moving in quick, even though there was nothing to find. Nothing but bodies and blood and broken innocence.

Ash came forward first. I sensed it as he stepped out of the woods and into the blackened hollow that was so seeped with blood that his footsteps squished.

Next came a gasp. Then another. And another.

Quiet descended. A silence so still that their heartbeats were thunder and I was the eye of the storm. Keyla shuddered against me.

"Selena," he said softly. There was a wary note in his voice as he stopped a few feet away. Keyla only cried harder.

It was then when her choked sobs rocked us both and her blood-smeared face popped over my shoulder that the Shifters started to come forward.

A primal urge filled my demon. Keyla was vulnerable

right now. Breakable. She didn't need them poking and prodding at her.

They came closer. Circling the hallowed ground. Words drifted from the edges of the trees. That coldness that had thawed for Keyla resettled as the people around us became threats. Targets.

The moment someone stepped around Ash to approach I turned my head and bared my teeth, letting out the slightest growl. Face painted, clothes soaked, and black ichor dripping from my chin and the ends of my hair, they paused.

"Stop," Ash commanded. "Her demon is protecting Keyla." The power of the Alpha ran strong and every Shifter inclined their head. His presence slid into my mind, brushing against my being. "Selena," he said with the same gentleness I used to rub Keyla's back while she cried. "They're not going to hurt her, I promise."

Hurt her.

Hurt her.

Hurt her—

A soft hand touched my sticky cheek. Keyla pulled back a fraction, her palm cupping my face. "It's okay," she said hoarsely. "We're okay," she repeated, convincing herself more than me. Congealing blood smudged her face, turning to black watercolors where her tears ran. "You were going to leave so they wouldn't hurt me but . . ." She trailed off and looked over my shoulder. Her swollen lips barely moved as she breathed, "You stayed."

You stayed. Those words echoed through my mind, drawing my demon back.

"You didn't give me much choice," I told her. Her lips pressed together in a watery smile.

"I couldn't let you go," she insisted with more force and less fear, already overcoming the shock of what she'd seen.

What I'd done.

"I didn't want to," I said, barely a murmur. Her eyes softened, and she leaned in to press her blood-splattered lips to my cheek. We were both covered in gore from what had taken place.

"I know."

My arms relaxed around her as I leaned back to brush the sticky strands away from her face as the rumors started. No one could come forward until Ash released his order, but that didn't mean they had to be quiet while they did so.

"Did you see the bodies?"

"Could they even be called that?"

"How did they even get this far?"

"Do you think . . ."

"What if she called them?"

"She protected our own."

"I heard she hunts the bloodsuckers for fun."

"Doesn't mean she—"

The rumors drifted through like leaves on the wind as Shifters went back and forth on whether I was the savior or the villain of this situation. I gritted my teeth and turned away, but Keyla caught my hand. "I get it now."

I paused. "Get what?" I asked, my eyes falling on the decapitated head nailed to a tree stump. I think I knew.

"Why you don't like to fight." She leaned forward, lowering her voice. "You don't like conflict . . . because in a dog eat dog world, you're not a dog at all." I turned my head a fraction, and her golden eyes caught mine.

"Oh?" I pressed my lips together, trying to find the words to say. To tell her that she's right. That the conclusion she had come to in not so many words was both the one I warned her of from the beginning and the one I feared she'd one day reach. "What am I then?"

"You're a god."

My lips parted, and I stared.

For all the evil in the world that I'd tried to stop, I never truly saw myself as much different. That evil and I shared many faults. While I fought it, I always knew that deep down it wasn't what made the monster I was. I was born this way. I was resigned to that knowledge.

But Keyla looked at me, and she didn't see a monster.

For all the dark deeds I'd done and beings I'd killed, she saw me kill sixteen Vampires and still looked at me like I was her hero. Some legend brought to life before her eyes.

"I'm not so sure about that," I said. Rocking back on my heels and into the blackened mud.

"If you're not a god, then what are you?"

Her eyebrows pinched together as she watched me, near oblivious to the Shifters around her as they silently judged our interactions.

I realized then it wasn't Keyla I needed to find those words for, but for the world who now looked on with far more fear and trepidation than the girl before me.

Anastasia was dead. Vampires attacked the Alpha's

daughter. The Court was crumbling, and nobody knew what was coming next.

Above all that seemed to be the question they asked. The question many would ask when word of the attack and the slaughter that followed spread.

I took a deep breath, knowing deep down how I had to answer, because I made a promise—that I would do what was needed to end this no matter the consequences.

Fate took a turn and Anastasia's life was stolen from me, but that didn't change the burden I had to bear. Both my past and my future.

I looked at Keyla, then to Ash, whose black eyes were only a shade warmer than my own when my demon was in control.

They were what I was fighting for.

And so I answered her question—the question the world didn't know to ask yet.

"Something so much worse," I said quietly. "I'm a Fortescue."

Ash watched as I fanned the ember that flew on the wind of whispers, where it would eventually land; the spark that lights the fuse.

The world was going to change with those words. Both his and mine.

But it was the things I left unsaid that troubled me most.

Because I wasn't just a Fortescue, but a Konig too.

And neither legacy was letting me go.

CHAPTER 6

WINDS WHIPPED THROUGH THE REEDY BRANCHES ABOVE. Lightning flashed in an otherwise clear morning sky, signaling that Blair had already learned about the attack before I could make it back to the mansion.

Warm fingers grasped my forearm, pulling me up short. A large group had left to hunt the single Born, but I knew as well as Ash did that he was long gone. Still, the Shifters' instincts rode them hard, and so he sent them hunting, and let the others be Keyla's escort home. I'd stayed in the clearing the longest, taking in the carnage. Embracing the viciousness that came from my choices. They might have been undead, but so was my sister. For the sake of the fight, I'd separated them into things versus people. It made it easier to not have to face the moral conundrum that I hated all Vampires, but my sister was one. Despite the things she'd done I couldn't hate her. But these people? These bits of rotten flesh and stolen blood? It was easy to hate them. Though a small part of me wondered if they were like her. People that had been turned against their will. Innocent people that had that innocence used against them and it made them monsters.

I shook my head, clearing those thoughts away because they wouldn't help me. Compassion was the death of justice, and too much had happened for me to question my actions now. I turned and left the clearing, tromping through the woods. Ash followed behind me.

"You were going to leave with them." There was a note that hung in the air between us; the words he said a dividing line. I didn't want to talk about it or feel the disappointment leaking down the bond.

Ash knew what I was going to do. He knew that I would have walked right off this property and into Hell if it kept them safe and led me to Lily.

I didn't do it, but I would have—if Keyla hadn't stopped me.

"I won't apologize," I said, not turning to face him. Unable to look at the accusation in his eyes.

"If you'd gone with them, they would have turned you before you ever set eyes on her."

"Oh, I don't know about that." Lightning flashed across the sky, catching my attention. Dark clouds rolled in from the horizon at impossible speeds. "Lily is angry and wants revenge for me not saving her, and Victor wants me to be a brood mare so he can sire powerful children. I don't think I'd have been turned, and that's assuming any of them could kill me. Something no one —not even Anastasia could ever manage."

I didn't have to look to know how much those words upset him. Heat sizzled through the bond, burning up any lingering disappointment with a scorching intensity. I might have staggered were I not expecting it.

"You're not invincible, Selena," he whispered. "They might not have been able to kill you, but you know as well as I do the dangerous depths you and your sisters hit in a rage. If Lily is as upset as you say she is, what are the odds she would turn on you? The Vampires aren't the only ones that can kill."

The scary part is that he wasn't wrong.

Lily was changing. Growing. Evolving into something I didn't know or understand. Even at my worst I hadn't done some of the things she had, and while I couldn't blame her for surviving . . . not every sin she had committed was in the name of freedom.

"You forget," I said. "I didn't want to leave, but I also didn't want Keyla getting hurt. It's not as if I'm wandering off into the first magical elevator I can find. I'm doing everything that you and Johanna have asked, including leaving Lucas to her. I've played by the rules for months now. And where has that gotten us?" I didn't raise my voice, nor did I need to. He knew the anger. He understood the fear. He felt the worry, the anxiety, and the desperation eating away at me every moment Lily was in that monster's hands. Because every moment she spent with Victor was one closer to the edge of no return.

I couldn't allow that. I wouldn't. And yet I had no choice, so long as I played by the rules.

"We're going to find her. We just need more time," Ash insisted.

"You know as well as I do where she probably is. We hope she's not, but we both know," I whispered. "And if she is, do you really think that anyone would follow me there to free her?" Silence. He wouldn't lie. Not to me, and so I got my answer another way. I chuckled under my breath, a dark sound, filled with a little of that madness I kept well hidden.

Even Valda looked on with concern.

"We don't know—"

"Yes, we do," I said, cutting him off before he could even pretend to feed me that sugar-coated bullshit. "You know as well as I that no one, except possibly Scarlett, would follow me there. No one except those with a death wish step foot in the High Council. No matter what name I have or the power I wield, fear will outweigh all if she's in that place."

The winds whistled again, harder this time. Smaller branches snapped under the force of those gales, and I took that as my sign to start booking it back to the mansion before someone ended up dead.

Ash released his grip on my forearm, falling into step beside me as I took off through the woods at a speed no other, except maybe Blair, could keep up with.

"If you really believe that," he said, breathing a little harder as he tried to keep up. "Why did you take on the Fortescue name?"

"Regardless of what others choose to do, the Supernatural council needs someone to unite it, and they won't respond to anything but sheer power. Which means the task falls to me." As much as I hated it, and I did. "Whether the world realizes it or not, we are already at war. The only question I have is who will be on the battlefield with me."

I wasn't sure what he made of my answer, but the training field behind the Shifter reservation was coming up fast. We moved from the trees into the grassy field, bounding through the horde of Shifters gathered around. They leapt back after I was already passing, the sight of my body covered in black blood and smelling like rot repelling them.

Well, it was that or the sight of Alexandra with her flaming black hair that bounded toward me. Her and her demon had merged, giving her two different colored eyes and flaming hair. While she was the same in her interactions with the Shifters, the hellfire that fanned from her head gave them pause, understandably so.

"I see you heard—"

Crack.

I blinked, not responding to the back-handed smack she delivered. Her chest rose and fell as puffs of breath came out white in the early winter air. Her hand curled inward as if she were debating between hitting me again and attempting to restrain herself.

She chose restraint.

"How *dare* you try to leave with them!" she shouted, anger making her one brown eye flash with fire and fury. The dark one of her demon zeroed in on me without emotion.

"I didn't try to leave," I said, catching her wrist as she brought it up to slap me again. My fingers curled, the flaking blood rubbing against her white cashmere sweater. "I didn't have a lot of options, and the daughter of the Shifter Alpha was in danger. I would rather be taken away than have them kill or turn her because I wasn't fast enough."

The fight drained out of her, and her fist unfurled. I dropped her arm, pointedly stepping around her as she stood there staring at the spot where I'd been.

"Wait—" she called. I paused. "I'm sorry, I just . . ." her words trailed off as her throat bobbed. Emotion becoming too thick for her to talk past, not without sounding weak. I nodded because I understood.

"If I wanted to leave, not a soul on this reservation could stop me. Remember that next time your anger slips." I strode toward the double doors that were splayed wide open. The panes of glass had been shattered. The wood splintered. Thunder roared overhead. I quickened my pace.

The foyer looked like a battle had taken place, and I briefly entertained the thought that Vampires attacked the residence as well . . . but that wasn't possible. I would have known, and the mansion would be in even more of an uproar were that the case.

Still, the broken vases and flowers strewn across the floors meant *something* had come through. Water dripped from the wooden end tables, speckled red. Splashes of blood painted the walls, but it was the blood of the living, which left few options. Beyond the main entry and through the hallway, the fighting had continued. It came to a stop before the front door.

I tilted my head, narrowing my eyes. There's no reason the fighting would stop here. That didn't make sense . . . I turned and looked up at the shattered railing on the second floor. That made more sense. The fighting hadn't stopped. Merely moved. I made the twenty foot jump in a single leap, my fingers skimming the broken and bloodied wood railing on the way up.

The shouts grew, as did the thuds of bodies being thrown around. I peeked down the hallway, and my blood froze. Whatever it was, it was coming from where Lucas was being held.

I cracked my neck and rolled my shoulders. Still coming down from the high of one fight, a second smaller one wouldn't be difficult. I strode around the corner and came to stand at the end of the hallway.

Blair stood, her blonde hair braided tight, casting the angles of her face in a severe light. Her eyes were black and wild. Furious. Oliver moved in an attempt to restrain her from behind while Liam screamed. It wasn't out of fear, but power. The sound that came from him was so strong it had the mansion quaking. Yet even as brick and stone quivered, Blair simply turned her head. Both arms were locked behind her—in Oliver's grips—and she twisted, bringing her foot up to slam into Liam's chest. The scream cut short as he went flying straight through the window at the end of the hall.

A roar of outrage came from Scarlett as she launched herself from Lucas's room into the hallway. While a powerful Supernatural in her own right, Blair was part-demon and one of the most powerful people not just in this city, but in the world. Scarlett, for as impenetrable as her skin might be, wasn't a match. Blair pivoted, taking Oliver's body with her. She spun around so that is was him Scarlett crashed into and attacked with a mad fury. By the time she realized, it was too late. She and Oliver went crashing through the wall and into the room on the other side.

Blair stepped out of the rubble and turned to face whoever stood on the other side of the door. I took a step forward, finally catching her attention.

She paused.

"They said you were taken." The disembodied voice of her demon came out cold and crass. Yet, hesitant. This rage wasn't just a random bout, but a reaction to pain. A pain the demon did not understand or know how to deal with.

"Vampires tried to. I killed them all," I answered, taking measured steps forward. I was careful not to be too fast, or she'd think I intended to attack. But they also couldn't be too slow, because caution meant I saw her as a threat.

Her demon blinked and replied, "Good." I nodded, strolling right up to her, close enough that I caught Johanna on the other side of the doorway that had been blown off its hinges. Behind her, Amber and Tori guarded Lucas with their lives.

It left a bitter taste in my mouth that after all he'd done, they would protect him like this and yet Lily was left to rot.

"So, what'd he do this time to warrant your wrath?" I asked with a feigned nonchalance. I didn't miss the way Tori narrowed her eyes, or how Johanna gave me an exasperated look—like how dare I engage her when she was like this.

But they underestimated one thing. I knew what it was like to be labeled for what you are. I understood how harmful it was to believe that you had no control over it. I didn't wish that on Blair. This transition was already taking its toll in blood and heartache.

"You were attacked by Vampires. I thought they came at his call." She raised her blade in his direction without looking, the tip of it dripping blood.

I nodded, crossing my arms over my chest and lifting one hand to my face. My thumb brushed over my bottom lip as I regarded her coolly. "Vampires did come, but they weren't at his call."

She blinked, giving away nothing. "You don't know that."

"I do, actually," I said with a heavy sigh, because I wish I didn't know or understand. I wish that we could all go back in time to when things were simpler. But they were never actually that way. It only seemed like it from the perspective of a child. Innocence was like that. Shielding the most horrid of things behind a veil of naivete.

Never mind that the monsters lurked in plain sight.

"He almost killed Aaron. He tried to kill Alec. The Vampires have never come before and now they happen upon you in the woods?" She let out a heartless laugh. I knew better than to show any fear; it would only egg her on, sending her deeper into this killing rage. "Don't be a fool, cousin." Her voice was almost mocking—if it had any inflection at all.

"I'm not a fool," I answered her sincerely. "Neither are you, but I hold more information than you do at this moment. There's no way Lucas could have called any Vampires," I assured her, even as a seed of doubt sowed its way in my heart. Could he have called them somehow? Could he have known?

Her allegations weren't baseless, but I needed him to be alive so I could question him on exactly that.

"Why is that?" her demon asked, voice dripping with disbelief and suspicion.

I did what I had to do. For her and for me.

I lied.

"Because I saw Victor order it last night." My voice didn't quiver. It didn't tremble. I didn't play with my hair or look away. I stared at her pitch-colored eyes and lied to her face, and her demon bought it.

The mansion held its breath for a moment.

She blinked twice, before the black faded into steel gray.

Taking a stuttered breath, she looked to the side where Scarlett and Oliver were only just getting to their feet—to Johanna who stood just on the other side of the door—to me, and Ash who stood behind me. Then finally, to the shattered window.

Her throat bobbed twice as she swallowed hard. The shouts down below didn't help as people raced to help the young Supernatural who had quite literally been kicked through a window and fell two stories.

That had to hurt.

"He's alive!" one of them bellowed, loud enough it carried further than our own more enhanced hearing. The breath left Scarlett's body momentarily before she was pushing past us and bounding for the stairs that would lead her down to the training grounds.

"You really did a number this time," I said quietly.

Blair only shook her head, because she'd pushed it this time, straying the line of how much the Shifter residence could handle.

She moved to step around me and paused. "Whatever your reason for lying, I hope you're damn sure about him."

Shock ran through me as she swiftly tried to retreat.

"How did you know?" I asked, hardly more than a whisper.

Blair didn't pause, nor did she yell as she replied, "You would never take Keyla into danger if you knew it was coming."

And then she was gone.

I felt her presence all the way to the third floor where she retreated to her room in self-imposed exile. Alexandra was already ready and waiting to watch her.

I cursed under my breath and turned to Johanna.

Lifting my blackened hand to point at Lucas as Blair had only minutes ago, I said, "Clear the room. He and I are going to have a chat."

CHAPTER 7

Tori jumped forward, throwing herself in front of Lucas's prone form. Bound to a chair with both arms behind his back and head bowed forward, he was not the boy I remembered. Neither was Tori the girl she used to be.

Determination and desperation collided head-on in her green eyes as she looked at me, ready to defend him. "You can't take him," she whispered. Those same eyes turning glossy with tears she thought she'd be shedding.

"I have no intention of killing him. You know that. Don't let your emotions cloud your judgement," I replied and waited. She slowly looked up and down my relaxed stance, to the knives I had stowed, and the flaking blood of the undead that filled every crack and pore of my flesh.

"Do you promise?" she asked, hardly a breath. Barely a whisper. I sighed softly.

"I promise I won't kill him, *today*." Her expression hardened again.

"How do you expect me to trust you when you put it like that?" she demanded.

I glanced to Johanna pointedly.

"I don't have the patience for this today. Keyla and I were just attacked in the woods, and Liam is likely in bad condition downstairs after being kicked in the chest by a demon and thrown two floors, yet we're wasting resources here. I've agreed to not killing him for now. You know why. You all know why." I looked to her again, a hint of anger lingering in my gaze. "But I have questions, and we are running out of time. I don't care if you trust me, Tori. I honestly don't. Not after you let Anastasia slip and the ramifications of that are going to result in the deaths of *thousands* of people before this is all over."

She paled. Her tanned skin going white as the Vampires we sought to stop. She lowered her gaze to the floor out of guilt. Perhaps I should have felt bad. It wasn't entirely her fault, but she had a role to play in it. One that if she'd stuck to the plan and done what she was told would have sent fate on a different path.

And maybe Lily's soul would not be hanging by such a slim thread.

"He's my brother," she eventually said, pulling out of a defensive stance. "Just as she's your sister. No matter what they've become."

If my face were not already a mask of indifference, I might have flinched at her words. She didn't know—none of them did—how true that statement was.

"Yes." I nodded slowly. "And it's because of him that my sister was tortured these last months and forced to endure *unspeakable* things." She swallowed hard, no doubt her imagination running wild with what those words meant, but she didn't understand. Not really. You couldn't know the horror of it. Unless you watched from Lily's eyes, as I did, while she killed a child that looked like Alexandra and reveled in it. "I will not kill him so long as she is trapped, because I need him to get her back."

"Ten minutes," Johanna said. She turned to them and pointed to the hole where the door had been.

"And then?" Tori asked, her feet dragging.

"I send Aaron in to keep her balanced," the golden-eyed woman answered. "She promised not to kill the boy in the immediate, and I trust she will withhold that judgement for another day." She paused, looking between Lucas and me. "I will stand guard at the end of the hall should it . . . escalate."

Tori strode by first, followed by Amber who didn't look as if she cared one way or the other how this went. Johanna paused at the doorway. "I can't get him to talk," she said softly. "I'm hoping that you can. Please don't make me regret this."

"You should check on Liam . . ." I spared a glance over my shoulder. "Alec too. I don't imagine he's taking this well." Given Blair was turning demon at least once a day and over half the time knocked unconscious, he'd lost it a few times and had to be subdued as well. It was hard on him, wanting to help but knowing that their history would always be between them. Blair's demon wanted him something fierce, but the girl herself couldn't let go of the past, and I didn't blame her. I don't think anyone did.

Johanna nodded once and left me to walk into the last place I wanted to be. Unfortunately, it was the very place I needed to be.

Lucas didn't stir as I plopped down into the rickety chair across from him. He didn't twitch as I leaned forward, resting my elbows on my knees, hands clasped together.

There was no indication that while his lungs still breathed and his heart still beat, that anyone was home.

"Lucas."

A single word, and his breathing paused, before resuming. His heart beat faster, whether from fear or something else I didn't know. *I didn't want to know.*

"I was attacked today," I told him. "Vampires. Sent by the High Council. You wouldn't have anything to do with that, would you?"

I waited for his breath to hitch and his pulse to race. I waited for a twitch of his fingers, or a glance of his jewel-green eyes, shattered like stained glass.

I waited, with bated breath, for his mind to sidle up to my shields and try to pry.

But it never came.

Eight of my ten minutes passed where we sat in silence.

Tumultuous, terrible silence. The only words spoken were those we left unsaid.

I almost stood back up again and walked out the door, metaphorically closing this one behind me where he would rot until the day came I felt like putting him out of his misery.

I almost did it.

Then he spoke.

"I dreamed of this day." His voice was raspy from disuse and probably bruised from my manhandling in the market. That felt like months ago, even though it wasn't.

"Of what day?" I asked, not allowing myself to overthink it.

"The day I would finally be rid of her."

Inside, deep down where I would never let him see—I shuddered. There were no tells as to how I felt. No clues to give it away—that I was suffocating on the knowledge that the same entity who drove Anastasia to madness was the one now residing in Lily.

"I never understood how you ended up with her to begin with."

His head shook. "No," he sighed. "You wouldn't." Lucas laughed bitterly and finally lifted his head. Several days of growth shadowed his jaw and dark circles lined his eyes. Exhaustion. I knew the sign well enough, even when it wasn't my face they showed on. "You never cared half as much for me as I did for you." The words didn't sting like they used to. "I wasn't sure if you were capable of caring for a man that way at all, until I saw you with the dog."

"Don't call him that," I snapped.

A ghost of a smile crossed his lips. One corner tugged up, reminiscent of who he was, but not who he is. My heart no longer squeezed at that smile. Certainly not when it danced the line of cruelty.

"I gave you everything," he said, still wearing that terrible smile. "Every piece of me there was to give and then some. I would have done anything for you—been anything for you. And do you know what you told me?"

"I told you I didn't want you to be my everything. I wanted to be your friend, and at the time I was still trying to figure my life out." His eyes darkened, that brilliant, jewel-toned green still holding an inkling of the darkness that chained him before.

"Exactly. You didn't want *me*—but you accepted *him*. From me you only wanted friendship, never mind how good we were. How great we could have been." He shook his head, as if trying to erase the memories.

"Never mind that you lied to me, right? That not only did you know he was my signasti—but that you two had a little deal going on the side. He got to play you sometimes, but you got the prize in the end?" I might have forgiven Ash, but I was still far from forgiving the piece of shit that sat across from me, wallowing in his own self-pity. "Get over yourself, Lucas. We were never going to happen, and that was before I found out about your lies, before you killed my sister, and before you tried to kill Ash."

"And yet I gave up everything for you—to save you from her—and it's him you forgive and end up with in the end." There was an edge of mania in his tone. Of the madness that crept in. "That's the reason you don't understand. You don't know what it's like to love someone so deeply that you give yourself up in the process. He will always choose you, whatever part of you he can have, just as you have clearly chosen him. But me? Lily? We're just pieces on the board that she moved. My love for you broke me. She swooped in and gave me hope. She preyed on those dreams I had of us. Showed me things that couldn't have been real, but they felt so real at the time . . ." He looked away, shame clouding his gaze. Once again he laid his feelings bare to me, but this time it was not in hopes that I would accept him. It was not rejection he feared. Oh no, I'd already rejected him. It was consequences of our choices, his and mine, that he now showed me.

"What kinds of things?" I asked, choosing to ignore the blame he placed on me.

"Visions of us." He looked at the ceiling now, not wanting to meet my gaze. "Of you. Of what we would become if *he* were never in the picture."

"There was never a picture he didn't exist in," I told him flatly. Lucas only shook his head. "You realize that, don't you? That whatever she showed you wasn't real."

"I know that now . . ." he breathed. "Now that she's gone it's like this fog has been lifted. I can see clearly again." His lips pressed together, like he'd said too much, but from my point of view it was too little.

"What did you mean 'see clearly again'?" I didn't want to say that he hadn't been seeing or thinking clearly since before his declarations of love. That would probably only aide to setting him off and right now he was at least talking and somewhat complacent.

"It's all a haze. Everything we did. Everyone we saw. I remember doing it, but I can't tell you what was real and what wasn't."

Dreams and illusions. Visions of us, he'd called them. Anastasia had fucked with him hard, and while I still didn't understand all of it, I understood enough.

Enough to know that he may be a lost cause.

There were some things people just never came back from, especially when they didn't want to.

And Lucas, for as much as he said he wanted to be rid of her influence—I wasn't sure he wanted to be rid of it all. He'd lived in a distorted reality for months. Coming back had to be jarring.

Reality meant he had to face the facts of what he'd done; something that he was not ready to do. Not when he still clung to that bitter resentment.

"Did you know I was going to be attacked today?" I already knew the answer, but I still needed to ask it. Still needed to have his words when Ash stood right outside the door listening but not interrupting, because he was well aware how Lucas would respond.

"No."

"You didn't communicate with the High Council in any way?" I asked, hoping for an expounded answer.

"You know as well as I do, maybe even better, what the limitations on telepathy are—probably more so given your father was a Fortescue."

So he'd heard about that already? Word traveled faster than the wind around here. Unless it was from Anastasia he'd first heard it . . . I steepled my bloody hands and settled my chin over my fingers.

"Do you know why they might have come after me?"

"Again, you're the Fortescue between us."

Another non-answer, but there was a flash of *something* in his face that told me Lucas wasn't completely out of it. "So is Lily," I replied, watching his haunted expression for further slips. "Who I know *you know* is alive."

"If you could call it that," he answered stiffly.

My fingers clenched, and I dropped my hands to my sides, leaning back. *I promised* them I wouldn't kill him. Unfortunately, a backhand to the face might do just that because I might not stop there.

"Where is she?" I asked, hoping, praying that it wasn't the place I thought it was. That it wasn't the one location on earth that might be unbreachable, even from me.

Silence was my answer.

Not yes. Not no. Not a smart-ass remark meant to piss me off.

Silence.

I asked three more times before I got the hint. Whatever reason he had decided to talk, he was done again. Which meant I was finished here, at least for today.

"He deserved what he got," Valda said from the back of my mind. Her cold, numbing presence unforgiving.

I didn't disagree, but I wasn't sure I agreed either.

That bothered me more than I let on, but not enough to stop me from coming back and forcing the answers from him if I had to.

I hoped for both our sakes it didn't come to that, because whatever shards of sanity Anastasia left him with might not survive me.

"Do you think he was telling the truth?" Johanna asked, pulling me from my own thoughts as she fell into step beside me.

"I think he doesn't know the difference anymore.

Truth and lies. Real or fantasy. He already had issues before she fucked with his head." I sighed, turning for the elevator. I needed to shower before I checked on Blair, then Keyla.

"It's a good way for her to take her secrets to the grave," she murmured to herself. I pressed the button, and the elevator dinged.

"What?"

"Even in her death he can't see through the lies she wove. It keeps whatever she was doing with the High Council secret. Probably the only reason they let her have him around since there was no chance of him running his mouth later. He didn't even know what was going on." I stepped into the elevator, and she followed after me. The doors slid shut when I finally responded.

"He knows something. I need you to find out what." In here was the only place that no one would hear us. The magical elevator transcended the boundaries of space unlike anything else—and therefore kept my words secret.

"He might not talk to me," she warned.

"Then make him talk." *Just don't make me the one to do it.*

"That would be easier if Blair wasn't insistent on wanting him dead," Jo answered dryly. The elevator dinged again, and the doors slid open.

"Liam alive?" I asked, both wanting the answer and not.

Johanna nodded. "Broken arm. Bruised ribs. He landed on a hippo shifter who broke his fall. Scarlett is with him now."

"And Alec? How's he holding up?" I asked quietly, stalling for a moment.

"Do you want the real answer?"

That was answer enough. "She can't help it," I said, needing to defend her.

"I know," Jo said. "That's the reason we're all putting up with this, but Selena—it can't last. Eventually, something will happen. She'll kill someone, maybe even Lucas, and with the fine line we're already walking with the Shifters . . ." She didn't finish it. She didn't need to.

This situation at the residence was nearing its peak. One way or another, something had to give. I just didn't know what.

CHAPTER 8

Yesterday he'd sent seventeen vampires for her.

Today only one returned.

"She killed them," the Born whispered. He was lucky he didn't have a heart to betray him now. To show his fear. "Slaughtered them in minutes."

I settled into the high-backed chair and swirled the crystal glass, holding the stem between two fingers. Blood dripped down the rim, mesmerizing me for a moment. "She let you return." My voice was soft, not ringing as it once had been. In this graveyard dressed in finery, words were a weapon and silence was treasured above all.

"What?" The man turned his narrowed eyes in my direction. Victor's cool gaze followed from me to him, and something dark settled there. Something wicked.

I tipped the glass back, swallowing the blood in two gulps. My tongue darted out to catch the drop that escaped me as I placed it back on the wooden finish and uncrossed my legs, moving to stand.

"If she killed them but you returned, it's because she

allowed you to return. I'm well aware how powerful my sister is and how she works. What's the message?" I asked, and his face could not pale, nor could his heart beat, but the chilling hatred that flashed through his eyes was unmistakable.

Victor got to his feet, a slight sigh leaving his lips as he set his glass aside. The Born didn't know what he'd just done. He didn't understand that in a game of survival, I would win.

I would always win.

Fingers touched my lower back softly as Victor came to stand beside me. He leaned in, his lips brushing over the small patch of flesh between my neck and ear. "He tried to lie," Victor said softly. Deadly. I kept my fingers laced behind my back and didn't shift a fraction. "You know how I don't like liars or failures." His whispered words were a command that no other understood, not like I did.

"But I—" the Born Vampire didn't blubber or cry. He didn't have time to as I strode forward and laid a hand upon his cheek. The darkness in my veins whispered of death as they trailed under my flesh, up my arm, to the point where our skin met.

His mouth fell open in a silent scream as he went to his knees. It had only been days since I'd sucked Anastasia dry, and that voice, that deep, devilish caress of the mind hummed in contentment at his pain. I was inclined to agree, not that it mattered.

Victor was not king in this castle, but he was prince—and the Prince of Darkness answered to no one.

"That's enough, flower," the devil himself said. My power recoiled when the red line that ran between us pulsed once, far too soon.

I pursed my lips where he couldn't see, but when I stepped back and dropped my hand it was the face of indifference that greeted him as I kept my eyes downcast. My steps were silent as I came to stand back at his side, the man I'd been torturing now splayed out on the stone floors. His eyes were glazed. Unseeing.

"Now," Victor said, wrapping his arm around me, his hand coming to rest on my hip. "You've had a taste of what lies in your future, should you try to twist this any way other than how it happened." Fingertips brushed over the edge of my shirt, and I felt nothing. Not revulsion for who he is and what he did. Not shame for staying right where I was. Not anything.

Numb to the judgements of others and uncaring about social constructs, I played his little games because freedom was my reward. But vengeance . . . that would be my prize when it was all said and done. When all of us were nothing more than dust on this earth.

My hands came around to lock behind my back, my wrist brushing his hand at my side. A shiver went through him, and I kept my eyes down and face forward, even as I sensed his attention beginning to shift.

The Born spoke.

"She was going to come with us, but there was a child with her that started screaming. Romulus moved before anyone could stop him and tried to silence the child, but the girl—she moved impossibly fast and took the hit instead." He pushed himself up onto his knees, eyebrows drawn together as he looked at the floor, recounting his mission. "Her neck snapped, and she simply turned around and slapped him back . . ." He hesitated, and I felt a sick sort of thrill run through me because you don't hesitate with Victor.

Ever.

"Flower," he said. It was the only thing he needed to say. I took two steps, and the Born's eyes went wide. He fell back, trying to scramble away from me.

"The girl you sent us for killed him with a single strike, my prince," he said in a rush. Victor held up a hand for me to pause, and I more felt than saw it because that damned line that connected a Made to its Born. He commanded me with that line. But his control was slipping. Slowly yet steadily. I obeyed, for now. "She slapped him, and his head caved in from the sheer strength behind it. Her eyes went black, and I —" He swallowed as I took another step in his direction, his eyes flying between Victor and I. "She looked like a demon, Prince. She moved as fast as a demon."

Victor examined him for a moment, evaluating if this low-levelled Born was simply trying to cover his tracks or if there was some truth to what he said. "Tell me more."

"After that s-she killed five of them," he stuttered but attempted to cover it. I barely contained the eye roll.

"You said she killed sixteen," Victor replied. Not a question, though there was a right answer.

"The first five she killed with daggers," the Born man continued. He'd said his name when he first entered, but I didn't particularly care. The chances of him surviving longer than this meeting were non-existent.

"And the other ten?" Victor asked. He was smart for that. Wanting to know more about the woman he sought. The one he believed he could sire heirs with, no matter how foolish that dream was. There wasn't a cell in this world that could contain Selena unless she wanted to be held.

"Their heads exploded."

That sounded more like it. Her telekinesis must have grown in the time I'd been gone. She might very well be a matter manipulator by this point.

"Exploded?" Victor repeated. There was a stillness to his voice that I didn't like. An undercurrent of violence that tinged the air and seeped through that crimson thread that tied us together.

The Born nodded slowly. Stupid, pathetic fool that he was.

When he was dead it would be me that would have to quell Victor's anger, and that was a treacherously fine line I hated to dance.

"Could she do that before you transitioned, flower?" It was uncanny how sometimes he seemed to be able to read my thoughts. I might have thought it possible if I didn't know any better. Still, I answered Victor without hesitation.

At least one of us knew how to handle him.

"She had the potential to," I said. "At that point in time she hadn't yet, but if there's any truth to the rumors we've heard, I suspect she may be a matter manipulator now."

If I'd had a beating heart, perhaps it would have squeezed at how easily I gave away her secrets. If I had a beating heart, though, perhaps I would not be here. Perhaps I might not have died and been imprisoned. Trapped.

Perhaps . . . I might not hate them so.

But there was no changing what had been done or the wrongs committed. Just as there was no prison that could hold her, there was no place she could not go—and yet she'd never come for me. Not once.

"She left you here to rot," *that voice in my mind said.* "They both did." *When I'd first awoken as a Made, I had hope. I had faith. Slowly but surely Victor stripped that from me. It's amazing the way everything you once held dear falls to the side when you've been starved on and off for months. When you've killed children from the crazed hunger that pushes you to the very brink of madness.*

And in that deep dark place, there was no one.

I was completely and utterly alone.

They'd left me here, abandoned me when I needed them most . . . and for that, they were dead to me. Perhaps more so given death was not the end for some. The whisperings of that voice in my mind agreed.

"What message did she send you with?" Victor asked. The lowly Born at my feet visibly trembled. I knew then that whatever Selena said, he didn't want to repeat it because everyone knew that Victor was prone to shooting the messenger.

His lips pinched together, and that mild pause was enough.

"Lily," my master said, oh so softly. The Born jumped to his feet, backing away further, and the two guards posted at the door simply stepped in front of it.

"Please—" He begged as I came to stand behind him. The idiot had the bad sense to look at me, and not the man whose lips curled back in disgust. Oh no, he'd rather stare at the hand that would deal the blow rather than the one controlling it.

How predictable. How stupid.

I lifted a delicate hand when the words left him in a rush. "Next time one of yours steps on Shifter land with the intention to use force, I will not be this merciful. Tell your liege —"

"She thinks of that as mercy?" Victor asked, his expression thoughtful. He looked from the soon-to-be dead man to me. A

ghost of something tender crossed over him before it was gone. "The rumors have always portrayed her as quite bloodthirsty. Is it true?" he asked.

"There was a time when no one was safe from her, but Alexandra or me." There was no inflection in the words, nor emotion on my face that might give away anything. Certainly not the boiling hatred I felt inside.

"And now?" he prompted. I stared into the endless depths of silver that were not my own. He had beautiful eyes. He always had. It was that face of an angel that fooled me once, but the devil was once an angel too—or so the saying went.

"She will defend those she loves with all her might. If you sent her into a rage over a child, then she's gone soft." It was the truth as I knew it, and it would damn her.

"Was there anything more to the message?" he asked without looking to the Born Vampire.

"Tell your liege if he wishes to talk, a letter will suffice. Allowing you to return is a kindness. Tread lightly. You may have just started a war."

Silence.

"I might have started a war?" Victor asked, softly. Deceptively.

"I mean—" I never looked away, but I barely saw it when Victor pulled a dagger from his jacket and threw.

The messenger only six inches from me tilted forward. His lips parted as gray bled through his veins and his skin began to crack. He stepped back, touching a hand to his chest before dropping to his knees and collapsing on his side.

Dead. A true death.

The strike must have been a hit to his heart.

Blackened blood splattered Victor's suit, but he didn't

seem to even notice or care as he said, "Are you angry with her, flower?" He didn't elaborate, but the cruel twist of his lips said more than his words.

His question would have stilled me had I not already been frozen. Looking away was not an option now. He would see that for what it was. Telling him the truth though . . .

"I was," I told him. Surprise flicked through his gaze so fast I might have missed it had I not spent the last few months memorizing every facet and feature of his face. Victor hadn't expected the truth. "I was angry with her when I'd awoken. I expected her to come for me."

"But she never did," he said.

"She never did," I agreed.

"And now?"

"No. I'm not angry anymore," I paused, lowering my eyes to his chin. It was easier to look there than into the pits of Hell where I was going when all was said and done and the scheming and games and lies finally caught up to us. I knew what awaited me now, and I embraced it all in the name of survival—and revenge. "The longer that went on, the more I realized that she did me a favor."

"Oh?"

"In leaving me, I was forced to find my own strength and learn that I could rely on no one but myself. Her greatest strength and weakness is her love for others, but in forsaking me, I learned to know better than to love or to hope. I realized that no matter what comes, I will survive it."

I felt his unflinching gaze on me as he slowly crossed the room. His oxfords left blackened footprints in his wake as he stepped through the pool of blood without care.

Two pale fingers came up under my chin, lifting my face and forcing my gaze back up to his.

What I saw there confused me.

After all the hours and all the days I'd spent watching him, there was an intensity to his features, but it wasn't the sort he had when in a rage. No, it was something else. Something I didn't want to put a name to.

Because this time when he looked at me, I saw it for what it was.

"Would you ever lie to me, Lily?" he asked, and that red line between us pulsed. I didn't grit my teeth for fear that would give me away. He was using the bond to manipulate me. To try to force the truth.

He didn't realize the more he gave me, the stronger I grew.

He didn't know that no matter how tight he squeezed, it wasn't tight enough to force veracity from my lips.

He didn't know that in this silent game of tug-of-war, I'd already won.

"No."

My answer wasn't too quick, nor was there any hesitation, and still the edge of his jaw clenched.

"Why is that?" he asked and then continued before I could respond. "If love does not fuel you, as you say. If fear does not intimidate you, as I know, then what is it that drives you? What is it that makes you loyal to me, Lily?"

And it was then that I understood both where I'd went wrong and what I had to do. I'd straddled too close to the edge of not needing him. In giving him the slight truth to stay under suspicion, I'd inadvertently led him toward something far more ruinous.

Once again Victor placed me on that precarious knife's edge, but this time I wouldn't simply straddle it. No. There was another way. A better way that could make the price of my truths worthwhile.

I took a step closer to him, and he didn't flinch away. I knew he wouldn't, not as I finally gave him what he wanted to hear more than anything. "The line between salvation and damnation is thinner than many like to think. You pushed me to desperation, and yet you taught me what it means to survive. Love and fear have no bearing because you taught me to think past those emotions. They were without use."

The more I spoke the more the ice in his expression thawed. Not an ounce of intensity was lost, but his rapt attention was shifting. Changing. "You forced me to walk that line and learn that I could. You made me into what I am. Anastasia signed my death, but you gave me a life again. I'm loyal to you because you have earned it, not just because you're my master."

The wind howled, sending flurries of snow about through the tiny window. The dead of winter had come, and the fief was at its fullest, but not a sound traveled through the corridors. It was utter silence as he stared at me.

The fingers under my chin disappeared as he ran a hand up my jaw and swiped his thumb under my bottom lip. A fat droplet of black blood sat swollen on the end. He paused and then lifted it to my lips.

There was a challenge in his gaze. He didn't want to say it. Victor preferred to command with silence, especially when it came to me.

It was just another game we played.

A game I couldn't lose.

My tongue darted out, sweeping over the pad of his finger to lick the drop away. Vampire's blood wasn't as bitter as one might think. While it wasn't as succulent as humans or the living, it was still a taste I'd acquired when I'd gorged myself on it after killing a guard.

A slight shudder ran through me at the memory, and Victor smiled. Misinterpretation was simply a manipulated miscommunication with the right gesture to guide it.

"Oh flower, you have no idea what you do to me." He leaned forward, his hand cupping my jaw. His lips loomed close, only a hairsbreadth away. "But you will."

Then he was striding away. The guards opened the door of his suite as he started down the corridor, not waiting for me but still expecting, nonetheless.

The blood seeping into my shoes was the least of my worries as I tried to separate what exactly was truth from lie.

The problem wasn't that I didn't know anymore.

It was that I didn't care, because in that small concession I'd found my endgame.

And with that, I turned on my heel and followed Victor out the door—the makings of a dark smile on my face.

With a single play, I'd just won this war of survival.

"Soon." *The dark voice inside whispered.* "Soon we strike."

CHAPTER 9

Cold sweat clung to my skin as I trembled from the dreadful reality I wished I could wake from. Gentle fingers brushed over my shoulder, but I didn't turn into him. I wouldn't console myself with his warmth, knowing that deep down, there might be no coming back for her. Not now.

"You saw her again, didn't you?" Ash asked. I pressed my lips together and took a deep inhale through my nose, trying to suffocate the terrible emotion lashing through my chest.

Failure. I knew it well.

Ash sat up, the sheets pooling at his waist as he leaned over and clicked on the bedside lamp. Outside the quiet night was coming to an end as the light of a dying star broke over the horizon, signaling a new day.

"I saw her," I nodded, brushing my hands over the cotton sheets before running them through my hair, fisting it and pulling tight. I didn't know whether it was

Lily's emotions or my own riding the action. Probably both.

"Do you want to talk about it?" he asked, trying not to push even though the same demons that plagued me would now be eating at him. Desperation. Depravity. Death.

I cursed the former because they made me crave the latter.

"She's changing," I told him, relinquishing my fisted grip on my hair to push the sheets aside. "For so long she wanted someone to save her, but I was too late. She had to save herself." I kicked my legs over the edge of the bed and slipped to the cool marble ground. "It twisted something in her. The things she's had to do to survive . . . I don't know if she can come back from them."

And there it was. The truth I didn't want to admit.

I'd abandoned my sister when I could have saved her and now finding her may be for nothing, because Lily didn't want to be saved.

"Being Made has changed her," he said, nodding slowly.

"Being Made, being tortured, being forced to become —" I broke off, swallowing those words down. "She's killed children, Ash. She murders with very little thought, because her only drive in life is to be free and then to get revenge against everyone."

His dark eyes saw my soul as the corners of his mouth tightened. "What happened to her isn't your fault."

Nothing. I said nothing because he was right, but also not. Anastasia brought it about, but I was the one that sent that wild shot that snapped her neck. My own grief had consumed me long enough that it was too late by the time I realized she'd survived Daizlei and was still alive, at least in some capacity. I searched for her without knowing where to look, and as the days turned into weeks followed by months . . . she'd lost hope.

I didn't blame her for that because I'd lost hope in her long before she did me. I didn't think to look for a Vampire. I didn't let myself entertain the thought because I assumed her being dead was the worst thing.

But she was turned, and I didn't realize until too late. That assumption cost her everything.

Maybe it wasn't my fault, but I was the one that pulled the trigger and then left her to face the consequences alone. That was on me.

"Selena," Ash said, his voice hard as if he'd been saying my name for some time. I blinked, and the press of his lips and heavy sigh told me he probably was. "What's happening to Lily is tragic." I paused, opening my mouth, but he barreled on. "It's more than tragic, and I am so sorry that she is dealing with this. But you—" I took a step away, and he slipped from the sheets and padded silently around the bed to stand before me. "You need to stop punishing yourself for sins you didn't commit."

"I killed her."

"You were aiming for Anastasia and missed," he grit his teeth. Warm hands wrapped around my forearms. "And you've been killing yourself since. I can't keep watching you tear yourself apart because of the actions of others. You may be a matter manipulator and the most powerful person on this planet—but you can't be everywhere, and you can't be everything." His words made sense logically, but the head didn't always think with logic. Sometimes it listened to the heart, and try as I might to be cold and uncaring and not feel so damn much—I couldn't stop blaming myself any more than the next person whose actions brought about the death of someone they loved so dearly.

"I know that," I told him. "I know I can't be everywhere and control everything—but in this one thing I wish I could. I wish that it had been me who died that day instead. I wish that Tori had never compromised our mission for her brother, but I know that in her place I would have done the same. I would pick Lily over the thousands that might die from that choice." I swallowed hard, my mouth dry and throat sore. "But she won't pick me, Ash. If this comes to a war, nothing will stop her because I'm the only one that can. But I won't do it." He pulled me to him and held me tight, holding my broken pieces together. I was thankful for his warmth when all I felt was cold and empty and numb. I was thankful for his steady presence when I didn't know what I did to deserve this kindness.

I was thankful for him.

But it didn't change that I wished it had been me.

Tonight showed me the stark clarity of truth that I hadn't wanted to face.

There was no saving Lily because she didn't want to be saved.

CHAPTER 10

I STOOD OUTSIDE THE ELEVATOR. TEN MINUTES AND THIRTY-eight seconds.

Thinking—struggling—with the need in me to press the button and step inside. One command. That's all it would take, and I could march right into Vilicky Novgorod, the Vampire capital of the world, and make my demands.

I could ask for my sister back and begin exploding heads. One for every second Lily wasn't standing before me. I was strong enough to do it. I knew I was.

I was strong enough to bring even the most powerful of beings to their knees.

But what if she said no?

What if I went, going against everything I promised I wouldn't do . . . and she didn't come back with me?

I wasn't sure if I could face it, because if I went—if she said no—there was a line in the sand between us.

One that would divide us forever. One that would be the death of one sister so that the other may rise.

I couldn't kill her. For all she'd done, for all she would do, she was one of the only people I would not be the end of. Not again.

My hands clenched into fists, knuckles white and nails biting into my palm as my arms shook slightly from tensing so hard.

"Selena?" a voice behind me asked. I blinked. I'd been so absorbed in my own thoughts I hadn't sensed the woman approaching behind me.

"Amber," I said without turning. My fingers uncurled as I stiffly stepped toward the elevator.

"I was looking for you. Aaron said you'd already headed out for your morning run, but Jo hadn't seen you . . ." The pause in her voice said it all. I could practically feel her gaze on my back, drilling holes through me.

"I was just on my way out," I said, taking too long to make it believable.

"Uh huh . . ." she drawled, stepping up to my side. She reached past me to click the button for the elevator. "Well, that'll have to wait for the moment," she said. The doors dinged before sliding open.

"Why is that?" I asked, stepping inside and turning to face her. Amber followed my suit, her gold eyes narrowing in suspicion.

"You've been summoned."

I froze, tilting my chin to stare at her. She lifted both eyebrows as I asked, "By whom?"

"The Shifter Alpha."

My lips parted as I inhaled sharply. Ash's father summoned me. His father never summoned anyone, not unless it was critical. He preferred to let the local leaders of each pack handle their issues in house, so to speak, and if they needed more, they were to defer to Ash. For him to summon me. . . this couldn't be good.

"Why?" I asked her, narrowing my eyes.

She shrugged. "Hell if I know."

"Does Ash know?"

Her lips pressed together. "No."

"No?" One of my eyebrows shot up. "Why not?"

Amber sighed. "I don't know, Selena. All I know is my mother gave me a direct order handed down to her by the Alpha, and when the Alpha gives an order, you don't refuse. Please don't make this difficult."

The doors dinged and slid open again.

We were on the lowest level.

Wood paneling and the scent of pine enveloped us as she stepped out first and began striding down the hall. I cursed under my breath and then followed after her.

"Doesn't this seem a little odd that after months of us being here, he wants to suddenly meet with me now? Alone?" I asked, lowering my voice so that it wouldn't carry down the empty hallways.

"I don't know, Selena," she said, sounding unconvinced that this was a problem in any way. She kept walking, her copper ringlets bouncing with every step. Gone were the makeup and miniskirts she'd worn at Daizlei. Here she dressed in cargo pants and T-shirts that didn't quite touch her navel. "My uncle's an odd guy. Not all there if you ask me, but nobody does."

"You're telling me," I muttered. The scent of orange and freesia tickled my senses as we turned a corner. The cracked double doors at the end of the hall gave me pause as my heart sped up and we loomed near.

I rested my hand on the door when Amber paused.

"About the elevator," she started, looking to the ceiling.

"It's nothing—"

"No. It's not," she replied, and I stilled. "I see the way you look at it sometimes. I know what you're thinking, and Selena," —she caught herself, blowing out a harsh breath— "when you meet the Alpha you'll understand. He lost Katherina almost fourteen years ago."

"When Keyla was born," I said softly. She nodded.

"She was the love of his life. His other half. His *signasti*." I swallowed hard. "If you go into that elevator searching for her and you don't come back out, that's what you're sentencing him to because he will *never* come back from it."

I had to look away from the weight of her gaze. Guilt ate at me, but not the kind she thought. I didn't feel terrible for considering it. I felt awful for once again choosing to stay because I was too scared of what I'd find on the other side.

"I understand."

"Good." She nodded and started back down the hall, then paused. "Selena?"

"What?" I asked, fingers tightening around the handle.

"Good luck," she said softly. Her words carried down the hall to my ears as did her footsteps leaving.

I turned the handle, and I wish I could say I was surprised at the man who sat in an oversized armchair, sipping tea from a cup. Warm brown eyes looked up into mine. His dark brown hair was longer than last time. It was pulled back with an elastic hair tie. A fine sheen of perspiration coated his skin, making his taut cheekbones appear sharper than they were.

Still he smiled, and it was kind.

"Hello, Selena," he said. I sighed, stepping inside the library. The door clicked shut behind me.

"Hello, Nate."

I stared at him, seeing the feeble Shifter in a different light than when we'd first met.

Around the reservation talk of the Alpha was common. Who he was, what he did, the things he said, but it was all hearsay. Shifters talked of him like he was some omnipotent being. All encompassing. All powerful. All knowing . . .

But he was none of those things.

The Alpha that they talked of was only a shadow of a man, and it didn't take long for me to understand Amber's words because I'd met him once. A night not so long ago where I stood beneath this very stained-glass window and watched the twirling shapes drift in and out in a never-ending series of color.

Nate had been here too, that night, under the guise of a mere man. Not a legend.

"I see you remember me," he said. That was a raspy draw of breath compared to what it had been not a month ago.

"You lied to me," I told him without thinking. Not that it would have stopped me. He smiled weakly, setting the teacup aside. There was a slight tremor to his hands.

I knew then that something wasn't quite right.

"You were not ready to meet me," he answered. Despite the fragile state of him there was a glimmer in his eye. A speck of hope that outshone whatever was slowly killing him.

"I did meet you."

"But not as me," he replied. I took a deep breath and let it go. My feet didn't make a sound as I started to circle around the library, not looking so much at the books, but at the ceiling. It was as fascinating as the first time I saw it.

"You called me here to meet you as the Shifter Alpha, but you didn't send or tell Ash. Is there a reason for that?" I asked slowly, my fingers trailing along the wooden shelves and cloth-bound spines of texts that hadn't seen the light of day in over fourteen years.

"He lets you call him that?" Nate asked, ignoring my question entirely. I allowed it, but it wasn't like I had much of a choice either. Of all the ways I expected to meet Ash's father, this wasn't it.

"He does," I said. "He prefers it."

Nate nodded and steepled his bony fingers together, resting his elbows on the arms of the chair.

"I don't think you realize how much you've healed my family in the short time you've been in their lives," he started. I didn't know what to say to that, so I chose silence. "You and my son have come a long way from the comatose girl he brought home."

"You knew about that?" I asked, not looking away as the window shifted from a cerulean blue to merlot. The color of blood.

A weak chuckle escaped him that turned into a cough before cutting off abruptly. Nate sighed before saying, "I'm weak, not blind. I know that you have been training with Keyla ever since you woke. I know that you pulled together the group of exceptionally young but powerful people that are residing in this mansion right now. I know you framed Anastasia Fortescue and that action inevitably led to her death." He didn't pause, even as I opened my mouth to speak. "Just as I know that my daughter was attacked, likely because of it—and that you chose to defend her despite the odds of you both dying."

I started to shake my head. To refute the claim, but he lifted a hand and motioned to the chair beside him across the tiny circular table. Swallowing hard, I walked on leaden feet toward it.

"What you did took courage, and it likely saved my daughter's life. I wanted to thank you for that." He dipped his head. The brown eyes that met mine were soft.

"You don't need to thank me. I would never let anything harm her." It was the God's honest truth.

"I know." He paused and then glanced up to the window above. The colors shifted from mercury to a royal purple so deep that it appeared to be night. "But that's not the only reason I brought you here."

I leaned forward, resting my elbows on my knees. My hands clasped together as I tilted my chin sideways so that I could see around the short curtain of hair. "Then what is?" I asked.

"Who are you?" he replied, the question coming out of virtually thin air.

"I don't understand," I said slowly.

"You are not the girl that arrived, nor are you the one that awoke, or even the one I spoke to last time. So . . . who are you?" he asked. There was something else in his expression this time. Not just that glimmer of hope, but a spark of something that was searching for an answer.

I took a deep breath, considering my words carefully.

He was right that I was none of those people before.

But there had to be a reason he was asking this.

It couldn't just be pure coincidence. I didn't believe in coincidences. Fate might be fickle, but it wasn't accidental.

"I am . . ." My teeth bit the inside of my cheek, but there was only one answer I could give. "Selena Fortescue."

Nate smiled, but it was a sad thing.

"You've chosen to take up your father's mantle." He didn't phrase it like a question, so I didn't answer it. Instead, I asked a question of my own.

"How do you know it was my father's mantle and not my mother's?"

The Alpha lowered his steepled hands and reached for the steaming cup of tea. It smelled like jasmine and orange, with maybe a hint of honey. "Your mother wasn't a Fortescue. Your father was. I know because I was his friend a long time ago . . . before life and responsibilities caught up to us." His eyes took on a misty look, as if he were seeing things that weren't there. "We went to school together, much like you and Asher."

Questions came to mind, unbidden and without permission. I wanted to ask what he was like, if my implanted memories did him any justice, or were they simply a fabrication of magic and childish hopes? But something stopped me because whatever he may have been like, I wasn't ready to know. I may never be ready to know. The mind was a fragile thing, and mine had been shaken by the games my family liked to play.

"Why are you asking if I took up his mantle?" I said instead. It was the safer question. The one I needed to ask. Judging by the pitying look that crossed Nate's face, my choice didn't surprise him. It seemed the old Shifter did know much of what went down in his home. But he didn't know everything.

No one did.

Nate took a sip of his tea, his lips pursing slightly as he swallowed with a slight hum. "Actions are what others use to define you. Your choices are what you use to define yourself. But your reasons—those make you who you are." I blinked, waiting to see the point. "Before I tell you, answer me this. Why did you take on the name of the very people that hunted you?"

"I believe there's a war coming. The Vampires in the woods weren't an accident."

"That doesn't answer why," he pointed out kindly. Prompting me.

I bit my cheek and tasted blood.

"I . . . I'm tired of the fighting. I'm tired of the running. I'm tired of looking over my shoulder anytime I leave these walls—but I can only imagine what it would be like to be someone who couldn't defend themselves against the Vampires. Supernaturals everywhere are dying. Black markets are open season for hunting, and throughout it all, the Fortescues did nothing. Anastasia was working with the Vampires for Christ's sake. My own sister was taken and"—I broke off, breathing hard—"I would do anything to get her back and end this. Anything. Even taking the name I hate more than anyone in the world."

By the end of my rambling, Nate was watching me far more intently. No longer pretending this was an idle chat between old friends or the father of one's significant other.

"You took up the name to change the world. To give them either someone to fear or someone to respect. Someone they could rally around," he said. I nodded slowly. "But so far you've done nothing but collapse a building, cause an earthquake, and destroy the Las Vegas black market."

"I wasn't at fault for what happened at Daizlei," I replied a bit terser than needed. He nodded grimly.

"No, but it was a Fortescue, nonetheless. I look at you, and I see hope. I see a person who is willing to do bad things for the right reasons—and that makes all the difference."

"All the difference for what?" I narrowed my eyes.

"You need allies, Selena. People who are willing to fight with you. Currently you have the name of a family that has done terrible things to Supernaturals and other paranormals alike. Some might get behind you out of fear, but if you want to stand a chance in winning this war before it really starts—you need whole factions of paranormals to back you. People that see you as the weapon and the wielder." I leaned back in my chair, brushing my hair aside to turn and stare at him fully. "I couldn't publicly support you as Selena Foster, my son's unbonded mate. I can support you as Selena Fortescue, the next co-Alpha, and a current member of Council—but without other allies it would be problematic." He looked away for a moment, letting out a cough.

"Shifters alone can't rise against the Vampires and expect to win," I surmised. "And without a guaranteed win, this would turn into an all-out war that would span into the human world."

He nodded. "You need backers. Enough so that the Vampires are willing to end this before it becomes a true war—one we might not be able to win."

It was smart, what he suggested. Enough groups of the paranormal community uniting as one front may just be enough to push them back into submission. Maybe.

"As you've so nicely pointed out, I don't have the greatest PR and the Supernatural Council is splintered. So tell me how exactly you think I'm going to get other factions on board with this?" I raised an eyebrow as he blew out a breath, readjusting in his seat.

"You go to them and you make friends. As the representative for the Fortescues, you still have a certain amount of sway. You're going to need that, because to stand a chance we have to do something that hasn't been done in a thousand years." A shiver went through me and the skin along my spine prickled. "We have to unite against a force greater than ourselves."

"And if I can't keep those promises?" I asked him.

A heavy pause stretched between us as I started to understand.

"Sometimes people do bad things for good reasons," he replied. I narrowed my eyes, curling one hand into a fist to rest my chin on.

"If that's the case, why aren't you out there doing this?" I asked him, and he gave me a deadpanned look.

"Look at me." He motioned to himself. "No one in their right mind would agree to go to war when this is what the Shifter Alpha looks like. Not even my own people would be on board if they realized how far I've deteriorated . . ." he trailed off, panting softly from the tension. "You're the strongest Supernatural that's ever been. Despite your name, that will count for more in this world. The other leaders will see you and think long and hard before turning away your alliance—because while you haven't proven to be the greatest friend, they do not want you as their enemy."

"So you want me to coerce them?"

"I want you to do everything possible to bring people to our side and try to prevent this from escalating further," he answered—non-answer that it was. I scowled.

"And if it doesn't work?" I asked. "If they don't back down and it does become a full-scale war?"

His lips pressed together and for the first time I saw some semblance of Ash in those features—in the strong jaw as it clenched—in the eyes that had a way of making it seem like they saw straight to your soul. In his youth, the Shifter Alpha would have been a sight to behold. He would have been Ash.

"If it comes to that, you're capable of doing bad things for the right reasons," he repeated. I blinked.

"Would you actually send the Shifters?" I asked him, needing to hear the answer.

"If it came to that, I wouldn't have a choice. Why do you think I'm bringing you here now?" When I didn't answer immediately, he continued. "My own home was attacked. My daughter almost taken. I wouldn't have been able to stop it if she had been—but you did. Some of my people fear you for what you are. Some respect you for what you've done. If war comes they won't fear or respect an Alpha that can't lead them into battle."

My heart thudded twice, a damning sound.

"If you can't . . ." I started.

"Then Asher will have to," he answered. "It's his duty as the Heir."

And there it was.

The real reason I was summoned alone.

If this escalates, then Ash will lead the Shifters because his father couldn't.

"You fear he wouldn't come home," I said. It wasn't an accusation, but he still answered.

"He's young, and he's cocky. While he may have more power than most of his kind, he's my son, and the last place I want to see him is in a coffin." The grim reality of his confession struck a chord. The night Anastasia slit his throat was still fresh in my mind, and it took all I had not to gag from the bile climbing up my throat.

I understood his fear. I understood it too well.

"There's no way either of us could stop him if it came to that. Not that I would try." He stared at me, and I continued. "He has never tried to stop me from being who I am. He wouldn't change me or ask me to be any different—and I wouldn't ask that of him. I understand your fear. I get it . . ." I paused. Both my hands fell to my lap. I looked at my fingers as they locked together. At the edges of my palms where the twin pentagrams sat. A reminder of what I'd done and who I was. "But if it comes to that, the decision will be his to make."

It was several moments before either of us spoke, both lost in our thoughts. Then he said, "You remind me so much of Katherina that it's painful. My son is lucky to have you." I nodded because I wasn't sure how people usually responded to that. Thank you didn't feel right, but neither did silence.

"I'm lucky to have him."

The Alpha nodded, the sallowness of his cheeks clearer when he moved. He leaned forward to grasp the cup and take another sip of tea. I tried to hide my frown at the not-so-subtle tremors in his hands, but those knowing eyes slid sideways as he said, "Go ahead. Ask."

I sighed. "Shifters aren't susceptible to illness. No paranormals are."

"Not a question, but yes."

"Why do you look like you're on death's door?" I asked him. He smiled up at the stained glass window.

"Because I am."

The truth of that statement shook me to my core. "Ash hasn't said anything to me." I paused, dread clotting in my stomach.

"He doesn't know."

My eyes slid shut, and I leaned forward, running a

hand down my face. When I opened my eyes again, he was back to watching me. "I'm going to take a guess that Keyla doesn't either."

"That would be correct."

God damn him.

"How are you even able to keep this from them?" I asked, pressing my lips together.

He simply smiled. "Being the Alpha has its benefits. Much like my son, I can choose to appear any way I desire."

I blinked, and his entire appearance changed. The hair that had been thin and lank, grew long and thick and shiny. His cheekbones filled and his jaw, while still sharp—looked healthy. His physique filled, and with it so did my dread.

He looked like Ash.

But it was all a lie.

Another blink and the illusion was gone.

"Why would you tell me this?" I asked.

The teacup rattled as he tried to place it back on the saucer. His movements were growing weaker by the moment. Using his power had clearly taken its toll.

"The same reason I brought you here." When I didn't respond and only gave him a half-attempted glare, he let out a chuckle. "So that you understand. Time is of the essence and Katherina whispers to me from the veil. I stay because he's not ready—and because I don't want to pass on a people at war. I saw the signs of what Ivan the Cruel was up to for years and chose to do nothing. The kidnappings. Paranormals being turned against their will. I was so deep in my grief and anger toward the

Supernatural community that I, and many others, let it happen. My complacence is unforgivable. As is the other leaders, but it doesn't change the fact that if we don't do something very soon—we won't have a choice. Go to the Witches. Go the Fae. If you manage to convince them, others will come forward, and we may be able to stop this before it starts."

I stared for a moment, taking in his words. Thinking on what he said. When I went to stand, my mind was made up. I walked to the door, pausing with my fingers on the handle.

"I'll do what I can, but coming from someone who lost both parents at a young age, you should talk to him. To both of them, before it's too late." I didn't wait to hear what his reply might be. The broken cough and scent of blood that followed me out said enough.

CHAPTER 11

Frozen blades of grass crunched beneath my boots. I clenched my hands inside my pockets as I approached the edge of a pit where Alexandra sparred with Ash on one side and Johanna on the other. Gathered together, Amber and Tori stood with Alec and Oliver, watching as the flaming whip snaked through the air with deadly accuracy, keeping them both at bay.

Her form was improving. The increased speed made up for the subpar footwork, and what she couldn't dodge with that she met head on with a strength that could take any Shifter in this yard.

I walked around the edge of the pit, coming to stand by Blair. She stood alone in the elements; her light blonde braid tucked into the hood of her jacket. Her hands were stuffed in her pockets and her expression bleak as she watched the fight taking place below her.

She was good, I'd give her that.

No one, not even Alexandra, would have noticed the way her gaze occasionally darted to the side. A flash of alarm and brutal gust of wind later and she straightened out.

Being out here was hard for her. Then again, everything was these days.

"Cousin," she said by way of greeting without looking up.

"How are you doing?" I asked, keeping my voice low.

"I've seen better days," she replied. It was the same thing she'd said every day for the past week. I let it slide. "How are you?"

"I've seen worse," I answered grimly. The corners of her lips turned upward at that. Just slightly, but they did.

Below us the fight grew fevered. Alexandra spun on her heel, the whip twirling like a streamer around her in a blaze of fire. Johanna, who had been diving in for a cheap shot, froze as Alexandra was consumed in a pillar of flame.

Both her and Ash took a step back, and the hands that reached for them were as red as the flame they came from.

"You never went running today," Blair said. Her eyes were still on the fight, much as everyone else. While they were watching the light show below, they wouldn't be thinking to listen in on what I had to say.

"No," I nodded. "I didn't."

"You told Aaron you were going running. Amber went looking for you and then showed up here shortly after without a word." Her analysis of it was cut and dry.

"I was summoned," I answered. Her eyebrows drew together slightly. Anyone looking at that moment would mistake it for her being worried about how carried away the fight was getting. Half of Alexandra's sleeves had burned away, and those tendrils of flame were still climbing when she grabbed at their clothing with hands hotter than an iron plucked from the fire.

"Summoned?" Blair breathed.

"By the Alpha," I answered in a hush just as Alexandra caught Ash. Her hands seemed to burn straight through his jacket and shirt in seconds flat. I flinched, waiting for the yelp of pain. Holding my breath for the second that she overstepped and branded his skin with her palms.

But it never came.

The whole training yard stilled as she slowly looked up, one eye black and one eye brown. Her copper-colored brows drew together in surprise.

His hands grabbed her wrists despite the fact they were on fire.

Ash smiled and then pivoted, tossing her into the side of the pit—a three-foot thick wall of concrete.

I cringed. That was going to leave a mark.

"She hesitated," I said.

"She overplayed her hand," Blair replied. I lifted both my eyebrows, and when I glanced back at her she wasn't watching the ring at all. Her sharp gray eyes were locked on my face. "Why did the Alpha summon you?"

"We had a little talk," I replied, glancing back to the pit as Alexandra pulled herself from the smashed-in concrete. "I know what needs to happen next." Shifters hollered and laughed. I narrowed my eyes.

"Oh?" she asked, tilting her chin. "Care to share with

the class?" I ignored the sarcastic edge to her tone as both of Alexandra's eyes bled black.

Shit.

"We're going to be taking a field trip," I told her.

"We?" she asked, and I could tell that she was pointedly looking at me now. Purposely avoiding what was happening down below. It must be setting her demon off. Well, that makes three of us, then.

"Yes. We," I answered, taking a step closer to the ledge. I tilted my head. Watching. Waiting as her demon peered out at them.

I reached in, using only my mind and plucked both Ash and Jo from the pit. One moment they stood there, looking uneasily between the two of them, and the next they were sailing over the rim as I stepped over the ledge, landing on the frozen sheet of mud.

It cracked under my feet, and Alexandra slowly turned her head in my direction as the Shifters took notice. My demon itched to come forward, and I let her.

"Careful, sister," I called.

Her demon blinked. She held out one hand and with a snap the flames that wisped off her skin turned black. Hellfire.

"He should have burned," she hissed. "But he threw me instead and they *dare* to mock me." Flames sprung from the frozen earth, melting the sheet of ice while simultaneously evaporating it and burning the ground itself. I stepped forward, keeping both hands at my sides.

"They aren't mocking you," I said. While they

laughed, I didn't think their true intention was to insult her. Not that she would realize it. "Were you guys?" I called over my shoulder.

A few grumbled *noes* were the answer.

"They're disingenuous," she replied. Her hand rose, and with it the flames did too.

Her eyes thinned into slits.

Everyone held their breath—and then a thud landed beside me.

I looked over at the five-foot nothing blonde that stood with her back straight.

"Alex," Tori said softly. It appeared she'd learned enough over these last months to know not to shout. "They didn't mean anythin' by it."

My lips parted as I opened my mouth to ask her what the hell she was doing.

"Don't," Ash's voice whispered through my mind. *"Let her talk."*

"They see how you control the flames, and that makes them scared," she said. Alexandra blinked, eyeing Tori with doubt. But the girl continued, for better or worse. "It makes them feel powerful if their Heir can stand up to a demon. It gives them hope."

Both my eyebrows reached for my hairline at that. Alexandra narrowed her gaze. Tori took a step forward, though, and those flames that danced perilously close twisted away from her.

"Don't," Alexandra said. Emotion colored her tone now as her demon started to lose sway. "I don't want to hurt you."

The wind funneled over the pit, sending Tori's shoulder-length hair back behind her. The ends were singed, but not burning. I wasn't sure if she noticed or not, but I did nothing to stop her as she took another step forward and the flame retreated further.

"You won't hurt me."

Alexandra shuddered. "You don't know that."

Tori smiled, taking another step, then another. "But I do."

She stood directly in front of my sister. The blonde ends of her hair smoking. Tori lifted a tan hand over my sister's. *I'll be damned.* Alexandra put the fire out. All of it.

Every flicker of black flame disappeared from sight as Tori twined their fingers together. Tears dotted the corners of her eyes as Alexandra exhaled sharply.

"I knew you could do it," Tori whispered, leaning forward.

Alexandra stuttered, at a loss for words the first time in her life as Tori's face loomed only a hairsbreadth from hers. Her eyes skated over the shorter woman's features, and I could see the choice weighing on her.

She looked to me for a brief second, as if I had some words I could give her. Like I could possibly tell her what to do. All I could offer was a slight smile and a nod of encouragement. She bit her lip—then she kissed her.

Both hands came up to cup Tori's cheeks. Tori let out a gasp and pulled back a fraction to simply stare.

Then the biggest smile I'd ever seen bloomed on both their faces as she kissed her back. The Shifters broke out in cheers, the tension from only minutes ago forgotten. That was the way with the paranormal world, though.

We could fight one minute and be kissing the next.

I shook my head, sensing that the danger had passed as I leapt out of the pit. Ash and Johanna stood off to the side by Blair.

His shirt had been torn. Holes burned into the chest where her flaming hands had touched. The outline of a handprint had gone straight through the fabric, but his skin was unmarred.

"Signasti," my demon whispered through my mind. Rarely did she separate our voices, but for this she did.

"How long have you known you're fireproof?" I asked him.

He smirked back. "About ten minutes."

I shook my head, fighting a grin.

Blair's cool gaze caught the corner of my eye, and I knew our conversation wasn't done. Tonight I would have tell them about the summons and the plan.

But today, for this moment, I was going to enjoy being alive.

However long that might be.

CHAPTER 12

I CLASPED MY HANDS TOGETHER, RUBBING THEM TO MAKE friction as I leaned forward, resting my elbows on my knees. We sat in the same suite we'd taken up when Anastasia got away and Lucas was brought back. Paper plates of half-eaten food and aluminum cans of orange Fanta lay scattered about as we all settled in to talk about what the Alpha had told me.

"He thinks the Witches and the Fae could get behind you and stop this from becoming a war?" Alec asked, prodding the fireplace with a poker. Blair stood off to the corner, stoically not watching him—or any of us—as she stared out the fogging glass into the field below.

"He does," I said and nodded.

"It's a smart plan," Johanna said, taking a swig from her soda. "They've both been oppressed by Supernaturals and preyed on by Vampires. If I were a betting woman—I'd wager the one thing they hate more than your kind are the bloodsuckers." She ran a hand over her braid.

"The Witches will not be inclined to trust us," Oliver said.

"No," Johnna agreed. "But if there's anyone that could convince them to come out of hiding, it's her. She holds the soul of the Mother, and for that, they would be willing to do a great deal." She swished the can, tipping its contents back. I licked my half-frozen lips and reached for the glass of water on the end table.

"And what of the Fae?" I asked, twirling the glass thoughtfully.

"They're going to be the harder won alliance," Amber answered from the other side of Ash where she sat with her feet sprawled over his lap, busy finishing off an entire fried chicken. "Cade's mom is full Fae and one of the three still reigning queens. His father—her husband—was a Shifter that was murdered by the Supernatural Council as punishment for conspiring against them." She frowned down at the chicken as if not feeling it anymore, set it aside, and wiped her hands clean.

"How?" I asked.

"Beheading."

I grimaced. That was unfortunate.

"So we're better starting with the Witches," I surmised. Amber nodded, her curly copper hair falling forward to obscure some of her face as she drew her legs up to her chest. She leaned forward and wrapped her hands around them, resting her chin on her knees.

"The Fae will be more likely to join if we already have the Witches loyalty," Ash said. "They tend to choose the side they think will win the war. It bit them in the ass a few times when they chose too early, but with the

Witches, the Shifters, and a decent portion of the Supernatural population we would be almost unstoppable."

Almost.

I didn't say it, but my brain snagged on that word. Twisting and turning everything over in my head.

"And if the Witches don't join?" Scarlett asked, her ice-blue eyes settling on him expectantly. Ash returned the stare without shying away.

"Then we hope that the Fae find us to be the winning side regardless," he responded. Her nose scrunched together like she found that answer distasteful. Scarlett leaned forward.

"And if they don't?" she asked.

His jaw tightened as his lips pressed together, but Ash didn't have an answer.

"Cade may be able to convince his mom," Amber started slowly, and Scarlett shook her head.

"That's not a plan," she hissed.

"Scarlett—" Liam started, putting his hand on her knee and trying to get her attention. It wasn't easy to do when he had to reach around his other arm that was still in a cast.

"No," she snapped. "Convincing them could take weeks—months—and that's time we might not have. What if they say no? What do we do then?" she asked, her voice rising an octave. No one had an answer. "Well?" She turned to look from one side of the room to the other, stopping on me. "What did the Alpha say he'd do then?"

"We'll cross that bridge when we come to it," I answered without flinching. She narrowed her eyes.

"You sound just like her. Making up bullshit excuses already," she said.

"Scar—" Johanna started to reprimand.

"No!" she yelled. "Don't you 'Scar' me, Johanna. This all started when we tried to break out of the Fortescue mansion, and you lost the balls to kill the bitch when you had the chance."

I blinked as Oliver turned a withering glare in her direction. "That's enough, Scarlett," he said. "We knew the risks and went ahead despite that. This isn't on her."

"Oh?" the Graeme heir said. "It's not?" She tilted her head, and that blonde curtain swept forward over her shoulder as she glared back. "If we hadn't done that, we wouldn't have gotten caught and sentenced to that school. Sebastian wouldn't be missing, and—"

"I'm sorry your brother is missing," Jo said suddenly. "I am sorry for hesitating as I did, and I will regret it for as long as I live."

"Regret doesn't bring him back," Scarlett replied.

"And your bitching doesn't solve anything," Blair said bluntly, finally drawing attention to herself. "We've all lost things. Some of us more than others, but holding it over each other's heads won't do us any good." She turned a fraction, leveling Scarlett with an apathetic stare. "So let's get back to the topic at hand, shall we?"

"I've yet to hear what the plan is if this doesn't work," she said stiffly, settling back in the loveseat but angling away from Liam. He sighed and looked to the ceiling, readjusting his cast as he settled back beside her, resting his hand on her knee and gently squeezing.

Scarlett didn't budge an inch.

I downed the glass of water and put it back on the wooden side table with a loud clank. Getting to my feet, I stood to face the fireplace with my back to the rest of them.

The warmth of it would never be enough to reach the chill inside me, though I tried. Standing only a foot away with my pale fingers curling and uncurling in the flames, I sighed softly.

Then I spoke.

"If all else fails, there is us." Silence was only so absolute when the beating of hearts and rush of oxygen was a sound unto itself.

"You can't *honestly* think that we could take on the High Council alone," Scarlett answered.

"I can," I said, facing the fire as I planned to face this war. "I do."

My fingers clenched around a wisp of flame, trying to hold onto that warmth even as the cold settled inside me.

"That's insane," she said in a hush.

I lifted my head and stared into the mirror over the mantel. Our eyes met, hers and mine, as I answered, "Is it?"

Crazy or not, it would be the only choice.

The only solution.

If all else fails, we would be the only thing that stood between this world and the undead.

The idea should have scared me more than it did, but the truth was—I was tired. I was tired of fighting. I was tired of losing friends and family to battles that weren't mine to fight. I was tired of living on the brink of war.

So I was going to do anything and everything in my power to stop it—except one thing.

There was only one line I would not cross, but if I had to walk to the edge of it to end this—so be it.

I think Scarlett saw that in my eyes. I think she realized just how far I was willing to go, because she didn't talk after that. Not a protest came from her as plans were arranged to get in contact with the Witches. Not a word.

Johanna stood and said, "I'll make some calls."

Three days later we received an answer.

CHAPTER 13

Victor went into the Council chambers three days and three nights ago. Alone.

I stood outside those doors as Made came and went, sneering as they did so. They made comments under their breath to the effect that my master had had his fun. They told me that Victor was tired of me. That I was a toy he used and then tossed aside.

I didn't let myself consider it for even a second as I stood at the end of the hall. He'd told me to wait for him, and seventy-two hours later I hadn't taken a single step from where he left me, despite their taunting.

A snicker so soft that a lesser being might mistake it for the wind sounded behind me. I didn't react as sour breath brushed over my skin and two fanged points grazed my earlobe.

"Well, well," the voice behind me said softly. I knew it immediately. "Seems that Victor has left his pet all alone."

I kept my eyes on the double doors ahead as I ignored her. She didn't like that.

"Tell me," Nikita whispered. This time her fangs nicked the skin and the sickly-sweet scent of my blood filled the hallway. "Did he drink from you before he had his fill? Or did he simply take his pleasure between your thighs before he grew tired?" The way she asked the question had me tilting my head.

"Is that what he did to you?" I asked her softly, knowing my voice wouldn't carry beyond those doors. "Did he use you as his blood whore before finding you without use?"

I'd never been brash in life. Forwardness was rarely rewarded when you were the weaker of the two parties. I let Selena and Alexandra do that, because they could back up the bark with the bite.

Now it seemed I could too . . . and yet it wasn't brashness that I desired, but the reaction.

Brashness would earn me a one-way ticket back to the dungeons, but patience paired with the right choice words . . . that would get me something far greater.

The darkness in my veins quivered with anticipation as that ancient voice stroked my mind into a calm that not even killing could break.

I felt her freeze. Funny how even those who never needed to breathe pick up the same habits as the living. It was a weakness. One that I exploited regularly given that Victor expected his pet flower to have the same tells as the monsters that surrounded me.

"You forget your tongue," Nikita replied, not answering me directly. It was answer enough. "Victor's protection or not, you'll be punished for that." Her nails trailed along my collarbone, and I knew she couldn't help herself. Not in this.

That was alright. I preferred the monsters without

restraint.

It made it all the easier to poke and prod just right—and the explanation took care of itself.

"Punished?" I asked, letting out a cold laugh so soft that I could have sworn she shivered. "I'm not sure you're strong enough to back up that statement given you've already been stripped of your position on the Council from the last time you thought to defy my master." I let the words drip from my lips like poison, and she ate them up like an apple from my palm.

Nails pierced the skin of my shoulder as a hand clamped down around the bone. A crack echoed down the hall, and everyone stilled.

Everyone but me.

A slight chuckle slipped from my lips even as the searing pain lit my body on fire. The physical pain of torture was nothing compared to the things my mind had already endured.

Victor ensured that.

Nikita stepped into view. Her dark hair framing her cold yet timelessly beautiful face. Monsters always did like to hide in plain sight. I was no exception, dressed in my stark white blouse and pale blue capris. A single drop of black blood landed on my cream-colored ballerina flats as Nikita pulled her hand back.

I knew what she was going to do before she did it, and still I didn't stop her as she slapped me.

For the second time in my life, my neck cracked.

The sound was an eerie thing, like an echo from a memory that I didn't want to remember. I lifted my pale hands, and they didn't shake, not for a fraction of a second as I twisted my head back around without faltering.

Nikita blinked, and a certain malice entered her gaze. She pulled back to strike me in the chest—her pointed nails tearing through flesh and muscle and bone. My body titled, but I kept my feet planted as she punched a hole straight through my sternum—and wrapped her cold fingers around my heart—useless as it was.

My lips parted, but I didn't breathe. Not a single word left me as the agony lit every nerve ending in my skin aflame. The tearing was sharp and brutal, but it was the ache as my skin tried to heal itself, only to feel her hand still lodged in my chest cavity that was a true pain.

The points of her nails grazed my heart as she toyed with pulling it from my chest.

And then a handle turned.

Seventy-two hours. That's how long I stood in the same spot when a clock chimed at the break of a new dawn and the double doors at the end of the hall swung open.

Just on time.

"What is the meaning of . . ." His voice trailed off, and I felt that cord that tied us together pulse once with rage. Nikita blinked, pulled from her bloodlust to realize her error.

Foolish, stupid woman.

Her face turned stricken as she tried to hastily pull away from me. Her arm shook as she tried to dislodge her hand from my chest cavity without making the damage worse.

The pain had blown through those shields of apathy I kept wound around myself as I smiled again. A dry rasp scratched at the back of my throat, making me cough, and black droplets splattered her face as it turned into a wicked laugh.

A gush of liquid ran down my stomach and pants, saturating my clothes as she finally managed to pull herself free.

I didn't stagger, though my vision blurred.

I didn't stumble even as she started to back away, leaving me to hold myself up.

"Lily," Victor said. My name was a plea on his lips, and it was the tone in his voice that pulled me from the edge of my own crazed mania brought on by the high of feeling something—anything—outside the numbness and rage.

I looked from her panicked expression to that of Victor's and despite the pain—despite the misery—I saw the world so clear in that moment. I saw the absolute terror in his expression as he watched me bleed out.

I wouldn't die—so long as I had my heart—but that didn't matter.

The game had changed because Victor now cared.

But he didn't realize it. He didn't see my actions for what they were.

No, as he crossed the marbled hallway with silent steps and came to a stop before me with equal parts murder and concern in his eyes—Victor didn't know that he'd played right into my hand.

They all had.

"Flower," he murmured, his wild eyes taking stock as he looked me up and down. An arm wrapped around my lower back as he used the other to hold the pressure on my chest—lest I bleed out entirely. But I healed remarkably fast, even for a Vampire. "My sweet, beautiful flower," he murmured, his lips brushing over my hair. "What happened, Lily? Tell me*."*

I didn't smile this time, though I was certain it didn't escape his notice before. "You told me to wait. I waited." His eyes narrowed slightly as he looked over his shoulder.

"You don't understand, Victor," Nikita started. "The girl

needed to be shown a lesson in insulting her betters. She's grown too bold. I was simply punishing her for her words while you and the Council—"

His lips were drawn back in a snarl before she even finished. A feral, uncontrollable rage in his eyes. They didn't call him the dark prince for nothing. Nikita and the others were going to be reminded why.

"Punishing her?" he asked. She nodded rapidly, taking another step back. The other Vampires in the hall stepped away, as though she were a leper and would infect them too. "For what?"

"She accused me of being a blood whore," the Born woman answered with only a sliver of the scorn she spoke to me with.

"After you asked her if I drank from her or simply took pleasure between her thighs." His words both delighted the monster in me and pleased the ancient voice. Not only those in the hall, but the Vampires beyond turned from the stands where they stood to bear witness. "Interesting how you twist your words, not knowing I could hear them."

Nikita spluttered between denying the accusations and asking forgiveness. Victor sighed, his silver eyes settling on me.

"Lily," he said. "Nikita attacked you first. I have the right to decide what her punishment would be." I didn't so much as twitch when he paused. "However, the High Council and I have come to an agreement that you are simply too extraordinary to be contained as a simple servant Made." I blinked, keeping my gaze on his chest, even as two fingers curled around my chin and tilted it up. "Do you understand what I'm saying, flower?"

Did I understand? Not quite. Not fully.

If they didn't want me as a servant . . .

"What am I to be?" I asked him.

The smile he gave me, so full of teeth and viciousness, was also sincere. It should have chilled me when he said, "Whatever I want."

My lips parted because I understood what he was saying.

He'd done the impossible. He'd found a way to all but free me, so long as I stayed by his side. So long as I became whatever he wanted.

There was a time when that would have scared me, but that time was long gone. The darkness hummed in excitement, and I had to work to hold it at bay while he was still touching me. Nikita gasped in outrage, but Victor paid her no mind as he reached into his pocket.

My lips parted when he extended his hand and his fingers unfurled. Set in a simple silver inlay was the symbol of a House that had ruled the High Council since the dawn of time beyond any living memory.

The Romanov family crest.

I lifted my hand and touched a single pale finger to the cool metal, running it over the edges of the ruby stones that had been kept uncut but polished. A single crimson thread was strung through it to make a necklace. A gift.

Not just any gift.

"Lily Fortescue, flesh of my flesh, blood of mine—" He walked around me, not relinquishing his grip around my waist as he did so, and if I had a heart it would have hammered like the drums at a funeral procession. Signaling the end of one life, and the beginning of another. "Never have I found someone so perfect as you. So pleas-

ing." The hand around my waist was lifted as he brushed my hair aside. Fingertips grazed the skin of my neck, and I shivered.

But not in fear.

A slight purr came from Victor as the cool metal touched my throat. Not a necklace, I realized, as he tied the ribbon tight—a choker.

How very fitting.

"From henceforth you'll be known as the Mistress of the Dark Prince." Every Made and lower Born dropped to their knees before us. He leaned forward, and the scent of fresh blood and fallen snow enveloped me as his lips grazed my neck in the same place Nikita touched. "And one day, once we settle the problem of heirs—you'll be my betrothed," he whispered for my ears only. I turned my head just a fraction, and his lips trailed down my cheek, kissing the corner of my mouth.

I didn't kiss him back, but neither did I pull away.

Today I'd laid plans for Nikita's death and my rise.

Little did I know that my prince was doing the same.

I could almost love him for that if I didn't want to kill him so.

He pulled away and stepped to my side, trailing his fingers over my shoulder and down my arm to clasp my hand in his. What a pair we made; him the picture of beauty and brutality—and me, the girl dressed in blood though it was my eyes that were the color of crimson. He looked like a dream and I his devil.

But Victor was drawn to pretty and terrible things.

"If anyone other than I so much as touches her"—he turned that feral smile to the only woman standing in the hall

beside me—"she has my explicit permission to kill them however she sees fit."

The darkness twisted violently with delight. My veins darkened down my arms as I squeezed the hand he wasn't holding, trying to push it back. Victor paused, his eyes flicking downwards and then to my face.

"Tell me, flower, is it my words or my touch that excites that power lurking under your skin?" His words were not loud, nor ostentatiously proclaimed, but the intimacy implied in front of the still kneeling Vampires and open Council doors had that ancient voice in my mind so very pleased with this turn of events.

I didn't disagree as I leaned inward and tilted my chin up.

"Both."

The obsidian pupil of Victor's eyes dilated. I didn't look away. He leaned forward, his lips grazing mine as he said, "So perfect."

The seconds ticked by and then he leaned back and motioned with his other hand toward the woman standing.

"You touched what was mine knowing the rules forbade her from responding because of your status. I'll allow my mistress to decide what it is we do with you now, and any others that can't seem to keep their thoughts or hands to themselves." Nikita's face contorted in a mixture of fear and disgust.

I stepped forward and the darkness sprung the moment Victor's fingers slipped from mine. A ghost of a touch ran down my back in encouragement. He loved it when I tortured. He adored me when I killed.

He didn't know what I did, though. He didn't realize that

every offering he gave was another nail in his own coffin when the time came.

Made can't kill their masters, but I was no ordinary Made.

I reached for Nikita, and she couldn't run. Not from me. I pulled her up by her neck, writhing and crying. My power would harvest her life force.

But there was something more I wanted this time.

I plunged my hand into her chest and ripped away her unbeating heart. Her deep sapphire eyes shattered from a pain too immense to truly convey.

I couldn't help the smile as I bit into her heart.

I couldn't contain the glee as I looked over her corpse to the Council beyond.

Vengeance is a virtue, and with enough patience—everything would be mine.

I JOLTED awake from a light brush of someone's presence against my own.

My eyes opened, hands balled into fists as I prepared to fight the intruder, but it was only Ash.

He gave me a tight smile, and the gold of his eyes was telling in the way he searched my face. Our hearts hammered in unison for a single, taut moment.

Then he whispered, "It's time."

And despite the soreness in my muscles, or the dryness of my throat, or tears on my face—I pushed all memories aside and prepared myself to meet the Witches.

CHAPTER 14

Colorful swaths of fabric drifted in front of me, blending in with the red walls of a bazaar in Marrakesh. Street vendors called out in Arabic. Men and women of all walks of life pressed in around me, unsettling my demon. Neither of us were massive fans of crowds, but we made do, keeping a careful eye on my cousin while we did so.

Blair walked stiffly, weaving around the others in the street without touching anyone. Every few minutes, though, her hand would twitch, or she'd go still. It was the only tell that not all was what it seemed. Her demon was restless and fighting, and we'd yet to reach the meeting point.

"How much farther?" I asked loud enough that it would carry to the front of our party, where Xellos was leading. As our only contact to the Witches, it fell on him to deliver our message and communicate their response. They didn't trust their location with outsiders, and because of that, Xellos' work with Tam was put on hold so we could meet.

"Not long now," he called back, still pushing forward. Fingers brushed my shoulder and I glanced over. Ash slowly looked from me to Blair and nodded in her direction once. He wouldn't say it out loud because she could hear us, but he wanted to know how she was. I pressed my lips together in a look that conveyed it all. He sighed and nodded.

On either side of her, Alexandra and Johanna trailed her like a parent did a wandering child. No one said it, but everyone here was keeping a watchful eye on her. Blair's fragile control was too weak for anyone to be comfortable bringing her, but they also realized we didn't have a choice. Without me or Johanna there to stop her should she go full demon again, she was a greater threat to the Shifters than we could afford—especially when we needed their loyalty. Bringing her with us was a far from ideal situation, but in this case we didn't have another choice.

None of us were happy, but for the alliance we needed we all made do.

Still, Blair's twitching was beginning to happen more frequently, and I knew her demon wasn't far. I subtly shifted closer, sliding up beside her.

"I don't like this," she said without looking at me.

"Me neither." I brushed a sweaty lock of hair from my face, tucking it back under my head scarf. "But we need this alliance, and they won't come to us, so we have no choice but to go to them. It's not like we have many options."

"I know," she said, her eyes scanning the balconies and the vendors as she wove through the crowd without paying it much mind. Like the rest of us, her blonde hair had been tucked away from watching eyes. "But I don't like it," she continued. "We're too out in the open and after the last few times we left the residence . . ."

She let her voice trail off, but she didn't need to say more for me to get the gist and agree with her. Every time we left the residence people died. This time we didn't even have Alec to disguise us. Given that his presence did nothing but aggravate Blair's demon more, and the connection with Anastasia as her ex-right hand, everyone thought it best to leave him home with Scarlett and Liam. While his arm was on the mend, he still wasn't in any real shape to fight just yet. Then there was the matter of Lucas's record at attempted escapes, so someone had to be left in charge. Scarlett's ability to hold a grudge made her the best one for the job since Johanna and I were needed for this.

Still . . . them not being here left us all at a disadvantage.

A cloud passed overhead, giving sweet relief from the burning heat. I wiped the sweat from my brow and took a passing glance over the crowd. A prickle up the back of my neck told me to be vigilant. This was a surprise mission, but that didn't mean our enemies weren't here watching.

Wind whipped through the street and my head scarf blew back, slipping from my shoulders into the open air. It soared twenty feet high, the dark blue material twisting and twining.

Then it happened.

One moment I was staring at the floating blue fabric and the next a sense of dread curdled in my stomach. It came out of nowhere and filled me so fully.

In the past, I'd felt it and bad things followed. But now I knew what it was.

"Something is coming," Valda said softly. My demon bristled, going on the defense to protect us. I looked every which way, sensing eyes but not seeing faces.

The crowd thickened. The scent of overripe fruit filled the air, sickly and rotten. My stomach churned because I knew. Something wasn't coming.

The undead were already *here*.

I reached out and grabbed Blair's hand, my fingers tightening in an unshakable grip.

Blair took one look at my face and her eyes turned black.

"Stay with me," I commanded her demon.

"What's going on?" Tori asked loudly, attempting to weave her way through the crowd. A hush settled over the bazaar for a suspended moment in time. My heart thundered in my chest.

"They're here," Blair's demon hissed.

Up ahead of us a commotion broke out in the street, and with the shifting of the wind, all hell broke loose.

Cloaked figures dropped from the balconies into the street with an unnatural grace. With so many people around us I had no way of knowing how many were dead or alive, and if this escalated it wasn't going to matter.

With three demons in play, any one of us could level the market and ignite a war.

"Stay together!" Xellos called out. I clung to Blair and hoped that everyone else had the good sense to do the same. Her demon took one look at me, silently seething but not struggling.

"If we are attacked you do not stop me," she said, making her only demand clear.

I nodded once, and she gripped my hand in turn, her demonic strength almost equal to that of mine. I let my own demon come forward, and we ran.

The wind picked up as the screaming started.

Men and women and children ducked and scattered like roaches. There were no explosions. No gunfire. No sounds that would cause mass panic to ensue, but the bloodsucking monsters that ripped through the crowd didn't need noise to make their entrance known.

Blood ran in the streets and it was all red.

I swallowed hard, ignoring the crimson tide that soaked the compact dirt beneath my boots. The scent of copper filled the air, and my stomach turned as Lily's own thoughts describing it as sweet wine flitted through.

Was she here now? With them?

I didn't think so, but I wondered.

Panic wrapped around my chest and squeezed, making my heartbeat race. Adrenaline filled me and the air thickened with power.

"This way!" Xellos yelled as he turned down an alley with Oliver in tow. A shield surrounded them that kept any Vampires or humans at bay if they passed too close, clearing the way for the rest of us.

I shot forward to clear the gap in the crowd and

stopped just as quickly. Pain flared in my shoulder where my arm connected to the rest of me. I turned, following my hand back to Blair who stood still as could be.

I quickly looked her up and down, but she hadn't been attacked or harmed. Neither was she trying to escape my grip.

My eyes slid past her to Johanna and Alexandra who were each dispatching several Made. Tori was handling her own fight one-on-one beside them. I frowned. *Where was . . .*

My heart dropped into my stomach as a hundred yards back a swarm of persons was closing in. While I couldn't see any of their faces, I could see their backs.

"Where's Amber?" Tori yelled, stabbing the blood-sucker in the heart. "Amber? Aaron? Where are—" She turned, and even beneath the splatter of black blood on her face, her tan skin visibly paled at the horde that had closed in around Amber and Ash.

A roar filled the marketplace as sheer energy shot down the bond. The embers of rage in my chest grew out of proportion as an inferno ignited.

"Get to Xellos, Tori," I said.

"But I can teleport into—"

"No," Blair's demon said coldly, cutting her off. "There's too many."

"But-but—" Tori spluttered. "We can't *leave* them."

"No one said anything about leaving them," I answered. My fingers slipped from Blair's, and her demon took one look at me. My eyes slid from the crowd to her.

"They will die if we do not do something," the demon said.

"No one is dying today," I whispered back.

Power flooded my system as my demon came forward. The world flashed between black and white as the valve on my ability opened. I took three steps toward them and lifted my hands.

Less than a month ago, I told my sister when I lifted my hands people died.

I told her that I was destruction.

And then I hid from it.

All my life I shied away from my power because of its might. I shied away from my demon because of her savageness. I shied away from myself, becoming a husk of the girl I was meant to be.

But power does not make you evil.

It's what you choose to do with it that does.

I lifted my hands, and I let go.

Morocco trembled.

CHAPTER 15

Magic lanced through the air.

Tendrils of black and purple took form as my raw strength rose up and I did not stifle it. I didn't hide from it. I did not shy away.

I channeled it.

"Last time I gave you a message." The words came from my mouth in a cold, calloused voice. I didn't scream or shout. There was no need. "Your master didn't heed my warning then, but he will now."

There was a flare of panic that shot through the bond in my chest, but it didn't matter. My demon had already made her mind up, and I agreed.

It was time to send them a different kind of message.

I would not explode their heads in a shower of blood and bone. I would not leave bodies to find.

Victor wanted to know if I'd finally become a matter manipulator. I planned to send him an answer.

And in the blink of an eye the horde crumbled.

It started as black cracks in their skin that would not heal.

Then the fear set in. The frenzy.

They turned from Ash and Amber, but with each step toward me the cracks spread. Their skin grew hard. Brittle. Breakable.

The red of their eyes was the last thing I saw before they disintegrated. Blackened dust plumed in a cloud that drifted through the bazaar. Where they'd been standing, only the scent of sickly-sweet rot remained.

My demon took in the scene before us, and knowing the job was done—she retreated.

I held my hands out, calling the power back to me, and it came readily. It slipped beneath my skin and settled inside me, lighting me up from within. Shadows of violet and obsidian danced under my skin as I contained it once more, slowly closing the valve on my power as it drained away.

Bone-deep exhaustion overtook me, but I remained upright. It wasn't unleashing the power that caused me to break out in a cold sweat, nor was using my ability. It was confining it and bringing it to heel that sapped my strength like nothing else. I stifled a yawn as my eyelids weighed heavy on me.

The bazaar was silent as the grave I'd made it.

Dust and death surrounded me.

Became me.

And as the weight of what I'd done settled over me, it was Ash's face that held me here. He didn't look at me like a monster. He didn't stare on with pity. He kept me grounded because he understood me. Why I did it and why I would again.

Slowly he rose to his feet, Amber by his side.

Her expression was shuttered, as if she couldn't believe what she'd seen. I didn't have to look to know that the others behind me likely shared her awe . . . and her fear. They'd known for a while now that I was a matter manipulator. They'd seen the levels of devastation I could create. But they didn't know how pure or how powerful my ability truly was.

I could make something from nothing.

Or turn something into nothing.

It was a terrible power to behold, but it was a burden that I bore so that when the world was remade, I could do it. I could be whatever I needed to be—and with Ash, I wouldn't lose myself along the way.

"It is done." I whispered those words over the market, and I could have sworn that somewhere out there, a presence was watching. Not one that was of this earth, but something older, something . . . god-like. It was almost as if the board had been set for a thousand years and the final piece put into motion.

The world would change because of it.

"We need to get out of here," Alexandra said from behind me, her voice firm. "Who knows what else could be lurking . . ." I didn't disagree.

Amber shook her head, as if clearing away the image she just saw. Still, her eyes lingered on the dust at her feet. Her lips pinched together as she and Ash strode forward.

They started past me and then paused. Warm fingers grazed my cheek as Ash put a knuckle under my chin to turn my head. His lips pressed against my temple, filling me with heat. It wasn't combustible as a firework, but comforting like candlelight. One of these exploded and fizzled in seconds. The other burned through the night, steady and sure as the sun did rise. His warmth spread through my limbs and pulled me from my own disoriented state.

"You did what you had to do. Thank you."

He didn't need to say it, but his words helped me all the same. I turned away from the market and toward my friends. My family.

Blair's demon stared on, her expression unfathomable as she repeated his words to me in a cold, chilling tone.

"You did what you had to do."

And then Alexandra said it.

Johanna said it.

Tori said it.

Oliver said it.

Amber said it.

With their words, something solidified in me. The pieces that were so slowly beginning to break, reformed—harder than ever. I nodded once to them and continued forward without a single look back at the mess I'd left behind.

There were going to be consequences for this.

I was ready for them. We all were.

The market was silent apart from the sound of racing hearts and windy streets. We grouped together, closer than before as we traversed the decrepit alleyways and came to a stop before a three-story red-walled building. If you could even really call it that. The outside was covered in clay, and there were no windows or doors. Only holes that opened up to the outside, covered by swatches of fabric that had been tied together.

Xellos swept an arm out and motioned for us to enter.

It was cramped inside, but clean, relatively speaking. Bits of sand had blown past the ragtag door and window covers, but given the only thing in the room was a group of circular pillows and a bowl of rocks, it wasn't exactly an issue.

"What do we do now?" Tori asked.

"We wait," Xellos said. "Take a seat. It's going to be a hot afternoon." If I hadn't been so exhausted, I might have argued or asked why we were waiting. As it was, I bent my knees and tilted back, letting gravity drag me down. I landed in a cloud of sand and dirt, but at least the cushion was soft.

Slowly, everyone took a seat. Everyone but Blair; she stood by the door. One eye on our group, the other on the market.

"We don't know that the danger has passed," her demon said, shifting restlessly.

"No one is going to attack us again, at least not today," I said with a heavy sigh. A slight frown graced her lips, and I continued. "Not after what I just did."

It wasn't completely true. There was one person that might.

I kept that to myself.

"She's right," Johanna said. "When it is not even a

real fight, the bloodsuckers will scuttle back to their masters and report what they've seen." She flicked her long braid over her shoulder, leaning into Oliver, who was very pointedly not looking at me. "What you have done is a blessing and a curse."

"And why is that?" I asked. I'd known for years that my power was two-sided. That you could not hold such brutal strength without paying the cost of it. I wasn't sure which way she would have interpreted it, and my curiosity was piqued.

"You have shown the world what you are, and that you can handle the war that's coming." Her eyes brightened for a moment, the golden hue becoming as otherworldly as that presence I felt in the market. "But your mere existence breaks the balance. You hold the mother's presence and cling to your own neutrality, but you are not as we are. They will see that."

"Who?" I asked.

"The Witches," Johanna said.

I looked away, licking my chapped lips once. What's done is done. I couldn't afford to harbor on whether what I did was the right or wrong decision. People were going to die. *My signasti was going to die*. Someone had to make a decision, and I did.

"What's done is done," Xellos said, as if reading my thoughts. "We can't predict what the Witches will do. For now you should sleep while you still can."

Johanna's words unsettled me more than I let on as I settled back. Despite my exhaustion, sleep didn't come easy. The adrenaline rush left me drained of awareness, but the buzzing pain in my temple kept me alert.

Darkness never closed in.

The world never faded.

I blinked, and it was not the red-clay ceiling I saw.

It was blood.

And it was *everywhere.*

CHAPTER 16

I ripped his heart out and tossed it aside. Blood ran down my arm and dripped from my fingertips. Lifting a hand, I licked up the smooth surface of my skin and then smiled cruelly. Five undead bodies. Five dead Vampires.

They were all Made, and while someone might have come after me for it before—no one would even look my way now.

Victor had made me all but untouchable. Invincible. Free.

Almost.

A dark energy hummed in my veins. I was close, so close to breaking the barrier. Just a few more . . .

"Flower?" a curious, inquisitive voice asked. There were no footsteps, but I knew when he stood behind me regardless. "I sent for you in my suite ten minutes ago."

I wanted to roll my eyes at the man that commanded me like a dog on a leash. Perhaps I was, for now. That ancient essence inside of me stroked the darkness. Soothed it. Soon . . .

Without bodily tells to give me away, Victor was never smarter than any of these other fools in the fief. In many ways, his infatuation made him even more blind.

More pliant.

I turned my back on the already decaying bodies to give him my full attention. He liked that. It made him feel important. Like my entire world revolved around him. In a way, it did, just not the way he thought.

"I would give my apologies, but regardless of reason, tardiness is unacceptable," I said by force of habit. "I accept whatever punishment you wish me to have." Never mind that I'd laid this trap, knowing he would come looking. Knowing what he would find.

"Lily . . ." he whispered softly. Dark silver eyes swept over my form, checking the spots where blood soaked my clothes thoroughly. "I am not angry with you. I want to know why these Made are dead. What crimes did they commit?"

I would have smiled could I have gotten away with it. He assumed that they did something to bring out my viciousness. There were any number of things I could have said that would have caused him to dismiss their deaths and my appearance without another thought.

Any number of reasons I could give that end with me being led back to his suite and some other nameless, faceless Made left to clean up my mess.

I was so close, though . . . I just needed more blood. More power.

And I had just the way to get it.

"They attacked me." I looked down at my ripped shirt and the lacy white bra that was stained black and was on full display. A trickle of blood ran down my cleavage, what little of it I had. "It seems that some Born do not like that I am your mistress. They think it gives other Made . . . ideas."

A flash of fury crossed his features before he masked it.

Cold fingers grasped my hip, pulling me forward and covering my exposed front from anyone that might wander down the wrong hall. "They touched you," he said softly, a madness creeping into his voice.

I reached up with one bloodied hand and cupped his cheek. "I didn't let them," I said softly. "The only thing that I allowed to touch me was their blood. No one disrespects you like that."

He stared at me intently for a full minute before reaching his other hand up to grasp my wrist. He turned his cheek and kissed my palm. "So perfect . . ." he murmured. Victor's upper lip pulled back just enough that his fangs could graze my skin.

Had I a heartbeat, it might have jumped in my chest.

As it was, I simply leaned in.

To take another's blood was to dominate them in Vampire culture. He never took that from me, though, much as he might enjoy toying the line. Only a few stolen kisses. Part of me wondered why. He had no moral compass. No concept of right or wrong.

Neither of us did.

But with me he was different.

The old me would have fallen for him. She would have given him anything, especially our heart. That piece of me was dead, though; he already killed it.

I was just planning to return the act in kind.

"In all of my seven hundred and thirty-eight years, I've never met a creature so pleasing as you, flower." His tongue darted over my skin, tasting the rapidly congealing blood. His eyes slid sideways, and a cruel smile crept up his lips. "I taste your tongue on your skin. You licked their blood away, didn't you?"

Most Made would have the good sense to be embarrassed. Apologetic even. Drinking another Vampire's blood was considered taboo outside sexual interludes.

It wasn't the first time I drank a Vampire's blood. After he'd half-starved me to death I'd snapped and killed his guard. Gorging myself on it then. Much like any other kind of blood, it was a life source, even if the thing containing it was actually dead.

"It's a taste I seem to have acquired," I said softly. Boldly. My tongue darted out to clean the slight sheen of black from my teeth. The sweetness of it, bursting with flavor in my mouth.

His eyes went hungry, and I knew the look. Before he acted on it, Victor released my wrist.

"If the Born think sending their Made after you will stop me from punishing them, they are so very wrong," he said darkly. Victor released me and stepped back, extending his hand. I took it, like the good mistress I was. Head up and eyes forward as he started to lead me down the ancient hallways. Winter had come. With it, ice and snow and a cold like I'd never experienced in life had settled into the fief. The cold did not bother us, as it did other, softer creatures. It did however make the days short, and the nights long.

Our night was only beginning as we strode toward the High Council doors. They opened without a word, both Vampires lowering their heads with acknowledgement.

Victor paid them no mind as he led me forward.

The Born that had been speaking paused.

"My mistress was attacked today." Even for Vampires, the entire Council chamber stilled. They knew what that meant. They'd seen enough shows of power from me to

know what was coming. It took everything I had to keep the smile off my face and the darkness complacent just a little longer.

"With all due respect, my prince—" one of them started. A man, two rows and three to the left.

"Lily," Victor interrupted, cutting him off. Shirt still ripped, most of my front bared to all—I walked forward without hesitation, my head held high. When I stepped off the first ledge, the Born started to scramble back. Those around him stepped away. Cowards, they were. They had loyalty for no one.

I stepped off the second ledge and turned. One of the Born shoved him forward and he fell to his knees before me.

I didn't need to look at Victor. He'd already given the command.

I lifted my hand to his throat and wrapped my slight fingers halfway around it. The mere touch of his skin set the darkness free and I couldn't have contained it if I'd wanted to.

In my head a voice was laughing, and it was twisted, dark, and so very cruel. It wasn't until the husk of a Born Vampire hit the marble floors that I realized that the voice wasn't in my head at all.

It was me.

The sound reverberated off the walls of the chamber and echoed back to me, a haunting, terrible melody.

Black swirls danced over my skin as I turned to Victor and smiled. The light in his eyes as I did so was nothing short of depraved.

"As I said," Victor continued. "My mistress was attacked today and some of the Born in this room ordered it." There was murder in his eyes as he took a single sweeping look

around the room. "I warned all of you what would happen if anyone touched her."

The room quivered under the intensity of his stare.

All but me.

I'd seen the madness that lurked within him, just as he saw the darkness in me. We fed each other. Fostered each other. Groomed each other—stroking the other's worst qualities to a fever pitch.

"No one went after the girl—" a woman dared speak.

The beautiful part about it is that she wasn't the liar.

I was.

I lured the five to where I wanted them and then slaughtered them before a word of my actions could reach the wrong ears. I had Victor and the Council all in one hand.

Just like they'd taught me.

Selena and Alexandra.

My darling, dear sisters.

They left me to rot, and rot I did.

It seemed in death that I finally understood what they'd been trying to teach me. What all of them had tried to teach me.

And now everyone was going to pay.

"Lily," Victor repeated.

Again, I followed his command. He was never the wiser about why I gleefully did so.

We repeated this five times. Five more dead bodies.

Five more dead Born.

The Council chamber was brimming with tension and hostility. All for me. All for him.

It was only when he commanded me to kill a sixth time that someone interrupted him. Another voice spoke.

This one old, so very old that the essence in me took notice.

"No more," the voice said. It came from above and below and every direction around me. Power unlike any in all of this place pervaded it.

Power I wanted.

Needed.

Victor stilled as if by command. "They were given orders. We had an agreement, Father, and they defiled it. I cannot accept that disrespect." His silver eyes dropped to me. Covered in the blood of the Made and the Born, I was a sight to behold.

"We cannot accept more death," that ancient voice spoke. "War is coming, and we need the numbers to be ready for it."

"A war that with her we will not lose," Victor replied coldly. "The same cannot be said for the cowards that hide behind their lessers. They are less than Born or Made. They are . . . without use."

There is no such thing as true silence.

If there were, I would know it. But even without heartbeats or breathing or any of those signs that point to the living, there will be something. *Be it the break of air as it stirs one's hair, the crunch of snow beneath feet, or the weight of silence as it speaks for you.*

This was the latter.

The already too tight tensions and repeated questioning finally came to a head.

On the floor of the chamber a man came forth.

His hair was whiter than snow. His skin the color of bone.

But his eyes . . . they were silver.

Just like Victor's.

"You've overstepped, my son," the man said. "Speak again and you will find that it is your whore who will be without use when I bleed her dry and let the Council feast upon her before I hand the scraps over to their Made to do with as they will."

The threat was for him, but it was aimed at me.

On another night, his threat might have made Victor eat his words. They might have sent him running with me back to his chambers. They might have worked.

But madness, it was not a thing that was rational. It did not make sense to those that were. Victor's possessiveness of me combined with his explosive temper . . . it was a terrifying thing if you didn't know how to handle it.

And me? Well, I pushed it just enough to get what I wanted.

"Victor," I whispered, and the sound was loud enough for all to hear. I didn't care. It was now or never. "They don't respect your commands. They talk down to you. They send their dogs after your mistress. It's no wonder they act this way when your own father will not give you the one thing you've asked for."

He tilted his head and slowly descended the steps, coming to stand before me.

His fingers—so pale, so cold—they touched my cheek.

"What would you have me do, flower?" he asked softly.

I reached up with both hands and cupped his cheeks gently. I went up to my tiptoes, balancing precariously on the edge with this monster that fate tied to me.

My lips pressed against his. Tentative, but sure.

His were far from it as he kissed me back fiercely. The intensity of it set my blood aflame. Were I living, I wouldn't be able to breathe for the fire inside was eating away at all oxygen. I kissed him back, matching him touch for touch.

The intensity of it rocked me to my core.

I'd never kissed a boy in my life, and Victor was a man. A man who spent months watching me. Grooming me. I hated him, and yet a part of me also craved him. Craved that strange cruelty inside of him, so like my own.

I didn't let myself think on it or analyze why I might feel that way. After spending so long in the dark, I didn't need to justify any feelings I might have to anyone.

He might have been born a monster.

But I was made one.

Perhaps that is why fate threw us together.

I didn't get to think on it because the next thing I knew a burning sensation spread through me as something sharp was rammed through my back.

I faltered, pulling away. Victor took one look at my face and his eyes dropped to my chest where the gleaming end of a long dagger protruded.

"Lily," he whispered. Panic began to set in. The edge of my vision darkened. "Lily," he repeated.

I stared down at the dagger as my knees buckled and my body folded. The last thing I saw before my vision went black were two thin glowing lines connecting Victor and me.

One was red.

One was gold.

"It's time."

A voice jolted me back to the present. I sat up,

gasping for air, panting from exertion. The sensation of blood pouring into my lungs and death closing in overwhelmed me.

"Selena?" Ash asked cautiously. "What's wrong—"

"She's dying," I said. "They stabbed her—she's dying, and they stabbed her and—"

Arms wrapped around me, but I couldn't register them. All I knew was that Lily was dying.

Again.

"Selena, I need you to calm down—" Johanna started. "Xellos can't open the portal if you're—"

"My sister just got stabbed in the heart!" I snapped. My hair lifted on end as fury flooded me. In the center of the room Xellos was chanting and magic stirred.

"Aaron, you're going to have to neutralize her. The Witches will spook if he opens a portal and she's going off." She'd barely finished speaking before I felt his presence in my mind.

He pulled on the bond that spanned between us, opening up himself to my rage—and me to his strength. The entire room grew still as Xellos murmured one last word and the note hung.

Behind me Ash began breathing harshly as my own breaths settled.

I was only just beginning to cycle down when several wisps of color snapped inward and then exploded out.

The portal opened.

A girl stepped out. I hadn't seen her in months, but even in my disoriented state I was able to make out her cloudy eyes.

Milla. The Maiden.

"The Witch Council is ready for you."

I heard the words, but they didn't register. All I wanted was for someone to knock me out so I could find out if my sister was dead or alive.

"Selena," Blair said. The curt drawl of my name pulled my attention to her. She came around to kneel in front of me. Her eyes still black as pitch. Her expression cold. "You made a promise to us that you would be what we need."

I swallowed hard around the lump in my throat, torn between what she was saying and the undead-possibly-dead sister I left behind in my nightmare.

"I made a promise to her too," I whispered, battling my own extreme emotions. "I told her I'd protect her and look how well that's turned out."

The sharp crack of her hand as it struck my flesh shocked me more than it hurt. I tentatively reached up and touched my cheek. The tension in the room was palpable as they held their breath.

No one wanted to engage her.

No one wanted to engage me.

"You slapped me," I said, dumbfounded by the action. Blair leaned forward, stopping when we were eye level.

"And I'll slap you again if you go back to that," her demon answered in a hard, unyielding tone. "You agreed to do whatever was needed to end this. You promised *her*." The demon snarled that last part, and I knew she was talking about Blair. "The Witch Council will not meet with anyone else. They will only see *you*."

"My sister might have just died—"

"Your sister is already dead," the demon spat. It hit harder than a slap would have. I froze, having to remind myself to breathe.

In.

Out.

In.

Out.

Her remarks were cruel, but the truth often was. Demons didn't bother with minced words. Kinder, though, they were.

I didn't want to listen.

I certainly didn't want to agree.

But deep down I knew she wasn't wrong. Lily had been dead for months now—in more ways than any of them knew.

"If it were you," I whispered. "If it were *her*" —the demons eyes flashed— "would you tell me to do it? Would you push me to continue on like I hadn't just watched her die?"

The response I got was short, but curt, and most importantly—it was the truth.

"Yes."

I closed my eyes and sighed heavily. My chest expanded and then deflated, each breath making my heart slow. Though it hurt painfully to do so.

"Why?" I asked her.

The demon didn't give me an immediate answer. Instead she looked past me, staring at the wall behind my back. "There is more at stake than you or I or your sister. The Vampires are a rot that have walked this earth too long—demons too. If I had the power to wipe it all out—even at the cost of my life—so be it."

My chest constricted tightly, crushing my newly found heart with it. Once, I'd lived for revenge.

It almost destroyed me.

And now . . . it seemed that love would finish the job.

A shiver ran up my spine and the hairs along the back of my neck rose. Lily might be dead. She might be alive. I didn't know, but falling asleep again to find out wasn't going to do anything but risk our best chance at an alliance—and with it—the best chance to win the war.

I looked past Blair to the girl that stood before the swirling portal. Milla. I didn't know her last name, or if I ever had.

"You can see the future, can you not?" I asked her.

The girl's cloudless eyes watched me as if judging what she could see.

"I can."

I swallowed hard and pushed forward onto the balls of my feet. Blair moved back, and Ash released his hold on me, handling the rage he stole with more control than I was capable of.

"Do you see her?" I asked.

She stared and not a kernel of truth revealed itself in her gaze. Milla was a child, and yet like the Crone already.

A true vessel of the Three-faced Goddess.

"I cannot say."

I bit the inside of my cheek and tasted blood, letting out a curse. "What do you mean you cannot say?" I clenched my fist and the building trembled. She didn't bat an eyelash.

"You're at a crossroads, and your decision will change the course of this war. It will change everything, but no one—not I, not your friends, not your signasti, not your family, not even the ancients—can make the decision for you." She spoke with the voice of three. Young. Middle-aged. Old. It was a voice I'd heard before, from a different set of lips. It was the voice of the Goddess speaking to me from the mouthpiece of a child.

"I don't understand why I can't get an answer. If you know she's alive, why not just tell me?" I snapped, my ire growing, the rage once again building. This time toward a Goddess and a girl. Heated fingers wrapped around my forearm as a crack ran up the clay wall and through the ceiling above me.

"A sacrifice is not payment without choice," Milla whispered. The words settled over me like the chill of frost in the dead of winter. They hit me with the force of a gale so strong it would shatter glass. I was once glass. Brittle. Breakable. The thing about glass is that once it's broken, it's sharp. Deadly.

Six months ago, this decision would have been the end.

Six weeks ago, I know what I would have done in a heartbeat.

Hell, even six days ago I might have hightailed it to a magical elevator.

But I couldn't do that. Not here. Not now.

I understood what the words meant, and even as dread curdled in my stomach, I walked forward on stiff legs. The anger drained away as such a deep, dwelling fear settled in its place.

It wasn't for me, but I didn't say that, even as I felt Ash's quick inhale of breath. His fingers slipped away as I went to stand next to Mila. She faced my friends. I faced her portal.

"If sacrifice is payment, shouldn't the person who bought it be the one to pay? Why don't you ask your Goddess that?" Her only response was a slight smile as if she found my answer amusing.

"I will not forget the decision you have made today," Milla uttered. "Remember that."

I had no idea what that meant, but given the girl liked to talk in riddles as much as the Crone, I wasn't inclined to ask. Daylight was fading, and with it, my time to convince the Witch Council that this wasn't just a Supernatural war.

It was *the* war.

The one that decided everything, if the ancients were to be believed.

I stepped into the portal.

CHAPTER 17

The wind whipped through my hair and sand stung my eyes. A sun brighter and hotter than any other I'd experienced engulfed me. Sweat formed beneath my tight jeans and long-sleeved shirt, slicking my skin and causing my pants to cling uncomfortably. Perspiration dotted my forehead in seconds, gathering at my temple. It trickled down the side of my face, over the curve of my jaw, along the sweep of my neck, and into my cleavage.

Voices sounded behind me as the others crossed through the portal as well. I heard them talking but didn't process what they said as I looked out at the world before me.

The Witches had gone into hiding over a hundred years ago. In the span of a few years they virtually disappeared off the map, and so few were seen after that. I had wondered before coming here what state I would find the highly reclusive Witch clans in.

Seeing tents in every color was not what I expected. They were tall and wide, and while I couldn't imagine living in this heat without air conditioning, I'd learned enough to not assume they didn't, given the crushing presence of magic all around me. A near-invisible barrier surrounded the immense cluster of tents like a dome. My eyes traced as far as I could see in one direction to the other, and it had to be over a mile wide.

"It's a protective shield," Johanna said beside me. "To keep people out."

There was no magical elevator in sight. No roads. No anything. I didn't even know what country we were in.

I glanced back at Johanna and replied, "Or perhaps, in some cases, to keep people in."

Her eyebrows rose at that assertion.

Milla stepped through the portal last, and it closed behind her as Xellos waved to us, awaiting our return.

The young Witch brushed past me, and I turned and followed her as she made her way down the line of tents. Their flaps didn't even twitch under the harsh winds, affirming my belief that strong magic was in play—a kind of magic I knew very little about. We approached a copse of trees where a river ran. Beside it, women dressed in purple skirts and blue tops chanted in a language I didn't understand.

Water lifted from the river in rivulets and the sand was magically pulled from it, leaving crystal clear liquid that deposited itself in a massive clay pot. Next to it, three others had already been filled. They smiled and waved to Milla, who nodded once respectfully.

I noted that they didn't address us in any way as we continued on.

A tent came into view, taller than the others. This one

was circular in nature and made of pure white cloth, despite the reddish-brown sand drifting in the wind.

We came to a stop before it.

Two men, both shirtless and wearing cream-colored baggy pants walked over. Mila gave them a command in the foreign language. They both nodded.

"These men will show you to your tent," she said to those behind me. Ash's fingers ghosted my lower back as he placed a kiss on my cheek and then walked away.

When they were gone, she said, "It is time."

I didn't ask her time for what as she strode forward into the tent and I followed behind.

The white flap swished to the side on its own accord and closed again behind me, exactly as it was before. The scent of cinnamon and myrrh tickled my nose. The tinkle of wind chimes rang in my ears.

An old woman sat on a cushion in front of the fire. Her teeth were yellowed as she smiled sadly. Her eyes changed color, the skin crinkled in the corners.

I cursed softly under my breath as Milla took a seat beside her. "Do you know who this is?" I demanded of her.

The child didn't even spare me a look as she replied, "The Crone."

I swallowed hard, pinching the bridge of my nose as I inhaled sharply and exhaled slowly, pacing a foot or two. "Let me get this straight—the supposed 'Witch Council' is literally this old hag—who I thought no one knew about—and a little girl?" The old woman—Livina—chuffed a laugh.

"Actually, it's just the girl," she said, cracking her

fingers and extending them toward a fire that burned without giving off smoke.

"Unbelievable," I whispered. "You two brought me all the way out here—for what? No offense, Milla, but I could have sent Xellos with a goddamn letter for just you and not made the journey all the way out here when we have very little time."

"You had to make a choice."

Her words stilled me.

A sacrifice is not payment without choice.

I shivered, though I was not cold.

"What are you talking about?" I asked her, but this time Milla didn't answer, as if I was below worthy of an explanation. I looked at the Crone. "What is she talking about?"

The old woman sighed and leaned forward. Her joints popped as she tried and failed to get up. Livina extended a hand and said, "Help an old woman, will you?"

I grit my teeth again but bit my tongue from lashing out as I silently extended my hand and she latched onto it, her bony fingers digging into the pads of mine. Despite the heat, hers were ice cold. Part of me wanted to ask. The rest of me didn't care.

"Why am I here, Livina?"

"Because it's almost time," she said simply. A blue as deep as the sea filled her eyes, and I knew from her expression it was sadness that caused it.

"Time for what?" I breathed.

"The end," Milla said. My eyes snapped to her. She was only a child, no more than thirteen, but the will of the Goddess she spoke to was strong. There was so little of that thirteen-year-old there now that it was hard to imagine any of her to begin with. "The final battle draws near. The price must be paid," the girl said in hushed words over the fire.

"No," I said before I could stop myself. It was a single word, and yet it condemned me. "I won't do it."

"Even if means an alliance?" the child asked.

My fist squeezed tightly as I tried to control my breathing.

"That's your price?" I spat. "You want me to kill myself? To kill her?" I pointed my finger behind me in the direction that Alexandra had walked.

"No," Milla said. "It is not *my* price. It's the ancients'."

"*Yours*," I corrected. "Not mine."

"Supernaturals and Witches broke the balance. It was the Goddesses of Supernaturals and Witches that set the price," Livina cut in.

"Funny how none of it could have happened without *you*," I replied coldly to the Crone.

"Selena . . ." Valda whispered through my mind. I ignored her.

"That's true," Livina said with a heavy sigh. "And my payment for that transgression will be completed when yours is."

I lowered my hand to my side. Flame and shadow filled the tent. But not smoke. Not safety.

"You took my memories. You took my parents. Now you're not just asking for my life, but also the lives of my sisters. Both my sisters—if Lily is even alive." I could hardly speak the words with the knot in my throat, but I pushed past it. "It's not fair what is being asked of me. It's not right. It's not balanced."

"It's not about being fair," Milla said. "Your ancestors condemned the world for a thousand years and both species have paid the price. This should not have been their burden to bear. The Witches are without balance, with only the Maiden to be reborn again. The Supernaturals are without their souls, blocked from finding their signastis. Was it right that millions and millions of people had to pay for this curse?" she asked me. My heart beat faster as anger and fear and guilt overwhelmed me. "Was it fair that the Fortescues slaughtered hundreds of thousands over the years because of what Cirian became?"

I was speechless.

My throat dry. My hands shaking.

I knew the answer. I understood what she was saying, but I didn't want to.

"No, it wasn't."

"No." Milla nodded, her voice slightly condescending. "It wasn't."

"Three deaths of Valda and Cirian's line is the cost that is demanded. Will you pay it?" the Crone asked.

Would I? Could I?

My life . . . perhaps. I didn't wish to die anymore. If anything my demon and I clung to life. Desperate for all the things we'd missed and the things we'd yet to experience.

If it were only my life that they asked for . . . maybe.

But Alexandra's? Lily's?

My lips pressed into a firm line as I looked at the fire,

at the tent, and the deep purple and red-colored pillows —at anything but them.

"No." I couldn't. I wouldn't.

Livina sighed, grasping her staff. The orb began to glow, its eerie light filling the tent. She lifted it and brought it down on the sand once. A ring of blue expanded from it. Her magic washed over me. My temples throbbed. Pain bloomed within my mind.

"What did you just do to me?" I asked as I stumbled back and then forward. The ground began to spin. The world tilted.

Just as it faded to black, I heard her answer.

"Made it so that the truth will find you. It is my last gift and your last chance."

I blinked once, and the tent was gone. The Crone was gone.

But the darkness, it consumed me.

CHAPTER 18

Silence. I'd finally heard true silence before it faded away.

My side lay against something hard and cold. Marble, my brain inserted. Liquid coated my bare skin and tattered clothes. Sticky, but drying.

Pain. It came from my chest.

I didn't understand why it was there. Only that I needed it to stop. I couldn't think past it. I put a hand to where it hurt, and had I needed air, the breath would have hissed between my lips as my fingers brushed over something sharp.

I opened my eyes.

It was disorienting at first. The stone block and splatter of blood, all I could see. I reached around and grasped the hilt of the dagger. My memories coming back now. Faster. Surer.

My hand still slick but stronger than ever, I held onto the hilt and pulled. A slicing sound so minute it was almost silent whispered through the Council chambers. My blood flowed again.

"You killed her," the voice roared. It took me a moment to

understand, given I'd never heard him raise his voice. Not once. Madness had him, though. I sat up, feeling eyes on me, beginning to take notice. Their expressions were horrified.

That was a difficult feat, but I'd achieved it by doing what no other had.

I'd died not once, but twice.

I'd had a true death . . . and I came back.

Again.

"She was a Made, Victor. There was never going to be more for her. You know that. She was without use." The ancient voice slithered over me. Parched, like paper. Powerful, but not invincible. "Be done with this conversation, Son. I tire of it. There are more important matters to discuss."

I looked down at my chest where two lines connected me and the man standing at the end of the aisle. One red. One gold.

He was my master.

He was my . . . signasti.

What an interesting turn of events. The essence in me agreed. It made things both more and less complicated.

My skin began to knit together. Muscles reattached themselves as bone fused back where it should have been. The pain receded.

I got to my feet.

And then the most peculiar thing of all happened.

My heart beat.

Just once. But it was enough.

Victor turned. His eyes widened. Black veins had crept into the white, making the silver around his pupils appear light in contrast. Blood splattered his clothes.

My blood.

"Lily?" he asked once, as if he couldn't believe his eyes.

I probably wouldn't either. Vampires didn't come back from true death.

Perhaps I wasn't just a Vampire.

Perhaps I was more.

I smiled, and for the first time I let him see the truth.

I let them all see the truth.

Because it was as cold and heartless as the marble floors he'd left me to die on.

"Victor," I said sweetly. Wickedly.

With the dagger in one hand, my shirt still ripped open, chest and stomach on display, I stepped forward. My heart beat again. It was slower than a human's but there was no denying what it was.

The sound like a battering ram to the council chamber doors.

The Born parted for me as I started toward Victor.

I came to stand before him and noticed how his fingers trembled. His expression stunned.

The golden tether between us shimmered then glowed as I reached up and placed a hand on his chest, over his unbeating heart.

"It seems not even death could keep us apart," I said almost thoughtfully as I dragged my eyes up his chest like the tip of a dagger. "Maybe that means we should stay together," I mused.

I had done the research. I had read the journals about signastis who lost their other half. The first thing to go was the mind, and if they were strong enough to outlive that—the sickness got them.

I couldn't die and the sickness couldn't be cured.

Oh, the irony of it all . . . I started to laugh.

For months I'd dreamed of the day I could rid myself of this man. For the day that I could destroy them all.

And yet . . . I couldn't.

Somewhere along the way I'd grown to crave his cruelty. To seek his dark smile as he applauded me for my wickedness. Those twisted feelings aside, I couldn't kill him because the bond would eat away at me.

"Flower." He licked his lips. The relief was obvious, as was the hunger and desperation in that word. "I don't know what to say."

I smiled again, and if he saw the monster behind it he clearly didn't care. Not anymore. "Tell me to kill him."

Some of the awe and disbelief faded in his gaze. His expression sharpened. Madness was still there, but now I knew it wasn't just his mind. Oh no, it was the bond.

He would do anything for me now. Just because of who I am. What I am.

If not because whatever feelings he may have, then because the bond will push him to—until I let him claim me.

"If I do?" he asked, already playing games again. Truth be told, I was starting to enjoy them.

I leaned in, lifting to my tiptoes. I put my lips to the hollow of his ear and whispered so softly no one else would hear. Not even a Vampire. Not even the ancients.

"I will be yours and you'll be mine. No one will ever take me from you again. No one will stop us."

The words were his undoing—and mine, in a way.

I just didn't know it then.

"Kill him," Victor said. His command didn't actually

work on me. It hadn't for a while now. It wasn't until tonight that I understood why.

Yet, I obeyed all the same.

Turning from my signasti, I looked upon his father, with skin the color of death and eyes like mercury. His hair was the purest version of white I'd ever seen. His lip curled in disgust, blasphemously obscene.

"Ivan the Cruel," I said.

"Made. Whore," came his reply. It didn't bother me anymore. I stepped forward, leaving black footprints behind me. Blood still dripped from the end of the dagger.

"King of Vampires, that's what they call you. You're so renowned for your cruelty it's in your very title. A living legend—as much as you can be. You're supposed to be the most powerful Vampire in the world." I took another step and called the darkness forward. This time it didn't stay contained beneath my skin, but instead surrounded me like a living, breathing beast.

"Just imagine," I continued, taking another step. "What they will say after a little girl kills you. A Made. A whore." There was no flicker of fear in his eyes. No signs that he thought I could actually do it. Just hatred and disgust.

I'd seen enough of both aimed at me to last a lifetime, even one as long as his.

My feet stilled as I came to the last step. Six feet was all that separated us.

"They say that legends never die, but they die all the time. Eventually we forget them." He sprang forward then, faster than even Victor could.

It didn't matter.

Before he could even touch my skin, the darkness engulfed

him. It drilled beneath his flesh and bone to the source of his energy and consumed it.

Seconds. That's how long it lasted.

But to a Vampire seconds were an eternity.

He didn't open his mouth in a silent scream. He didn't make a sound, nor a motion. The only thing that betrayed his thoughts were his eyes. I couldn't decipher what that emotion was in them as I killed him.

It wasn't fear or anger or disgust.

The thing it was most akin to was the same emotion I read on Anastasia's face before she crumbled into a pile of dust and bones.

Relief.

That perplexed both me and the entity within as his skin began to break apart into flakes. They peeled away and began to drift as more crumbled away. Muscle. Tendons. Organs.

Ivan the Cruel had been ancient. He'd been a true legend.

And now all that would be remembered of him was the girl who killed him.

They would tell stories about this day—about the look on his face and mine. About the blood on my hands and the dagger that should have been my end. They would make me immortal with their words, but it was my strength that would make me a legend.

And I would stay one, because I could never die.

I turned, power thrumming beneath my skin. My body was but a mere vessel for the immense darkness I contained, and I loved it. The power—the way every nerve ending came to life—the looks on their faces as they realized how very sorry they were going to be. It was this feeling—this single sensation—that I loved, and it was probably the only thing I loved.

I lifted my head to the Vampire High Council and opened my mouth, preparing to say those final words that would be etched into history books.

The elevator pinged. Were I not so used to controlling my expressions, mine might have soured at the interruption. As it was, I lifted a single eyebrow at the metal doors as they slid open.

The lack of a heartbeat gave away the Vampire that stumbled through them, falling onto the floor of the amphitheater. Loose white pants and a long-sleeved shirt covered most of his features. A turban had been wrapped around his pale blonde hair, but there was no mistaking the red eyes that looked upon me.

This was going to be good. Made never came into the Council chambers. Not without the greatest of reasons.

"We found her," he said, getting to his feet. His eyes squinted as he looked at me, as if unsure whether I was the one he should be addressing.

"Found who?" I asked, knowing already of whom he spoke. There was only one person that could strike fear into a Vampire's heart.

"Selena Fortescue."

A light touch skimmed by back, the only announcement that Victor gave as he came to my side. His cool fingertips gripped my hip, pulling me closer. The gold thread between us flared to life once more. My chest squeezed, though I assumed it had more to do with the precipice I was on.

This night had been a glorious night. I'd died and come back. I'd killed Ivan the Cruel. I'd cemented my place.

And now, it was time for the most important thing of all.

Revenge.

"Where is she?" I asked, my voice high and ringing with authority. Victor's nails bit into my hip but he didn't reprimand me.

"Marrakesh," the Made said. A hint of indecision ran over his features, and I narrowed my eyes. "We believe she was trying to make contact with the Witches, and we attempted to intercept . . ."

He hesitated, and Victor stiffened against me. I kept the smirk off my face with some effort. If there was one thing my signasti despised, it was those that hesitated. It made him think they were weaving lies. His paranoia had climbed to an all-time high these past months, and while that likely wasn't the case here, I wasn't going to tell him that.

"Attempted?" Victor asked, his tone hard and biting. I pressed closer, letting one hand rest on his abdomen.

The Made opened and closed his mouth twice before finally finding the words. "She is a matter manipulator. One moment we were upon them, and the next the entire horde crumbled into dust. There was nothing of them left. I've never seen anything like it—"

Victor cut off his rambling by pulling a dagger from his inner coat jacket and throwing it.

The bit of metal landed with a thud and the Made collapsed, rambling no longer.

"Flower," he purred in my ear. I tilted my head and looked to him. "She's seeking an alliance against us, and she would not answer my summons. Your sister is quickly becoming without use, and dare I say—a problem."

My heartbeat didn't betray my excitement, much to my satisfaction. I nodded twice. "Yes, she is."

"What do you propose as a solution?" It wasn't just a

question. It was a challenge, and likely not the last one I would have placed upon me. He was giving me everything. Power. Revenge. Freedom.

He wanted something, and it didn't take a genius to figure out what it was.

He wanted to be my all. My everything.

He wanted me to pick him against all odds.

What he didn't realize was that I already had. I chose myself. I chose to survive. In choosing that, I chose him.

"If Selena truly has reached her potential, then it's best to hit her where it will hurt most," I said slowly.

"Where is that?" he asked once.

I stared into the empty elevator that still hadn't closed. My thoughts beginning to take form. My sister never valued herself as much as her loved ones.

I smiled, and it was one born of blood and pain.

Vengeance was a virtue, and now it would be mine.

I WOKE WITH A START, gasping for breath. My heart hammered in my chest, a sound that was quickly becoming a comfort on its own. Blood rushing roared in my ears and the sounds of the Witch camp winding down for the night followed it.

I blinked once and sat up. Firelight bathed my face. Shadows danced over the two women before me. At least they'd had the decency to put a pillow under my head after what Livina did.

"You put me to sleep."

"Not quite," the Crone answered. "I let the Mother's

visions take you, hoping that you will see the truth and make the right decision."

"Right dec—" I cut myself off and exhaled heavily. "She's alive."

Neither the old woman nor the child appeared surprised as they continued to stare into the fire like it held some kind of answers.

"She's neither dead nor alive," Milla answered. "She is something other. Something that has never been."

"And will never be again," the Crone added. The age lines on her face were stark in the low light. The shadows making her features harsh.

"I watched her die. I *felt* it. Now she's back and her heart beats again—maybe there's a way to save her. Maybe I can—"

"She cannot be saved."

The Crone's words stilled me.

"What do you mean she can't be saved?" I asked, my brows drawing together. "If her heart beats, I can still do something. She can still come back."

"So long as Cirian's soul resides within her, she is lost," the Crone answered. "I am sorry, Selena. Truly, I am. But it's the only way." My lips pushed together as heat licked through my veins and the pounding in my head worsened.

"You've already said she's something that's never been. Maybe she can beat him. Maybe she can—"

"You know what she is," Milla said. "You have seen what she has become. You have not told them, though" —she pointed in the direction of the tent that Ash,

Alexandra, Blair, Tori, Johanna, Amber, and Oliver had been escorted to—"Why?"

I looked away and closed my eyes, inhaling then exhaling slowly. So, she knew.

I wanted to berate myself for that. Of course she knew. She was the Maiden. She could see the future.

"They wouldn't understand—" I started.

"They wouldn't let you pretend," the girl spat with more venom than I expected. My eyes snapped open, and I regarded her. "You're risking the lives of millions for the life of one that's already gone. You know what she is. You know her heart is poisoned. It would be a mercy to end her and yet you won't."

My lips parted and then my jaw clinked shut.

"It's not just her you're asking for, though, is it? You want me. You want Alexandra. And what about my signasti? What about the people that we'll leave behind?" Anger coursed through me, but I did not let it control me. Instead I funneled it into words. "The best part about this is I can't tell them. I can't tell anyone about the curse or the price, but you're asking me not just to kill myself, but both my sisters—and no one will even know why. Thanks to your Goddess. But you—you could tell them. Couldn't you?" I took a step forward, and a flash of that younger girl peeked through. Her innocence. Her uncertainty. Yes, she could tell them, but I wasn't wasting my breath begging her to because she wouldn't.

"I'm the Maiden. What the Goddess tells me—"

"That's a bullshit excuse and you know it. Your Goddess is demanding an unfair price for a debt your own Crone racked up." I jabbed a finger in Livina's direction. "So don't sit there and tell me what's right or wrong. Don't act like I'm the only one making selfish decisions here. Mine are just for people I love. Yours is for your bitch Goddess. At the end of the day, we aren't all that different."

Mila surveyed me with caution, her face betraying what her eyes didn't.

"Is that your final answer?" she asked stiffly.

"If your price for assistance in a war your people started is me killing my sisters, I'll find another way without you," I said curtly. "Without either of you," I added in Livina's direction.

The Crone shook her head, the sadness of a thousand years in her eyes as she watched me. Regret and sorrow were the baggage she carried on her shoulders.

I turned my back on her, on both of them, and started for the tent fold.

"You can't outrun a curse ordained by the gods, girl. It's impossible."

I paused, fingers gripping the thick fabric of the flap.

"We live in an impossibly possible world. Nothing is impossible. If you two cowards won't help me, I'll find someone else that will."

I let the words hang between us like a noose as I stepped out into the night. The wind shrieked, blowing sand everywhere but with a flick of my hand it all scattered. The Witches that were still awake and about glanced my way, but I ignored them. Following my link with Ash, I came before a maroon-colored tent and flung the flap to the side.

"Time to go," I said without even getting in the tent. From this angle I could see a ladder that went straight down and a room with wood floors, thick rugs, and plush pillows. A chilly breeze hit me from *inside* the tent, confirming my suspicions about magical air conditioning.

"What? Why?" Alexandra asked, getting to her feet. Tori scrambled up from her spot where she'd been lying next to her.

"Because we're done here," I replied. Johanna and Oliver shared a look.

It was Amber who chose to read the tone of my voice and said, "You didn't get an alliance, did you?"

I scrubbed a hand over my face, dragging it through my sweaty roots and dirty hair. It came back streaked orange and brown. I sighed. "No. I didn't."

At that they chose to climb the ladder one by one. I waited until they'd all filed out to start toward where the portal had been. I could hear Milla already there and chanting under her breath.

"But why?" Tori asked. "You're supposed to be this Mother person. Why wouldn't they—"

"The Witches are cowards," I tossed the words callously over my shoulder with the same precision I'd throw a dagger. Tori deflated a bit. "They wouldn't give us an alliance without the one thing I cannot give. They refused to see how asking for it was unreasonable."

"What did they want?" Blair asked. I noted that it wasn't her demon as I turned to look at her.

"I can't say."

Her expression didn't falter. "Can't or won't?" she asked. It wasn't a challenge and the question was valid.

"Both. I'd rather not talk about it." She nodded once, but Oliver stepped forward.

"This alliance affected more than you. If they asked for something and you wouldn't give it—"

"Did you not just hear me?" I cut him off, my tone eviscerating him before my words even could. "I cannot give it to them, but even if I could, I wouldn't. I've done everything you lot have asked. I watched my sister get stabbed and still came to this goddamned meeting and it was all for nothing. I'm not playing games, and I'm not keeping secrets. So can you back the fuck off for a second?"

Stunned, Oliver blinked and did just that. Johanna placed a reassuring palm on his shoulder and nodded once for me to continue on. I gladly did so, eating up the distance between us and Milla.

Three sparks of light swirled through the air. Red. Orange. Yellow. They twisted and shot toward each other. Upon colliding, the colors exploded outwards—the portal coming to life, Xellos waiting for us on the other side.

"Let me know if you change your mind," Milla said stoically. Pissed and tired, I couldn't contain my response.

"So much for you remembering the choice I made and helping me," I scoffed. A flash of hurt crossed her face, but she closed it away before the others got to us. With her kinky black hair tucked beneath a wrap and her body adorned in the bright colors and riches of her people—she looked like a high priestess, and I wondered why it never occurred to me or anyone that she was actually the Witch Council. While a child she may be, it was clear her people regarded her as more than that. She was their Goddesses incarnate. A vessel for great power.

I shook my head as she hugged and said goodbye to Johanna and Oliver. They went through the portal first, followed by Alexandra and Tori. Then Amber and Ash.

Finally, when it was just the two of us, she came to stand beside me again.

"I know it is hard for you to understand, but soon you will. I haven't forgotten the choice you made today, just as you must not forget a sacrifice is not payment without a choice," she told me a third and final time.

Dread thickened in my gut. My skin broke out in a cold sweat despite the cool temperatures of the desert. I didn't think it was her words, but I didn't know what else it could be.

Exhausted but feeling at a loss for what to do, I stepped into the portal. For a brief second, I let the universe carry me and my thoughts away.

For some reason, it was the end of my nightmare that I thought of then.

The way Lily smiled and the silent promise of revenge.

If I could have, I would have shuddered. In the back of my mind I knew something was wrong, but for the life of me I couldn't figure out what.

CHAPTER 19

THE ELEVATOR DINGED. THE DOORS SLID OPEN.

Inside, the scent of sweat and alcohol filled the strip club with just a touch of depravity. It hit me full force as I stepped out onto the cheap carpet, the soles of my boots sticking to it. After a day in the desert, the air conditioner was a blessed relief, chilling my sweat-coated skin faster than the perspiration could evaporate.

"Friends!" Tam came striding forward from halfway across his club. He wound in and out of people, catching a shot girl that bumped into him and balancing her tray before sending her on her way again. He beamed a thousand-watt smile at us, still just as sneaky as it was the first time. Tam was the Las Vegas pack Alpha. He also ran an execution ring in the black market that was strictly off the books. I had no idea what he was hiding in that smile today, but for once, I was too tired to care.

"Where's Cade?" I asked him, speaking just loud enough his paranormal hearing would catch the words over the techno music blasting through his club.

"He's around," Tam answered vaguely, his smile freezing in place. "What, by chance, do you need my second for?" His electric blue gaze wandered between Xellos and I, searching his partner for the reasoning behind my mood.

I lifted both eyebrows and gave him the look.

The look that said I'm at the fucking end of my rope so stop playing with me.

"The Witches fell through."

Those four words made him freeze and the glint in his eyes died. His smile dropped a fraction. Passersby wouldn't notice, but the air of personality left him as the creeping chill of what was upon us washed over him.

"That's unfortunate," he said softly, looking away.

"You're telling me. So where is Cade?" I asked.

He sighed. "He's finishing up a transport for me at the moment. I'm assuming you want him for a stepping point to his mother?"

"You would be correct."

He nodded twice and then motioned for us to come forward. "I'll give him a call and tell him to wrap it up. In the meantime, feel free to take a seat and—"

"Tam," Ash said in a harsh tone. The lesser alpha paused and took note, unable to ignore the command in Ash's voice. "The Witches aren't coming and the situation with the Vampires . . ." He trailed off, trying, but failing to not look at me. I knew what was on his mind. My teeth clenched, and I looked away, both of us keeping that truth to ourselves.

Milla was right that I hadn't told them what Lily had

become, but Ash wasn't an idiot. He saw glimpses of the nightmares I lived. He felt the emotions—her emotions—roll through me like a tidal wave in my sleep. While we didn't speak on it, the truth of my sister was a heavy one that sat between us.

"I understand it's dire." Tam stepped forward, trying to assure him.

"It's quickly progressing, and I'm not sure we have much time. Please make sure Cade knows this is more than business for us." His hand clasped mine. Warm and safe and right.

It only barely stopped my stomach from roiling as I thought of the way Victor's hand clasped Lily's. They were so far removed from what Ash and I had . . . but he was her signasti.

My head dipped, and I blew out a breath, running a hand through my greasy locks. My fingers got stuck in the tangles, and I let it fall back to my side, too tired to care about how it looked.

"Of course," Tam said. He turned, pulling out a cellphone and dialing before his back was even to us. I tilted my head back, but the bright flash of lights made my demon and I wince. I squeezed my eyes shut and shook my head, attempting to shake the steady throb building in my temple. All it did was make things worse.

"How are you holding up?" Blair asked, coming to stand beside me.

"Shouldn't I be the one asking you that?" I replied without opening my eyes.

She chuckled low. "I've had better days."

I snorted. "You and me both."

"Can I ask you something?" I opened my eyes and looked at her sideways. Her light blonde hair was braided harshly, pulling the skin around her face and giving her gray eyes a slight slant. Like the rest of us, brownish-red dirt smudged her skin. The Vampire's blood on her black clothes had already dried, but a cloying scent still stuck to all of us. Despite her haggard appearance, it was the expression on her face that struck me most. So sharp. So lethal. I nodded, raising a hand to my temple once more as the buzzing grew. "Do you think it's worth it?"

I blinked. "Do I think what's worth it?"

"This." She motioned to Tam on the other side of the club, his cellphone practically glued to his ear as he spoke in rapid-fire Spanish.

"Tam?" I asked. Tension verging on pain radiated through my head like an electric current but I tried to block it out.

"Allies. Do you think the time we're spending doing this is really worth it? I mean, if we couldn't even convince the Witches, what reason does the Fae queen have to side with us?" she asked, shaking her head. "She doesn't, and frankly if I were in her position, I'd probably try to sit it all out and hope the Supes and bloodsuckers would just kill each other off so we're no longer her problem."

I groaned, turning to give her my full attention as best I could. "You're not wrong, but what choice do we have? The Supernaturals are scattered. The Shifters can't face this alone. If we fail, there's no one to help her when the Vampires turn their sights on the lesser threats. I'm hoping we can convince her with that."

Blair pressed her lips together. She wasn't the only one that thought it was a long shot, but at this point it was the only shot we had. I wasn't willing to pay the price asked.

Darkness crept into the corners of my vision. The room started to spin. I stumbled.

"Selena?" she asked. I blinked several times in rapid succession, trying to clear my vision. It didn't work.

That's when I felt it.

The muscles in my abdomen tightened. My stomach turned. Nausea swept through me and a cold sweat drenched my skin in seconds.

Fear. Dread. Knowing.

I'd had this feeling all my life right before something terrible happened.

The only warning I could give before my vision completely went was, "Something's coming."

It wasn't something.

It was someone.

I STEPPED out of the elevator and into the world beyond. Laughter was the first thing that assaulted me. It was quickly followed by the ting of metal hitting glass. A clinking of plates and silverware, my brain quickly supplied as a dull roar of voices threatened to overwhelm me. There were so many

voices. So many hearts that beat like a thousand tiny drums. They called me to war. My own beat too, only slower, quieter.

It was more sound I'd heard in so long, and in that time I'd grown to prefer silence. Solidarity.

The wind whistled and had I not trained myself to not respond to pain or surprise, I would have flinched. For while only death held true silence, this place was sensory overload compared to the fief. As it was, I strolled forward into the foyer, an army of the undead at my back. I didn't take many foot soldiers with me. Only the fifty or so I needed to achieve my objective and send a message of my own.

One my sister couldn't ignore.

Couldn't deny.

I flicked my gaze up over the three floors before me. Most of the noise was not coming from the upper levels. They weren't empty, though. I motioned once with my hand and the Made at my back sprang forward. They leapt the twenty feet that allowed them to clear the railing on the second floor. They jumped once more to clear the third.

My army clung to the shadows as they broke into rooms and killed those that lived. The sounds were still muffled as I moved away from the foyer and down the hall. I followed the dull roar that was only just beginning to quiet. Soon I would hear doors being flung open as some would escape my weaker counterparts. It wouldn't be long before I could hear the shrieks.

I approached a set of double doors. Blood was starting to scent the air as silence rolled over the dining hall before me.

I paused, inhaling deeply. Tonight would be a feast for me unlike any other.

Many of the Shifters before me looked on with either

confusion or distrust. They had yet to hear the sounds of death from the floors above us. My Made were being careful. I'd asked for peace and quiet so that I could have what I wished. Because of that, the Shifters hadn't yet realized that they were under attack.

Still, the talking had come to a complete stop. The clings and clanks of silverware hitting plates muted. Even the laughter, as boisterous as it was, had died out right as I came to stand between the wide-open doors. Silence had regained its footing once more.

But very soon it would yield to their screams.

A single girl got to her feet. She had long chocolate brown hair and golden eyes. Her tan skin was flushed and her expression hopeful. Her body language was open. Her heart beat faster with each second, like the pitter-patter of wings.

"Selena?" she asked, squinting.

Understanding dawned on me. With my hair now black, we looked almost the same. If not for the eyes. Perhaps Shifter sight and hearing was not as good as the rumors foretold.

I stepped forward, a cunning smile drawing my lips upward. Her brows came together as she squinted. I continued walking, making it halfway to her before I saw the moment it clicked.

"You're not Selena," she said, stumbling back.

"How did you know?" I replied softly.

"Your eyes are wrong," she started, stating the obvious. "Your heartbeat is wrong. Your face is wrong. Your blood smells wrong." She sniffed once, and a hint of fear crept into her gaze. "You look like her, but you're not her. What are you?"

I kept my smile plastered to my face with the same ease I used to remain subservient for so long now.

"I'm her sister," I told the girl, taking a step forward.

"She only has one sister and you're not Alexandra," the girl shot back. Adrenaline hit her system, giving her some fight to combat the fear.

"That's where you're wrong." I shook my head. "I'm her other sister. The one she forgot about. The one she left to rot." A hint of ice crept into my tone, so cold it burned. I was not the sister that burned though. I was not fire, or ice.

I was death.

Destruction.

"Lily died," the girl spat, her expression growing angrier. "If you were her, you'd know that."

I paused, cocking my head.

Intriguing. How very intriguing.

"I did die," I told the child, looking her over. "Twice. Selena didn't come for me then. She was too busy protecting this place. You . . . people." I couldn't help the disgust that coated my tone like bile on my tongue. "She's not here to protect you now, though, is she?"

All at once, the Shifters around the room jumped to their feet. It seemed they'd finally realized the danger in their wake.

I'd seen executions happen faster than they'd reacted.

It was almost sad in a way. How pitifully weak they were to the rumors.

And the great Alpha? Well he was nowhere to be found.

My dear, sweet sister had left to find them friends. She'd wiped out dozens of soldiers in Marrakesh. Selena, being who she was, would have thought herself above reaction. Above consequences. It was time to teach her that she wasn't the only predator on the playground now. Teach her that when the shepherds are gone, the wolves shall feast.

The darkness within me crept forward beneath my skin. It slithered through my veins and created shadows on my skin. I lifted a hand as several Shifters closed in around me, still in their human form.

Pathetically ignorant is what they were. They should have shifted on sight. Either they'd grown complacent or they were never as powerful as I'd been led to believe. It mattered not. The sheep were mine.

Closer, I beckoned them silently.

Like beasts driven by instinct, they obliged.

It was only when it was too late they realized their error.

The darkness broke free.

The screams began.

The next few moments slowed for me as I took in my carnage. Several of them shifted before my darkness reached them. A man jumped into the air and landed on one of the tables as a lion that roared. A woman pushed two smaller children behind her and then morphed into a hippo. A gaggle of younger Shifters, no older than myself, turned into hyenas. All of them, despite their different forms, human and animal alike, zoned in on me as my cloud of darkness settled over us.

It only took a single second before they started to charge.

There wasn't enough room for it. Too many bodies. Not enough space.

Even if there was, it didn't matter.

The lion got to me first. He was only three feet away when blood and tissue and muscle were leached of all essence of life as my power burrowed within him.

Bones slid across the gap between us. All that remained of him when I was done.

The hippo rushed for me, the hyenas backing her up. The Shifters still in human form dove to the side, allowing her a shot.

A chance at hope.

The hippo thundered forward, her gaping jaws wide. Saliva dripped from a tooth onto my shoulder when the darkness consumed her. The hyenas followed.

I turned, my arms extended wide, and with the added power that those Shifters gave me, I sent my dark power for the rest of them.

One by one they began to drop. They fell to their knees and then to their faces, and by the time I took a step toward the rest of the room, they were nothing but husks of skin and bone. The same as all others who had tried and failed to beat me.

I took another step toward the girl, her face now pale. Her lips trembled. Her skin began to grow faintly, like a sun trying to eclipse my night.

I tsked, sending my power forward.

"Protect the Alpha's Daughter!" a young woman cried. She ran forward, her light blonde hair flying behind her. A boy not yet a man followed swiftly. His hair an orangish yellow, and his arm was in a sling. Panic filled his eyes as the girl went ahead of him. Grim determination filled her features. The Shifters that were still alive fell in line behind them, forming a wall between me and the child.

The one Selena protected.

My power hit the young woman in the chest. While not a

corporeal thing, its energy slipped past her clothing and skin, penetrating her being deeper than the stab of a knife.

She grit her teeth, and that intrigued me.

It had been a long time since someone could hold against my strength.

I'd killed humans and Vampires alike. Mortals and immortals. Legends.

None of them could hold onto consciousness or presence of mind when I'd unleashed it upon them, but this girl did.

Even as her strength was failing, she went to her knees, but she did bow. She did not simply die. It was as if something stronger than iron had been suffused in her will to live and to fight.

I knelt before her even as the darkness ate at the men and women behind her.

"What's your name?" I asked her.

"Graeme," she spat, her German accent thick. I recognized it from my past life. She was the heir to a great house. One that would soon be dead.

"I'm pleased to have met you. When they tell the stories of how you died and your house ended, I'll make sure they honor you."

Her eyes went wide. It appeared that power didn't scare her, but those words did.

She was probably used to being powerful. Being respected.

I'll give her that in death, but the rest of them . . . I couldn't say the same.

Dark energy flowed, and with every person's essence my power only grew, suffocating all that dare touch it. The woman before me sat in the thick of it, and yet she didn't scream or cry or plead. She simply grit her teeth and accepted her fate.

It fascinated me enough I almost wanted to let her live, but what kind of message would that send? I came here to make it a graveyard like the one my sisters left me to rot in. I came here to make a point.

But I couldn't help the strange thrill that filled me as her expression fractured when the power drilled too deep. Everyone had a tolerance of what they could take. I wondered where hers was.

I couldn't stop the twisted desire I had to see her break.

Just like I broke.

My hand moved on its own accord, blackened fingertips skimming her lovely porcelain cheek. Power surged as it funneled deeper. Against her will I harvested that energy, and her fight against it made it all the more delicious. My desire to see just how deep her core of strength went only grew as she struggled.

Too soon she shattered.

A sigh of sadness whispered between my teeth as her eyes turned dull and glassy. I waited for a moment as the screams continued and more shifters rushed forth, both in front of and behind me.

It'd been a long while since something interested me. Since someone was strong enough to interest me.

Frustration chipped away at my calm exterior. Irritation that my fun was over so soon.

I lifted my head to see the boy in the sling. I hadn't noticed how close he'd gotten or that he was still standing. His free hand held hers as she walked into death. The other, the one in a sling, had come free holding a dagger. He lifted it, poised to strike.

That hand came down before my power crushed him.

A burning started in my throat as pain clawed its way through me. If I weren't already kneeling, I would be then. My power reacted past the hurt, eating away at him. He only got one swipe where he chose to slit my throat. It wouldn't have worked, even if I had been a vampire still. It was a grand notion though. A beautiful attempt at avenging his beloved.

My throat was mostly healed by the time he hit the floor beside the girl he'd tried for.

Somehow, through it all, he was still holding her hand.

Months ago regret might have filled me at the sight. All it did was cause the anger to blossom. No one was there when I died. No one held my hand. No one tried to avenge me. No one cared.

Only Victor, this past time.

Before that though . . . I looked at their linked fingers again and the darkness began to pulse as it started to build.

I'd been so alone that the only one to hold my hand was a devil in a suit. I'd sold my soul for this path. For this freedom. I'd be damned if my pity let it slip away.

Heart hardened, I turned to the double doors as an impeccably dressed man came to stand before them. He walked quietly, but not silent. Lush brown hair, tanned skin, and eyes that crinkled; his face was Aaron's, or what it would be in twenty years.

"Alpha," I said softly. "I'm happy you decided to grace me with your presence."

"You didn't give me a choice," he answered tersely as he

scanned the room—searching for something among the carnage. I shrugged my slight shoulders and strolled forward.

An odd scent washed over me.

Orange and freesia were prominent but there was something else . . .

I kept the grimace from my features. Underneath the beautiful exterior he wore, the scent of rot permeated the air. Sickness. Weakness.

"You allied with my sister, and she, along with her merry band of children are all over the world trying to find allies now." Sweat dotted his brow. "Allies that you think will win you a war."

His fingers twitched once and then again, a slight series of tremors that couldn't be hidden. "You and your kind brought this upon us all when you attacked Daizlei. I've been complacent for too long, but you don't get to enter my residence and try to kill my daughter without retaliation."

"This isn't about that." I narrowed my eyes. "If it was, you would have marched on Vilicky Novgorod by now. You haven't . . . which leads me to believe you can't." I raised an eyebrow, carefully noting his responses. "Without allies, that is."

The Shifter Alpha didn't portray his feelings through his features, but like all living things he had tells. The slight uptick in his heartrate and tightness around the eyes. "You attacked my residence; this will not go unpunished by the Court." He spoke firmly, like he believed what he said. I didn't think that was quite true.

"The Court hasn't been active in months. Anastasia has fallen, and without an heir the Supernaturals are scattered. The Witches are in hiding, and despite my sister's attempts, I

don't see them leaving their desert anytime soon. Which leaves you." I cocked my head and let my long nails tap along the tops of the dark wooden tables. The beating of drums had calmed with the deaths of many. My own power perfumed the air as it sought for more but found only bones.

Most everyone in here was dead now. Yet the Alpha stood here speaking calmly. I could only assume why.

"Do your Shifters know you're sick?" I asked him.

His lip trembled.

It appears I hit a nerve.

"No."

"Pity," I murmured under my breath. "They don't realize how weak they are. Your complacence, as you call it, will be their downfall. You've let them believe you're healthy and they're safe, but without the power of a true Alpha they're crippled." A fine sheen of sweat broke across his forehead. The dewy drops reflecting under the harsh lighting. Within the moments he'd been standing here the illusion of health waned. Sallow cheeks and sharp bones started to jut out. The larger frame he carried shrank more and more as the seconds went by.

"Why have you come here?" he asked through gritted teeth. He was clenching his jaw in an attempt to keep his now chattering teeth at bay, but I saw through it. "What message do you have from the High Council?"

I smiled and began to walk toward him, leaving only footprints behind as I stepped in the dust created by the dead.

"It's not for you," I said, coming to stand before him. The Alpha . . . the almighty Alpha . . . he didn't even lift a hand to stop me as I pushed my fingers through his flesh and cracked his bones. His heart shuddered, trying to beat, even as my

hand closed around it. I clenched my fist around it and the soft tissue yielded in a small explosion of blood.

"Katherina . . ." he breathed out, dying in seconds.

If he felt any pain, he didn't show it. Sick and already at the door, death welcomed the Alpha into its arms like a lover.

I pulled my hand from his chest and the old man's body tipped backward. It fell for a suspended moment and then hit the floor with a dull thump.

I didn't feast on his energy because I wanted this one to be intact.

My message clear.

No one was safe, not even the Alpha.

An elevator dinged in the distance. A single set of footsteps ran. I tilted my head. I was just stepping over the body when another appeared in the doorway. Brownish-red dust coated his skin in uneven swipes. His body stank of sweat and maleness, but there was something underneath it. Something familiar . . . I peered up at him silently as his expression turned from stunned to feral. Rage pulsed through his skin and the black surrounding his pupil bled away to a brilliant gold.

I realized it then that the familiar scent that clung to him was my sister.

I'd come here to return her message.

It appeared that luck was finally on my side.

THE SCENE SHATTERED. My vision cleared. Bright lights assaulted me. Hands touched my skin. Faces I recognized but couldn't place in the moment were bathed in blue and red light. They spoke to me, but I didn't hear the words.

A tidal wave of emotion built in my chest. It held me suspended in time as it rose and fell. I didn't understand the nameless emotion that consumed me in the moment. All I knew was that the impossible just happened.

A roar filled my ears. My chest tightened painfully.

I took a single gasping breath and the bubble popped as Valda whispered, *"I'm so sorry."*

CHAPTER 20

"What happened?" I asked. Too many people tried to respond, and I raised my voice to a shout. "Why did he leave? Why was he there?" They quieted then.

Only one of them spoke and the words were my undoing.

"He got a call from Keyla. She was scared and crying; said something bad was happening. He charged into the elevator—"

I moved in a suspended state of shock. They were still talking. Still trying to explain to me. To calm me even though they didn't know what I'd seen. Not really.
Not yet.

I got to my feet and shoved past them all as I headed for the elevator. I had to get to him. I had to get to her. To stop what was about to happen, even if Valda was simply shaking her head. My demon was desperate. We shared the feeling.

Four gray metal walls surrounded me, the sounds of protests and shouting ceasing as the doors shut.

Power filled my being, lifting my hair from the nape of my neck. I could sense the dark tendrils as they caressed my skin.

The elevator dinged. The doors slid open.

Silence.

It was the first thing that greeted me, and my heart began to beat. Blood rushed in my veins and a pounding filled my ears. I raced down the halls. A sickly-sweet scent filled my nostrils. I wasn't even to the double doors when my stomach plummeted. Nausea made my head swim as I stumbled forward the last few feet.

Death. So much death. It filled the room—filled the residence. Blood and dust and bone scattered the empty tables. I spotted Ash's father. The gaping hole in his chest said it all. Beyond him, Scarlett and Liam lay together. The end of their houses.

In all the carnage, Ash was nowhere to be found.

His scent was here but fading.

Our bond was weak, but not gone.

I searched inside myself, looking for that other side —but found only darkness. The sudden loss overwhelmed me. I fell to my knees and the sound of a creature in such immense pain startled me at first, because I didn't realize the sound was coming from me.

My fists clenched against the wood floors and panels broke apart beneath my fingers as I clawed at them. I screamed and the windows shattered like pieces of my heart. I shook, and the residence trembled with me. My grip on my power—my sanity—was slipping.

I'd lost my parents.

I'd lost my sister.

I'd lost my signasti.

I'd lost my *home.*

There were so many words that could probably describe what I was feeling. There were certainly so many thoughts. Feelings. Overwhelming wasn't a strong enough description of the literal soul-crushing experience.

A floorboard shifted.

I didn't realize what it was at first. I saw, but it didn't register as a brown head popped up.

It was only her voice that brought me back from the edge of ending it all.

"Selena, is that you?"

My breath caught in my throat. My vision cleared. She sat in a hidden compartment under a wooden table. Her golden eyes glowing. Her fear bringing her ability out, stifling my own power.

I'd thought she was dead. I thought everyone that had been in this room was dead to my sister's all-consuming power. I didn't realize she hid.

I didn't know there was hope.

The mansion stilled and without the rush of power, my grief-stricken haze lifted.

"Keyla?" I whispered.

Her face crumpled as she crawled out of the hole she'd hidden in. Tears streaked her face and red rimmed her eyes and she tried to scramble out from under the table, avoiding the bodies of Shifters as she did so. I stood up and walked toward her. Keyla pulled herself free of the table and stumbled forward, her legs picking up speed the closer she got.

She barreled into me, throwing her arms around my shoulders as she buried her head in the crook of my neck where it met my shoulder. Wet tears soaked my shirt as sobs racked her body.

"He's dead," she moaned. I held her tight, clinging to her as she clung to me. "She's killed him!" she continued in a strangled cry. "She k-killed my dad."

"Shhhh," I breathed. Her pain resonated with my own.

The difference was she was a bystander in all of this. A child who did nothing and couldn't have stopped it.

I could have . . . but didn't.

I pressed my lips together and rested my cheek on her hair. We stayed like that for a few moments, rocking back and forth as she let it out and I held her together. It was painful to see her this way. Not as much as what came next, because deep down I knew . . . this was it.

The final straw.

She stole Ash from me, and I had to find a way to get him back before it was too late. For months now the signs had been pointing to this, but I didn't want to see it. Even when the Crone asked it, when Milla asked it, when the ancients asked it—I denied them all.

And once again, it cost me more than I was prepared to pay. It wasn't right and it wasn't fair, but I was the only one with the power to change that.

Keyla's sobs slowly quieted. Her spasms stopped. She leaned against me as the numbness of grief sunk in, and I knelt, sweeping an arm under her knees. I curled the other around her back and turned, cradling her to my chest as I walked away from the dining hall where the worst of the crimes against the Shifters had been committed.

She didn't need to see this anymore. There was nothing that would bring back that room or the dead Shifters in it, her father included. I wished he'd taken the time to tell his kids he was sick while he was still here. I wished he'd warned them of the inevitable. Maybe it wouldn't be so hard for her . . . for Ash. Then again, death was death. Whether by sickness or slaughter it was the permanence that made it so difficult for the living when their loved ones were gone.

I knew a thing or two about that kind of loss. I felt it myself, even now. Not for the Alpha or Scarlett or Liam, or for the hundreds of Shifters that died today in the dining room alone . . . though I should. I felt it for Ash, though he was still living. I felt it for Lily because I knew she wouldn't be able to any longer.

I felt it for myself because the truth was staring me in the face.

Fate would take everything from me for the recompense it was owed. My debt or not, the ancients would find a way to reap what my bloodline sowed.

Either I paid the price, or the world did.

Milla had all but told me that, and I would laugh if it wouldn't lead to crying, because it was my choices that brought us here. I'd suspected long enough she was in Vilicky Novgorod. While near impenetrable, it wasn't impossible. Nothing was.

And yet I didn't go to her.

I didn't save her.

So she damned herself instead.

Keyla sniffed, the air between the nostrils whistling like a screech as she wiped her nose on my dirty shirt.

"Keyla?" another voice asked as we turned the corner, the group pouring out of the elevator. Keyla turned her head and her eyes began to water when she saw Amber standing there, her expression that of relief. "I'm so happy you're okay—"

"He's gone," Keyla whispered, her voice scratchy. "They're all gone." Amber's face started to fall as Keyla made no move to go for her and instead turned and clung to me further. Golden eyes chiseled into hard gems; Amber looked up at me.

"What happened here? Why are so many people dead?"

How did I answer that? How did I tell them my sister was the reason so many friends and family were torn apart?

"The residence was attacked while we were gone," I started, my voice hoarse from screaming. I kept talking while I still could. "The Alpha was killed. Scarlett and Liam were killed. Ash . . . Ash was taken."

"Taken?" Amber whispered. She looked from the broken railings of the second and third floor, to the bloody handprints that decorated the walls here and there.

"By Vampires."

"This is why Ash took off. This is what . . ." Alexandra turned away from me, trying to collect her thoughts as she was already coming to the conclusion I didn't want to say.

"The visions . . . they're getting worse the—" My

words choked to a stop as I started to explain what the Crone did and how it affected me. Valda's curse inhibited any who didn't already know from being told, and the words sat on my tongue.

"The?" Alexandra repeated. Anger coated her tone.

"I can't say," I answered, swallowing hard. "All I can tell you is that the Vampires attacked, and a large number of Shifters were killed. They came here to send a message."

"Killing the Alpha isn't sending a message—" Alexandra started.

"The message wasn't for my father," Keyla said. "It was for her." She looked up at me, and it amazed me that this child who knew the truth about why Lily came was clinging to me. I couldn't understand why she would find any comfort in me anymore, but she clearly did, and I wasn't going to turn her away.

"What's she talking about?" Amber asked, her voice splintering apart as she took in the reasoning why her home had been attacked.

"While we were away, something happened in the High Council. My sister was killed . . ." I paused, not knowing how to continue. How do I tell them the truth I've been holding back for so long? "She came back."

"What do you mean she came back?" Johanna asked.

"I mean she pulled the dagger from her heart and it started to beat again."

"That's not possible—" Oliver started.

"But it *happened*," I said without an ounce of spite in my voice. We were beyond the anger and spite. Despera-tion was all I had left. "Ivan killed her, and she came back and destroyed him. She's in control of Victor and the High Council now."

"Did she do this?" Alexandra asked. I bit the inside of my cheek because I didn't want to say, but of course that's why she asked.

"Yes."

That single word was her doom. I knew after this there was no coming back. They wouldn't support me, and I didn't know if I could even support myself.

"How?" Alexandra asked. Her expression was shuttered, her words harder than steel.

"How doesn't really matter right now when we need to help the people—" I started.

"How. Did. She. Kill. Them?" Alexandra said, her voice rising. I swallowed hard as her dark flaming hair fanned higher and the demon's apathetic tone crept into her voice.

"Her power's grown. After all that's been done to her, something twisted. The Vampires broke her and the way the pieces came back together again . . . she's not who she was. She's vengeance and death and ultimately—she's destruction." With every window in the mansion shattered and the cold of late December seeping into the walls, a chilled breeze drifted through and Keyla shivered.

"How long?" Alexandra asked. "How long have you known what she really is?"

"A month . . . maybe more," I said under my breath. Guilt and shame ate at me.

"You knew the road she was going down for *a month*

and let us believe she was some sad, lonely Vampire being tortured—"

"She was," I snapped.

"She just killed hundreds of Shifters!" she screamed at me. "I don't have to run through the rooms to see that when I smell it." Fire erupted up her arms, and if she noticed she did nothing about it. "We don't even know who's all dead yet—"

"She was tortured!" I shouted. Alexandra stepped back. The fire winked out. "She was starved and beaten and forced to eat children to survive. Her master—her signasti—is the Dark Prince. She was abandoned and left alone in the High Council's clutches for months. Of course she turned down a dark path. After what's been done to her I don't blame her for hating me. I hate myself enough for not saving her while I still had a chance." My voice cracked at the end, and I looked at Tori. "You asked me if it were my sister instead of your brother how I'd feel. Despite what she is, I love her—even though I am the reason she became this way. I love her, and I wanted to save her so badly . . ." Tori's eyes watered and there was pity in them. "I didn't tell anyone what she was becoming because I wanted to believe she could come back from it. I'm sorry I lied by omission and this is what it brought down on us. I didn't mean for this to happen . . ."

No one said anything as Alexandra took one look at me and turned on her heel. The front door slammed. Tori didn't look at me as she ran up the stairs and took off down a hallway, leaving Alexandra to stew on her own.

"I need to go find my mom," Amber said, shaking her

head. Her eyes were glassy and her steps shaky as she bolted from the room at a speed the rest of them likely couldn't follow.

"Someone needs to check on the Shifters. There will be injured that need tending to. Dead that need to be buried. The children without a parent need to be gathered together until we can find out who is dead, missing, or alive," Johanna said. Her golden eyes stared at me intently.

"If the Alpha is dead and the heir is missing, it falls on you to lead them, Selena," Blair said. I was already shaking my head before she finished her sentence.

"I'm a little busy with—"

"Selena," Blair said. I sighed, adjusting Keyla as I turned to directly face her. "His people were just killed. His father was killed. You and Keyla are the last things they have to hold onto. With the Alpha dead, that makes Aaron the new Alpha—and you by default." My teeth clenched together but I didn't argue with her. "Keyla isn't old enough to lead them, but someone has to. They won't accept me or Johanna or Alexandra or even Amber. You are his signasti, and the only one with a claim to lead that's strong enough to make them listen."

I didn't want to, and if we were all being honest, I wasn't the ideal choice for a leader. I never have been. Almost any one of them was better suited. Blair and Johanna and Alexandra and Amber, all included. Amber wasn't strong enough to take on the powers we were facing, though, and Keyla didn't have the age or fortitude to handle what was coming.

I hated it because I never wanted to lead. It seemed

like so long ago that I was just a girl trying to protect my sisters from the world and from themselves. That I was no one, just a girl bound to exceptional power.

Now I was a Fortescue. I was a matter manipulator. I was a Konig. I was an Alpha.

I was the world's last chance.

Keyla leaned in and whispered, "I believe in you. If anyone can get my brother back, you can."

The words hurt me as much as they solidified my decision—if it could even be called that. I'd made a lot of shit decisions that led us here. Time and again the Crone told me a choice would have to be made. I chose wrong before, and now I was going to fix it.

I had no other option.

It was time to go to war.

CHAPTER 21

Sleep called to me around six in the morning, but I couldn't do it. I couldn't close my eyes and see what was becoming of her. What she was doing to him. Maybe it made me a coward that I couldn't watch the consequences of my actions. I wasn't sure, but of all the horrors I'd seen, something told me if I closed my eyes that these would be the worst.

That these would truly break me.

Keyla slumbered in a fitful sleep beside me in the large canopy bed. I laid on Ash's side where it still smelled like him. I let his scent wrap around me and comfort me and my demon while we watched over Keyla. Her brown hair was splayed out and she looked so innocent. So meek. If I didn't know of the immense power she hid I would never have guessed. If I hadn't felt it myself, I'd never have believed it.

Footsteps approached the door and I pulled myself from the soft mattress and padded toward it. My fingers grasped the cool metal. It slipped in my clammy palm as

I turned the handle. Johanna stood in front of it, hand poised to knock. She lowered it to her side and raised both eyebrows.

"Have you slept at all?" she asked, peering past me into the dark room.

"No." The word was curt and the response probably rude, but I didn't have enough working brain power to do better. Her brows drew together in concern. I stepped out into the adjoining living room and closed the door behind me. Keyla didn't stir.

"If you don't sleep—"

"I won't have to see things I can never unsee," I replied, crossing my arms over my chest.

Understanding flashed in her golden eyes. She nodded once, tugging at the sleeve of her long shirt. "You won't be able to avoid sleeping forever, you know," she said eventually.

"I'm aware." I sighed. "But it doesn't mean I won't try. Why are you here?"

She looked like she wanted to say more but decided against it. Johanna extended her hand. In it was a folded piece of stationary.

The scent of sickly-sweetness that faintly drifted from it made me tense.

There was only one thing that smelled that way.

I swallowed, but my throat was dry. My arms dropped back to my sides.

"Have you read it?" I asked. Johanna nodded. Her expression was solemn. "And?" I prompted, hoping for better but knowing it was only worse.

She handed me the note. I grasped the stiff paper

between my index finger and thumb. The texture was rough, almost chalky. It absorbed the dampness from my finger as I flipped it open. My stomach clenched as I read:

My Dearest Sister,

I trust you've received my message by now. You left me to die. I wonder if you will do the same for your signasti. I'll be in Central Park in three days' time when the sun goes down.

Every second you're not there is another drop of blood I take from him.

I look forward to seeing you again. Tick. Tock. ~Lily

My teeth threatened to crack from how hard I clenched them. I'd known she was planning to play games. They'd become her favorite pastime in recent months. Her only real joy. I'd known I only had so long before she turned her sights my way and finally enacted this grand ploy she'd been dreaming up.

I thought I'd be able to stop her before it came to this. I thought I had more time. But now we were here, and in three days I had to come face-to-face with my sister and kill her. Again.

Somehow.

"She wrote this in blood," Johanna commented. I didn't need to lift it to my nose to know she was right. Even dried, the note stunk of their undead scent and made my stomach turn.

"How was it delivered?" I asked.

"She sent a messenger. I found him first. His head has

already been removed," she answered pragmatically in a detached voice.

"Have you told the others?"

"Not yet." Her answer surprised me. "I thought you deserved to be the first to know." I nodded but couldn't find it in me to tell her thank you.

"We need to figure out a plan," I said. "She's moving pieces on the board so fast I can't keep up, but now that she has Ash I have no choice but to try."

"If you slept you might see what she was actually planning," Johanna said, testing the waters.

I nodded, releasing a strained breath. "I know, but I'm not prepared for what I'm going to see. She slaughtered a room full of Shifters without trying. She killed the Alpha with barely any effort. All these months I've been planning to get her back and she's simply been biding her time, growing stronger . . ." I let the words trail as I shook my head.

"I won't pretend that I'm thrilled with you right now," Johanna murmured, taking a step back and turning to survey the fixed windows and clean space. "I understand why you did it though. We often overlook the worst qualities in the people we care about. It's a flaw unto itself really. You wanted to believe that given enough time you could find her and fix her."

I nodded, slipping the note into the baggy sweatpants I wore. "I have a problem with willfully believing what I want because I want it to be true. So many people have died because of that. Because of me." My chest tightened.

Johanna looked at the ceiling, stuffing her hands in

her pockets while she did so. "The things the world is asking of you right now aren't right. The sacrifices you've had to make and will have to continue to aren't fair. It's too much to expect one your age to handle this well." Slowly her attention drifted down the walls, coming to settle on me. "Regardless of all of that, the gods and the world are asking it, and they're asking it of you—the one of us who is the most capable and yet struggles the greatest in turn. You're an interesting choice for them to make. I can't help but wonder if they chose someone who's neither good nor bad for a reason."

"Would you do it?" I asked her.

"I'd like to think I would," she answered softly. "But I can't say for certain. The truth of it is none of us have had to give as much as you and none of us are being asked to make the choices you are." The pressure around my chest eased its grip. "Jayma was my best friend. I loved her as much as you love your sisters and Anastasia killed her. If she hadn't actually died... if she'd come back as something else ... I can't say I could be the one to put a dagger through her heart. I'd like to think I could. That I would do it for the old her, but the truth is I don't know, and I don't want to know."

I nodded, moving to take a seat on the cushioned leather couches. I sat near the edge with my legs open and my elbows resting on my knees. I leaned forward, letting out a yawn into my hands and then running them through my hair.

"I don't even know if she can be killed," I admitted.

"Everything can be killed," Johanna answered, coming around to sit across from me.

"I'm not so certain of that," I murmured. "She was stabbed through the heart and healed herself. She has a heartbeat again. I don't think she's even Made anymore. She's something else. Something," I paused, trying to grasp for a word that could explain but came up short. "More. She's more than you or me."

Johanna sighed. "She's a part demon that was turned Vampire. She could heal herself before death. It's not a stretch to say that she might have found a way out of it."

I reached for the brandy on the end table and poured two fingers in a crystal glass. Johanna eyed me with distaste when I extended it to her.

"It's six something in the morning," she said.

I shrugged. "It's five o'clock somewhere."

The liquid burned going down my throat but the heat that spread through me, it was a mockery of what heat could be. I frowned down at the decanter and set it aside. This was a hard conversation to be having this early with no sleep, but with three days and the clock ticking, it wasn't one I could avoid.

"We're going to find a way through this," Johanna said. I grimaced at my glass, turning it round and round to watch the two drops of amber liquid run around the rim.

"You can't guarantee that," I said.

"No," she nodded. "But I've been in a lot of difficult situations before. Seen a lot of bad and good. More bad than good, if I'm being honest. I have to think that the ancients wouldn't ask this of you if there wasn't hope at the end of the line."

I thought about that. It was hard to believe she'd

have hope if she knew what I knew though. Assuming I could find a way to send my own sister to the grave, I had to follow her.

If there was hope, it wasn't meant for me.

The only thing that waited on my horizon was death.

CHAPTER 22

"Three days?" Alexandra repeated. We stood around a long conference table, none of us using the chairs. On one side of the room, a wall of windows overlooked the field that had once been where Shifters trained. Now it was barren; the odd mechanical contraption they'd used to train sat quiet without the gears turning to make the scythes swing. It looked sad. Desolate. About the same as the people around here felt.

In front of it a pile of bodies had been stacked and was growing higher by the hour as Shifters brought their loved ones before it. I should have counted my lucky stars that Ash wasn't in it. I was grateful, but all I could think about was where he was and what my sister may or may not be doing to him. I wondered if death would have been kinder.

I wondered about a lot of things.

"Yes," I answered, almost absentmindedly. It was strange how fast things were happening that I was being forced to take it in stride. People dying. My signasti being kidnapped. My sister coming back. The inevitable end. I should have been screaming or crying or tearing apart mansions and causing earthquakes. Instead I stood eerily quiet, watching over the cold ground, once so full of life . . . like me.

"How do we even plan for that?" she asked. "There's what" —her eyes flicked from one person to the next— "seven of us. That's it. What kind of plan involves seven of us?"

"We're not sure yet," Johanna said. "That's what we need to figure out—"

"I'm inclined to agree with Alexandra here, Jo," Oliver said. "I want revenge for our friends too. What happened to Scarlett and Liam . . ." His voice trailed off, and we all looked at anything but each other, especially me. "The missing Alpha is a problem, but how do you expect us to even make a dent when they killed almost a third of the entire residence?"

"She doesn't," I answered him. "While a third of the residence is dead, two thirds very much aren't, and they want justice for their friends and family. I can have Tam put out a call and I guarantee there will be even more Shifters that will rally around us when they hear what's happened." Was it a great plan? No. No, it was not. At the moment it was all I had to go on.

"What are more Shifters going to do when they only managed to even kill a handful of Made during the attack?" he asked, his voice dripping with condescension as he forgot one little fun fact.

"Hey," Amber snapped, bristling. A trail of fur started to line her arms as her eyes glowed. "Many Shifters died in that attack because they were taken by surprise. My mother included . . ." Her voice trailed off as the fight started to leave her as fast as it came. Alexandra put an arm around her shoulder and stared pointedly at me. I ignored it.

My guilt had already suffocated me so thoroughly I was forgoing breathing at this point.

"The Shifters were not prepared for the last attack. They would be for this one, and there will be more of them from Tam's estimates," Johanna inserted diplomatically. "We'd also be able to use Selena and Alexandra's Fortescue heritage to call on Supernaturals for aid."

Alexandra scoffed. "The Supernaturals hate us as much as everyone else does. While the Fortescue name holds power in persuading other courts to do shit, the people are tired of it. Too many died at Daizlei and they think Selena did it. Too many have been kidnapped and turned or worse." She pressed her lips together as her thoughts took a darker turn.

"She's not wrong," Blair said. "We'll be lucky if we get even a few hundred Supes willing to join the fight, and even then, there's no way of knowing if their powers are useful for this."

"And that's not even our worst problem," Alec said. He stood at the opposite end of the room from my cousin. I noticed her tense in my periphery. Her demon kept its thoughts and opinions to itself for the moment. While we'd been out trying to form an alliance with the Witches, Alec stayed here to guard Lucas. Something that saved both their lives during the attack.

Fortunately, him being alive kept her demon

appeased. Unfortunately, this situation was testing her small modicum of control.

"Our worst problem?" I found myself asking. "I don't know how we really quantify what's better or worse here. People have died and more are going to before this is over. Ash is gone. The Shifters are crippled. The Supernaturals just as much so in their own ways. We haven't even heard anything from the Fae since this happened—"

"Actually, we have," Amber said. "Cade's mother laughed in his face when he pleaded for our cause."

"His father was a Shifter." I frowned. She nodded.

"And the Shifters didn't rise against the Supes when he was killed."

Well then.

If it were even possible, the situation just went from bad to worse.

"That's still not the worst problem," Alec said, interjecting again. I turned, looking at him pointedly.

"Please, tell us what the problem is, then," I said, losing patience with this.

"Central Park."

I blinked. "What?"

"Central Park," he repeated.

"Yes, I have quite good hearing. I heard you the first time—"

"Humans," Blair said. I paused mid-sentence, my lips parted and jaw hanging open. At once, I understood what they were getting at.

A string of expletives tumbled from my lips. One look

around the table told me I wasn't the only one who missed that.

"She wants to start a war in Central Park and expose magic and paranormals to the world," Alec said after the shock started to wane. "Anastasia had suspicions this was their plan for a long while before she started keeping me at bay." His attention strayed toward Blair before he corrected himself and turned back to address me directly. "If we do meet her there and a fight breaks out, there will be no way to keep this from the media. If we do this and lose? It becomes open hunting season for the Vampires."

My insides curdled at the thought, but once he pointed it out I knew he was right. This was her move. To give us too little time to plan. To force us into the open. For so long Vampires had been sequestered away from the world because of what they were, and strict laws placed on them for feeding. If the people who enforced those laws were no longer around, then Vampires had free rein, and with the Born able to create new Made, it wouldn't take long for them to have a true army. One that not even the entire paranormal community could hold back.

"She's in Vilicky Novgorod," I said. "What if—"

"We can't march on the High Council," Johanna sighed. "There's too many Vampires and no way of getting that many of us there in time that the first wave wouldn't just be slaughtered."

"I never said anything about getting *us* there," I replied tersely.

"Then what—"

"It's her." I cut her off in a harsh tone. "She's the one leading them. If we take her out, then we stop the brain. She's the Dark Prince's signasti. If she's out of the picture, he won't be able to function. The Made can't think for themselves because they've been too subjugated and the Born have lost their confidence ever since Ivan the Cruel stabbed her through the heart and she came back again."

"Selena . . ." Alexandra started, some unnamable emotion coating her tone that I didn't understand.

"What? That's what you wanted, isn't it? Her to be taken out?" My sister swallowed, her lips pressing together. "I can go by myself. I'm faster and stronger. If I can get to her, then maybe—"

"No," she said. "You made a mistake in not telling us, and I'm still unbelievably pissed at you for it, but I'm not letting you go on a suicide mission because you've decided to take this on yourself now—"

"Then what do you want me to do?" I asked her, leaning forward and placing my hands on the conference table. "She is where this begins and ends. I hate it more than any of you—but she is what we need to focus on. If she comes out of this alive, it doesn't matter how many Vampires we kill. She will never stop."

"Why?" Blair asked when Alexandra didn't speak fast enough.

"She blames us for not saving her. She knows I stayed here and protected Keyla. She thinks that we left her to rot."

"We didn't leave her—" Alexandra started, anger surging forward.

"It doesn't matter what we did. All that matters is what she thinks."

"The girl I knew was soft. Gentle. Even after you started training her she held onto her compassion. For her to do this . . ." Blair said and shook her head as if perplexed by the situation.

"She was desperate. People do crazy things when they're desperate." I sighed. "In Lily's case, she had to find a way to survive what she'd done and the only way she could was to normalize it." My hands formed fists as I thought of the way she'd killed the girl that looked like Alexandra. She'd told herself a great many lies since then. Lies that she started to truly believe. "She told herself that's what survivors do. Her thoughts have quickly descended into madness ever since killing Anastasia, but she bordered on it before that."

Of course, Cirian's soul had a part to play in that. While my sister had already lost so much of the battle before she'd killed Anastasia, the ruthlessness developed after, as did the grandiose thoughts. I hung my head, watching the strands drift back and forth.

"That's very curious that it was Anastasia's death that tipped her over . . ." Johanna murmured, her thumb brushing over her bottom lip as she stared too hard at the mahogany table.

"No matter what brought it about, I don't agree with you going there by yourself. It's what she's going to expect because that's what you've always done," Alexandra said.

"I second that," Blair chimed in.

"I do as well," Johanna concluded.

"Which brings us back to square one," I said, lifting my head again. "We have to be in Central Park in three days and have as many allies as possible. It's our only choice."

A knock came at the door. I lifted a hand and the knob twisted on its own accord. The wooden panel swung open, revealing a red-eyed Keyla in mourning clothes.

"Everything's ready," she said. Her lips were chapped and her tan skin pale. Her slender form was covered head to toe in black, formless clothes. Her bottom lip quivered as she waited for an answer.

"If this is the best we've got, then I think we're done here," I said to the others as I walked around the table and went to her side. I linked our arms together as we headed downstairs.

"Selena," she started softly.

"Hmm?"

"Are you really going to kill your sister?" she asked. I took a deep breath. No one had asked me quite so directly. No one deserved an answer more.

"I am," I told her as we came to a stop before the open double doors that led out to the training field.

"I'm sorry," she said.

I don't think I'd ever heard something as kind as those two words. My sister took her father from her. She took her brother from both of us. Somehow, Keyla managed to have empathy for me despite it all.

I pulled my arm away just to wrap it around her shoulder and kissed her hair as I whispered back. "Me too, kiddo. Me too."

CHAPTER 23

The scent of burning flesh cloaked the residence as the fire burned past the midday sun and into the night. Our first day was over. The second had yet to come.

Thoughts of the future and what I had to do weighed heavily on me as the flames licked through skin and muscle and bone. While Lily's victims were largely ash as it was, the others that had died were not. Keyla gripped my hand in hers as she stood with me, staring into the flames. Her sobs had broken hours ago. The tears had run dry. Now all that remained were her long fingers linked tightly through mine as she numbly gazed forward.

On her other side, Amber stood, looking like an older version of grief. Keyla lost her father. Amber lost her mother. Now they were orphans like me.

The thought was almost as gut wrenching as the smell. I'd never forget either as long as I lived.

Across the pyre, my sister's dark eyes watched me. While the Shifters and Supernaturals around her stared into the burning remnants of their loved ones, she stared at me and only me. Her jaw set in a hard line. Her lips pinched. She was still angry with me for keeping secrets and for the outcome they brought.

I couldn't blame her for the anger, but she also didn't know half the things I did. I could thank the Crone for that.

"*It's not her fault,*" Valda said.

"*Her actions brought this about,*" was my reply.

"*And mine. And Cirian's. I'm as much to blame as she is,*" Valda answered. She shook her head, and I couldn't help but wonder how much she suffered through the ages—watching the outcome of her actions as I watched mine now.

"I wish there was another way," I whispered.

"*I know.*"

The sun set and the moon rose. The fire weakened as the last of the bodies burned to ash. When it was only soot and charred bones that glowed like embers, the flames winked out.

Through it all I stood there. Even after Shifters began to leave. After Amber escorted Keyla back. After there was not a soul in the field, except mine, Valda's, and the ancient presence I felt watching over me through the funeral.

"Did you know?" I asked, my voice quiet but still loud in the dead of night. A sweep of cloth over the frozen blades of grass was the only indication that she'd stepped out of the trees. I turned and repeated my question again. "Did you know that this would be the outcome if I went with Milla to the Witch clans when given the choice? Did you know while I was with you it gave my sister the reason and time to attack, whereas if I had never gone with Milla, this would have never happened? Did you know that in choosing to try for an alliance, Lily was going to attack and I wouldn't make it back in time?"

Her kaleidoscope eyes smoked over with a hazy blue as she let out a sigh. The Crone lifted a hand and beckoned me forward, her joints cracking with the motion.

I stood my ground.

"Did. You. Know?"

Her eyes fell to the pile of ash where grass had once been. The stench of death still filled the air.

"Yes."

My eyes closed, and I pinched the bridge of my nose. "Why?" I asked. "Why would you lead us into the Witch clans just for this to happen?" I threw an arm wide, my eyes flying open as the anger returned. It was only a shadow of what it once was, though. I was too tired. The fight was too long. The costs of this war were too steep for me to continue to hold onto only rage. Before it had been all-consuming, but now there were grief and guilt and such a deep sadness there to keep it company.

Misery. That's what they called it.

"You had to make a choice," the Crone started. "It's hard to see, and I don't think you even understand what you were choosing between, but ultimately you chose right."

"My sister—"

"What little good that was left in her has already been corrupted by Cirian's soul," the Crone replied. She wasn't harsh or cruel, but the words didn't hurt any less. "You know this. You've known it for a time now."

"I'm tired," I said eventually after a long pause. Her aged skin fell as she looked at me with pity. "I'm tired of the secrets and the lies. I'm tired of fighting and losing. I'm tired of people dying—of being the reason they die. I'm tired of having the weight of the world on my shoulders."

"I know, child."

"Regardless of whether it's right or fair, I don't want to kill her . . . but I don't think I have a choice." I stuffed my hands in my pockets as the chill settled over us. A light misting of fog blew across the grounds of the residence, sweeping the ashes and smoke across the land.

"Come," Livina said, her knobby fingers beckoning me forward. We walked into the forest together. "A sacrifice is not payment without choice, Selena," she said after we had walked a bit. Her thick cloak drifted over the dirt and twigs and leaves without ever snagging. She used the staff as a walking stick. "It may not feel like you have a choice, but there is *always* a choice."

"It doesn't feel like one when my options are find a way to kill her or let the Vampires take over and kill everyone."

"I never said the choice wasn't hard," the Crone continued. "Only that it's there. It can't be a sacrifice if you don't choose to make it." Those words struck me, and I didn't know why. "The gods punished us because I refused to sacrifice the person I loved most in this world. Valda and Cirian and I have played this eternal game because of that choice. Cirian burrowing into the

Fortescue minds, using them as his puppets to create evil. Valda, watching each of her line die as a result of her actions. Whereas I'm trapped here, in this body of an old woman trying to move the pieces to where they need to be—when they need to be there." She stared past me, but I got the feeling she wasn't really looking at the forest. Like she saw something beyond. Something that hadn't happened yet, or perhaps something from long ago. "I can taste the end. I know it's coming for me. For us all. Milla sees a great battle on the horizon, with too many endings to count. They all come down to you and what you choose to do."

"I don't even know *how* to kill her," I said. "Or if she can truly be killed."

"Nothing is impossible," the Crone said cryptically.

"You're not going to tell me more than that, are you?"

She smiled. Aged and yellowed as her teeth were, bleeding at the gums, clearly in pain—she smiled.

"I can't," she said. "It's not the ancient's wish."

"I wish the ancients would come down here and tell me themselves what they want and how to do it," I griped. She chuckled.

"We're all pieces on a board to them, Selena. You, me, Valda, Lily. They created the world and its children." Red bled into her eyes, making her look like one of the Made. "I broke the balance and they chose to punish us all. You are the opportunity that has been a thousand years in the making."

"Here's the thing I don't understand," I said, my breath creating puffs of white. "Why me? Why does the killing have to be by my hand?"

"*Because of me*," Valda said.

"You hold the Mother," the Crone said. "If one of your sisters had been born first, then they would hold the Mother, and the duty would have passed to them."

I shivered. The idea of Alexandra or Lily being forced into this . . .

"It has nothing to do with me being Nyx's Blessed?"

The Crone shook her head. "The mother goes to the first born, regardless of your power . . ."

"But?" I asked, sensing the unspoken word.

Livina sighed. "I find it interesting that it was you. I have wondered many times these last years as I watched you struggle and grow, if it was intentional on the ancients' part that you were chosen and not one of your sisters. You've always struggled the most with who and what you are. The ancients picked the child who would have the most difficult time with this choice, and I can't help but wonder about that . . ." Her voice cracked as it often did, using aged vocal cords. "About you."

"I don't know if that really makes it better or worse that it could have been someone else. One of them instead of me." Above me the night sky filtered through the trees. Bright stars lit the night. Burning prisons for the ancients of old, if my father was right. "I suppose it doesn't really matter in the end. Nothing can change it."

"Would you change it?" she asked. The question startled me. "If you could?" I thought for a moment as we walked deeper into the night.

"I don't think I would," I said. "Whether it's me or them, someone has to do it. I'm not selfless enough to say if it were someone else or some other family—that I wouldn't push it on them, but my own sisters? No . . . I don't think I could." A light wind blew, whipping the strands of hair from my face. It made the trees restless as the branches shifted and the leaves rustled.

A raccoon scampered by as we approached the lake, though we certainly hadn't walked twenty miles with her limp. The corner of her lips drew up as I cast her a wary glance.

"Magic," she said mischievously. Livina shuffled forward to settle on a rock, her staff laying at her side. The wide expanse beyond was a void of black, dotted in light by the stars' reflections.

"Why did you bring me out here?" I asked cautiously, approaching the flat rock next to her.

"To give you a gift," she said, turning toward the water. It wasn't an easy movement for her old limbs. She kicked one leg up at a time before scooching toward the water's surface.

"What kind of gift?" I asked, no less wary. The Crone had an odd way of being. Last time she gave me a gift it was a riddle foretelling of Lily's fall.

"The only thing I can give you." She reached for her staff, falling six inches short. With a wave of my hand the staff lifted and met her fingers. She gave a grateful chuff before facing the water once more.

Livina lifted the wood and the orb at the end began to glow. My chest squeezed.

"I don't want to see more of Lily—"

"I'm not showing you your sister," she said. "At least not this version of her."

The clenching around my heart lessened as I shuffled

forward over the rock. As soon as my own reflection was staring back at me, she touched the orb to the water and a ripple spread. In the center, a picture formed.

A baby with gray eyes and blonde tufts of hair that turned black.

Me.

"What is this?" I asked as a second child came into view. Auburn hair marked her as Alexandra.

"My memories," she said, smiling fondly. "I can't give yours back, but I can give mine from those years."

This time when my chest clenched it was for a different reason. Emotion stuck in my throat, making it hard to swallow. "Why are you showing me this?"

A third child came into view. She had honey blonde hair and dark brown eyes.

Lily . . .

"For what you've done," Livina said in a cracked whisper. "For what you will do."

"This is it, isn't it?" I asked, barely able to pull my eyes from the lake. "You're not coming back."

I read the truth in her eyes before she nodded. "It's almost time. I must ready myself and make sure Milla is prepared."

I didn't know how to feel about that. While I'd only ever met her a handful of times, something about it just seemed so wrong.

"You'll die when it's done, won't you?"

"Yes." She sounded relieved by the idea. I couldn't imagine. I wanted to cling to my life and hold on with everything I had. The concept of dying was so permanent.

For a person that could change even matter itself, that permanence was a difficult thing.

I didn't know what I was supposed to say to the woman who ruined and simultaneously saved my life. It wasn't every day this sort of thing happened to me. I told her the only thing I could, for the gift she gave me.

"Thank you."

She smiled, and it was filled with sorrow.

"I've done many bad things in my life and most of them I can't make right, but you can. For that alone I owe you everything." My lips parted, but she didn't pause for me to speak. "I've wronged your family so deeply in trying to save them . . . that debt isn't something I'll ever be able to repay you, and I'll go to my grave knowing that. Don't give me your thanks, girl. I don't need it. Save it for those that do."

I pressed my lips together as she started to turn away. I wanted to say something but didn't know what. Valda nudged forward, and I stepped back, allowing her this moment.

"Goodbye, Livina. I'll see you on the other side," Valda told her, the words coming from my lips.

The Crone paused, looking back over her shoulder. Her eyes swirled once more, the color turning violet. "Until we meet again, my old friend."

The Crone brought her staff down once and disappeared in the blink of an eye. Valda stepped back, and I came forward. The memories of my childhood were still playing across the surface of the lake.

I went back to the flat rock and climbed on top, settling in for the long night while I tried not to sleep.

The bitter cold kept me awake enough as the temperature started to plummet. I shifted, resting sideways on the hard stone while I watched my youth play out from the eyes of a stranger.

By the time the dawn approached, the memories faded. The only problem was that it wasn't the pleasures of the day that awaited me.

Only nightmares.

CHAPTER 24

His heartbeat was an echo in a chasm.

A war drum before the battle.

A signal to all that were dead and undead of what I'd done.

And they loved me for it.

Ivan the Cruel had ruled for so long that the Vampires didn't believe he could bring about a new age. They'd lost hope that true freedom was on the horizon. After so long of being in the shadows and told that's where they belonged . . . the craving for retribution against those that confined them had reached a fever pitch. The need for blood and violence too great to stifle.

I didn't want to stop them. Oh, no. I wanted to bring them out—bring us all out—into the light. I wanted to upend the very fabric of society that had imprisoned my mind for so long with their morals and conventions.

I wanted to be the harbinger of a new age.

One where I was free. Truly free. Unable to be restrained or controlled ever again.

My attack on the Shifters was only the beginning.

The attack I planned for New York?

That would be their end.

A door slammed behind me, sounding like a gun shot fired into an abyss. Aaron jumped, his wide blood-stained eyes narrowing on the man behind me. The gag in his mouth prevented him from speaking, though he'd tried many times. Cold iron bound his hands behind his back, and metal chains linked his feet to the floor.

Victor strode forward, and I could feel the anger riding him as he came to my side and then stepped in front of me, blocking my view of my prisoner.

I didn't lower my chin or look at his black oxfords as I once did. I stared straight ahead, his chest filling up most of my view, the darkened bricks of the dungeon in my periphery. Water dripped through one of the cracks in the stone ceiling, falling in a rhythmic beat with my prisoner's even breaths.

"Flower." His voice was hard. Victor was in one of his moods again. "I let you have your fun and went to sleep expecting you to wake me on your return . . ." He reached out, grabbing my hip. It would appear forceful to most people, but Victor's strength was only a fraction of my own.

"I've been busy," I answered, still not looking into his eyes but not looking away. It was as much a power play as anything we did.

His nails bit into the flesh at my side. The edge of them cutting through the soft cashmere sweater without effort. The prick of pain brought my senses to awareness. It made me want to sigh, almost content. I wouldn't tell him, but the rough way he handled my body made me feel alive again.

"I said you could strike back. Not return with a prisoner. A

male prisoner." The cutting edge of his tone almost brought a smirk to my lips. The bond madness rode him hard. The urge to claim me growing harder to resist. "You've been here all day with him. You reek of him. Is there something I should know about?"

I didn't answer immediately. The truth was my sister's signasti did nothing for me. The only man that ever had and ever would stood before me, my devil dressed like a dream.

He liked to play games.

Once upon a time those games almost destroyed me. But I learned. I grew.

Now it was my turn to play.

My turn to win.

I kept my eyes glued to his chest and lifted one hand to let my pale fingers trail over the hard planes. Thin material was all that separated us, and the tension in the air was palpable. Delicious.

His strong hand trailed up my side and over the curve of my breast. He ran the tips of his fingers over the choker. His thumb brushing across the metal insignia. Cool but not cold against my skin. He took my chin between his index finger and thumb and lifted it, forcing me to look.

"I asked you a question, flower."

"I've yet to decide if it deserves an answer."

Ire flashed across his features. He didn't like that response. For once, I didn't care.

He changed his grip, and to someone else it might look like he was cupping my jaw. His thumb swept under my chin, the pads of his fingers softly pressed into my throat.

My heart began to pound. Loudly.

The noise surprised me, and I stepped back. He stepped

forward. Again we repeated the movements until my back touched the rough bricks of the dungeon wall.

Firelight bathed our features, casting it all in pale hues and dark shadows.

Victor leaned forward, his lips skimming my jaw. Warmth heated my core.

"Why are you toying with me, Lily?" he whispered.

"Because I can," I answered, unafraid. Victor didn't scare me anymore. He might have once, but now we walked in the darkness together. We played in the night.

He was a monster, but so was I.

Victor inhaled sharply, and I knew what brought it on.

The scent of my arousal filled the air.

"Lily," he breathed through gritted teeth. "My control is fraying, mistress."

"Queen," I corrected him. My Vampire stilled.

Right that second the Shifter managed to get free of the gag and started to speak. "You don't have to do this, Lily. Your sister loves you. She only wants—"

"Silence." Victor's voice cut through Aaron's speaking. He pulled back enough to look me in the eye. Our noses were close enough the tips nearly touched. My breath fanned his face. "Who is he?"

"My sister's signasti."

The way he smiled should have scared me. The silver of his eyes gleamed like that of a blade.

"Oh flower, you please me so. More than anyone ever has." His eyes dropped to my lips and while Aaron was still speaking, yelling, really—all of it faded.

Victor leaned in, pressing his lips to mine. I licked the

seam of his mouth, and he opened up, brushing his tongue against mine.

He leaned in, and I reached for him, sliding my arms around his shoulders to twine my fingers in his pale white hair. With one hand he gripped my throat possessively, and with the other he lowered it to my backside, lifting me and pressing us together in one motion.

My feet came off the ground. I hardly noticed we were moving until the metal locks on the dungeon door clicked as he kicked it shut behind him.

Aaron's yells faded into the distance as he strode through the castle without a care, my body curved around his. Within seconds we were at his door. I knew it from the scent of fresh snow and silk sheets. He paused, pulling back from kissing me.

"You're excused from duty," he said to the guards. "Tell the other Born to make their Made aware that no one is to enter my wing."

"For how long?" one of them asked. I leaned inward and tentatively licked the skin of his throat. Desire blossomed inside me like a flower at first light.

"Indefinitely," was his only reply.

The sole of his foot made contact with the wooden doors and they burst open. The two guards made themselves scarce.

I kissed his throat and then tested the waters once more, letting the tip of my fang skim the surface. Victor groaned.

"You will be my undoing," he murmured. My back touched the bed. Black strands of hair fanned around my face as I looked up at the canopy. Victor pulled away. I frowned as he dragged himself off my body.

"What are you doi—" I didn't get to finish the words as

he stood at the end of the bed. His gaze raked over my prone form. He removed each of my ballerina flats with care and then paused. I laid there, silently challenging him to do it. The silver turned a shade darker as he reached for the button on my black jeans. A flick of his thumb and a pop sounded.

He pinched the zipper between his forefinger and thumb, slowly dragging it down.

I lifted my hips silently, urging him forward.

Cool fingers grasped the edge of my pants, dragging them down but leaving the lace panties in place. Once they were pulled free of my thighs, he flung them away from us, my legs now bare to him.

Victor placed his hands on my knees and pulled me forward. I slid to the edge of the bed and then stopped.

He spread my legs wide, settling between them.

My heart stuttered. My breath grew uneven.

"What—" I started to ask again.

"Don't ask me dumb questions, flower." I pulled myself up so that I was sitting and able to watch him.

Victor wrapped his hand around one bare foot and pulled it toward him. My eyebrows drew together, but I said nothing as he kissed the instep, the sensation running through my body like a shock of desire. My breath caught as he gently massaged circles into the path his lips took.

By the time he reached my calf, my eyes were hooded.

His lips kissed and licked and nibbled at my sensitive skin. His hands followed, creating a dull ache inside of me before he even reached my thigh.

Vampires didn't need to breathe, but he chose to—fanning those sensitive nerve endings as he approached the apex of my thighs.

His lips skimmed the outside of my panties. He breathed in.

Then he pulled away, beginning the process again on my other foot.

It was maddening. Lust filled me, hazing my brain so that all I was, was a reaction. An emotion. A response. He stroked, and I moaned. He licked, and my breath hissed between my teeth. When he drew near the place I wanted him again, his eyes met mine. A slight smirk curled around his lips.

Beautiful and incredibly cruel. My chest warmed.

"You asked me what I'm doing," he said, running his nose up and down the silk fabric that barely covered me. "I'm treating you like a queen, because that's what I'm going to make you." His teeth bit the fabric, but not my skin. He pulled once and with a twist of his neck the silk piece ripped free. "My Queen."

Then he pressed his lips against me, and I trembled.

My body shook as he kissed me there. When he licked that sensitive place, my vision became unfocused. That gold tether that spanned between us started to shine. My core wound tight as he continued with his ministrations and my fingers dug into the sheets. They ripped instantly, and I leaned forward, wrapping them in his hair instead.

He pulled away and blew out a breath of cold air. My thighs shook.

He leaned in again and sucked once. I detonated.

An anguished garble slid from my lips as my body tightened around the fingers that were now replacing his mouth, pushing their way in and out of me. Wave after wave of ecstasy washed through me as I ground against him, riding it out. When the last of my pleasure left me, he stood.

We stared at each other long enough the sun could have rose and set. For this moment, he was all that existed. He and the havoc he wrought on me.

I knew he was waiting. Despite his cold, calloused ways—he was giving me a choice in this.

Just as he'd taught me, I chose myself and I chose him.

I spread my legs wider and a growl of approval escaped him when I reached for his pants. The girl that died would have been embarrassed to be this forward with a man, having never done it.

But these hands were not white as they once had been. They were stained so red that the color was almost as black as my heart. If I could kill men and women with my bare fingers, I could give and take pleasure with them all the same.

He'd seen me at my lowest, as a dirty, grubby Made in a cellar.

He'd seen me at my worst, half-crazed by starvation, but useless all the same when I held onto the idea that someone would save me.

He'd seen me die, and agonized over it.

Now he would see me bare myself to him and the winter air as I claimed him while he claimed me.

I slid my fingers over the edge of his trousers and tugged. They split apart at the seams. I reached for his shirt, pulling on both sides. Buttons popped as it split up the middle.

My hands dropped to my own sweater. I tugged it over my head, tossing it away. My bra came next, and then it was only us and the all-consuming need that only grew.

I scooted up the bed and leaned back. Victor didn't ask me if I was ready.

My actions showed him I clearly was.

Victor crawled onto the bed, settling between my spread legs, the tip of him skimming my entrance.

I met his stare and nodded once as he braced himself over me. His hardness slid inside, not painful in the ways I'd been told it would be.

Full? Yes.

Uncomfortable? A bit.

Needed? Completely.

I writhed in his grasp, but he held tight, going slowly at first. I planted my arms behind me, using the firmness of the mattress to gain purchase as I dug my heels into the bed and worked my hips against his.

"Flower, I'm trying to make this easy on you—"

"Don't," I gasped, shoving forward and taking his full length.

Victor groaned and dropped me to the bed, following me down. His forearms caged either side of my face as he held himself over me, pushing in and out. He stroked that carnal flame he'd created into an inferno. The golden tether of our bond grew impossibly bright. My eyelids started to droop as I fell into it.

Victor gracefully moved one hand to slide his fingers through my hair and pull sharply without losing pace. "Don't close your eyes," he commanded.

I growled, arching my back off the bed as I fought to keep pace with him. His lips skimmed my neck, the tips of his fangs pressing hard enough I knew what was coming. "I want every part of you," he breathed.

"Then don't ask. Take it."

His fangs cut through my flesh and the scent of sweet wine filled the air. He moaned against me, and my pleasure height-

ened. That pressure was building again but its peak was elusive.

I needed more.

Using my own strength, I flipped us and straddled his waist. He sat up, bringing us chest to chest. My hands wrapped around his silky strands, pulling them taut and tilting his head back. My blood wet on his lips, I kissed him, savagely grinding my body against his own.

He grasped my hips, guiding them for what I needed but I didn't know how to find. The climax drew near again. A moan was already building in my throat as I sank my fangs into his bottom lip and sucked hard.

He groaned, uttering my name like a prayer as the bound flared. My core tightened as the tension shattered. Golden light blinded me entirely as it snapped in place around us.

A noose and a lifeline. An unbreakable tether.

I was his and he was mine.

Several seconds of silence spanned between us. Our breaths were heavy, and the wind roared. Shadows played under my skin as my power danced in my pleasure with me, but didn't harm him.

He scooted back to lay against the pillows, bringing me with him. Bodies still connected, I laid my head on his chest.

"I love you, Lily."

It was the first time he'd said those words and I believed him. In his own way, he did love me. "I know," I whispered back without saying it in return.

When my eyes closed, it was still darkness I dreamed.

Beautiful, glorious, darkness.

And death.

I WOKE WITH A START. My throat was scratchy as sandpaper. Cold wind whipped my face. I groaned, rolling over. My joints were stiff from sleeping on a rock. I didn't have to look at the lake to know that Livina's gift was gone. Light shone from the west telling me that most of the day had come and gone.

"You're awake."

I jumped. "What the—"

"Relax," Alexandra said, rolling her eyes. She sat on the rock next to mine, where Livina had been the night before. She wore jeans and a thick sweater. Her fingers were displayed in front of her and a tiny fire rolled along them, moving with the wind. She sighed and the flame blinked out, a wisp of smoke going up before being blown away. "Dream of anything interesting?"

A subtle way of asking what was going on with Lily.

"If I could unsee it, I would," I groaned, rolling my shoulders to work the knots out.

"I'm going to assume Aaron is still alive given your state," she said without looking at me.

"Yeah," I answered on a sigh. "He's alive. Surprisingly whole, all things considered."

"Don't do that," she said.

"Do what?"

"Think." I blinked, but she continued. "She's killed hundreds of people. There's no coming back from that."

"I've killed thousands." The hard look she gave me said it all.

"You killed thousands *on accident*. She walked into

the residence with an army and the intention to kill. The Alpha is dead because of her. Scarlett and Liam are dead because of her. Mothers and fathers and children and babies are dead because of her—"

"I get it. You don't need to—"

"But I do," she interrupted. "I know you. As much as you say you will do it, you'll try to find any way out. I don't like this any more than you. Honestly, I don't even know what to think. All I know is that my sister died at Daizlei, and what she is now" —she paused, swallowing hard— "whatever this is now, it's not her. It's a monster, and it needs to be put down."

She didn't even understand how close to the Witches version of the truth she'd just come. She didn't know about Cirian or Valda or Livina or the history that brought us here. She didn't know that Lily wasn't the only problem.

She didn't know the ancients demanded her too. Demanded me.

"She can't be killed."

"Does she bleed?" Alexandra asked.

"Yes, but—"

"Then *it* can be killed." The way she struggled even referring to her as more than an *it* was quite telling.

"She heals herself before she dies," I argued. "I could stab her in the heart and she'll pull it out and stab me back. How do you kill someone like that?"

"The same way you did the first time."

I blinked. "Say that again."

"Say what?" she asked derisively.

"Repeat what you just said."

She turned, looking at me like I was crazy. “You kill her the same way you did the first time.”

I looked up over the water, and for the first time, I felt hope. The sun was setting and with it the final day was upon us.

I jumped to my feet and turned my back on the lake.

“Where on earth are you going?” she called over her shoulder.

“To make a plan,” I yelled back.

My heart sprinted with me as I raced through the forest and back to the residence. I was onto something big. I could feel it in my bones.

CHAPTER 25

"Hey," Blair called out across the foyer. "We've been looking for you everywhere. Where have you been—"

"No time," I panted. "I'm calling a meeting. Round up everyone you can to meet me in the second-floor conference room." Her mouth opened then closed. She nodded once and walked away, off to find the others. I took the second to get my head together. This was it. I could feel it.

The Crone said nothing was impossible. The pieces were there; I just had to figure out how they were supposed to go together.

I started for the conference room. Not paying much attention to who was coming and going around me.

Three deaths by my hand.

That was the price . . . and Lily already died once.

Which only left two.

If I could figure out a way to stop her from healing herself—my shoulder knocked into someone. "Excuse me," I muttered, already trying to continue on. Fingers wrapped around my bicep and I paused, looking back at the girl I'd bumped. Her golden eyes drilled into me.

"I've been looking for you," Keyla started. The rest of it was lost on me.

Like a flash of lightning the idea struck.

I stood there staring at her as one by one the shards of information I'd gleaned slid into place. Like pieces of a puzzle, I knew broad details about them. It was only once it clicked that I saw the bigger picture, and my answer to fate's call.

"You're the key," I whispered, almost dumbfounded. Keyla frowned.

"Are you okay? Did you hear what I—"

"I'm fine," I answered on instinct, pulling myself from my stupor. "What were you saying?"

Keyla chuffed, shifting back and forth. "I was saying" —she started, with only a hint of her usual attitude— "that with my father dead and my brother . . . gone . . ." She struggled with what to call it, and I didn't blame her. "I'm the last of the line. I'm young and can't fight as good as you guys—though I am damn good with a mace—"

"Keyla, can you get to the question? I'm assuming there is one."

She sighed, taking a deep breath. "I want to be in on the planning. I want to be there when it happens. He's my brother, and I want to help save him."

I stared at her and all I could think was that Ash would kill me. If he knew what I was planning, he'd tell me to leave him. To let him die.

That wasn't an option.

No matter the risks, I was getting him back and ending this once and for all.

"Come on." I grabbed her hand and pulled her with me down the hall. She blinked and opened her mouth, then closed it, clearly having expected there to be more resistance. She started walking beside me, keeping pace.

"So, what's the plan?" she asked, adding a little pep to her step. "Are we dropping into Vilicky Novgorod and going to slink around the High—"

I opened the door to the conference room with a flick of my wrist and motioned for Keyla to go first. She gave me a sheepish smile and stepped inside. I followed behind her, pleased everyone was already here.

"I want to return to planning," I started.

"What's she doing here?" Amber glowered. "Keyla's in mourning right now. She shouldn't be—"

"You are too," Keyla shot back. The glare in Amber's eye deepened as she looked between the two of us.

"Why did you bring Aaron's sister to the war meeting?" she asked me, ignoring Keyla now. The mention of my signasti was a blow to the chest, but I grit my teeth and kept my temper in check.

"I've figured it out."

"Figured what out?"

"How to win this." No one said anything, but they waited with bated breath.

"What does she have to do with this?" Amber jutted her chin toward Keyla.

"Everything," I replied softly.

That really got their attention and even Keyla stood straighter, preening under the compliment. Johanna exhaled heavily and leaned forward, resting her hands on the mahogany wood surface. “I think it’s best you start explaining then.”

I nodded.

“I’ve told you guys time and again that Lily is the one we need to focus on—”

“We’ve already been over this,” Amber snapped, cutting in.

“Yes,” I said in a hard tone. “Except now I know how to kill her—and more importantly, I know how to keep her from killing all of us.”

Amber lifted an eyebrow, prompting me forward. “This better be good.”

“Before she died, she could heal. If she stole energy from someone else, she could heal herself. When she became Made, that power amplified. She healed herself from death—and even from Vampirism, in a way.” On the other side of the table, Alexandra stared at me intently. “She couldn’t be killed because there was no way around her power.” I looked at Keyla, the latent Shifter born to a forfeit. “Now there is.”

“You’ve got to be smoking something if you think I’m going to let you take Keyla into battle,” Amber growled.

“We don’t have another choice,” I snapped back. “Lily can’t die, and without canceling out her powers, she’ll kill everyone in *minutes*.”

“Minutes?” Oliver asked. I nodded.

“Her power doesn’t just include those that touch her anymore. It’s like a cloud of death that spreads out and kills any who touch it. No one, except possibly me, will even be able to get near her.”

"Whether or not Keyla's power is useful, I don't know how you could ever consider bringing her into battle when—"

"Because I don't have another choice!" I shouted at her. Amber's jaw hung for a fraction of a second before snapping shut. "You think I want to kill my own sister to begin with? It almost killed me the first time I did and that was an accident. Now she has Ash and is hell-bent on unleashing Vampires on the world. I don't have a goddamn choice here anymore, Amber." She had the good sense to look away. "Without taking her power out of play, this is all for nothing. We can gather as many people as we want. We can call on the Shifters and the Supes and the Fae and the Witches—and she will *kill* them all. I love Keyla just as much as you, but she's the only one with an ability to stifle others, and she's strong enough to even cancel out my power. We need her there or this is it."

Let it be known that I was not the motivational type. I didn't come up with rousing speeches. Helping others emotionally was never my forte, even with my own sisters. I was the girl that got shit done. Unfriendly and antisocial as I may be, I was the one that found a way. And this? This was our *only* way.

I could feel it in my bones, as deep and true as my bond with Ash.

"I think she's right," Alexandra said, being the first one to break the silence. "If Lily is strong enough to kill that many Shifters in minutes, then she's strong enough that throwing sheer numbers at her won't do anything but fuel her more."

“And you’re talking about bringing my cousin into that,” Amber said. “How do you know she can even get close enough without succumbing to your sister’s power?”

I looked at Tori. Her face went pale.

“You want me to—”

“Yes,” I answered. “If I can get close enough to push her power back, you can teleport in with Keyla and cancel hers out.”

“But,” Keyla started. I glanced at her, and she shook her head. “I want to help, Selena. I want to be there. But . . . I don’t think you should rely on my power. I don’t even know how to control it.”

“Exactly,” Amber piped up. “She doesn’t even know if she can do it. You could just be sending her in for no reason.”

“Make no mistake, Lily is planning to show up in full force. What she’s become . . . it’s terrifying.” I shuddered at the memories and how they flashed through my mind like a movie reel. “Keyla used her ability when Lily invaded the residence. It’s why some Shifters couldn’t shift. They were too close to her. On a battlefield where people are dying around her? It’ll happen again.”

“How do you know that?” Keyla asked, her voice quiet.

“I see things . . . when I sleep; things my sister does.”

“How do you—” she started to ask, but Amber cut her off.

“So you want to gamble that she’ll be scared enough to use it and shut Lily’s powers down?”

I hated myself for the answer I had to give. At the end of the day, it was our only real shot.

"Yes."

"I think," Johanna said, tugging at the sleeve of her long shirt, "that Keyla should get to choose. She knows the risks and what's being asked of her."

The young girl considered it. Her porcelain white teeth nibbling on her bottom lip as she stared at the table in great concentration.

"I want to do it—for Aaron."

Amber stared at me stone-faced, and I knew in that moment, regardless of what did or didn't happen to Keyla, she would never forgive me for this.

"Then it's decided," I said. "Tori will teleport Keyla in, getting as close as she can."

"If she does this, you won't have your powers either," Blair said.

"I won't need them," I replied. "Lily may be undead, but I'm also a demon. If you take both our powers away, I will win in a hand-to-hand fight."

"You don't have to," Johanna said. "I can fight as well as you. Let me deal the death blow—"

"No," I said.

"But—" Alexandra started.

"No," I repeated. "It has to be me."

"That makes no sense," my sister shot back. "Your issue this entire time is that you don't want to kill her, and now you won't let Johanna take the—"

"I said no."

They didn't understand, and they never would. Valda

hung her head in sorrow alongside me because she was the only one who knew what was being asked.

Three deaths by my hand.

That was the price, and only I could pay it.

"I can't believe you," my sister said. I didn't respond. At this point there was nothing I could say. It wasn't like I could tell her about the prophecy.

"Moving away from the topic of who is killing Lily, where do the rest of us need to be for this?" Blair asked, re-anchoring the conversation.

"Someone needs to be guarding Keyla," Amber said. "I'll do it."

"I can protect myself," Keyla piped up.

"No," I shook my head. "Amber's right."

"Finally, you see reason—"

"But she shouldn't be the one guarding you."

Amber slammed her fist down on the table. "What is your deal?" she demanded.

"When Keyla's power turns on, you won't have your speed or be able to keep up with the Vampires that go after her, and believe me—once someone realizes what's happening, they will go after her—except vampires don't have abilities. We all retain the strength and speed of what we are. Without your ability, you'll no longer be faster than them."

"Which is why she shouldn't be there," Amber chided. "If no one has abilities, then—"

"Blair should be guarding her," I answered through gritted teeth.

"Blair?" Amber asked incredulously.

"Me?" my cousin asked.

"You," I replied. "You don't need your powers for this fight. An ice storm will only hurt our people as well as theirs." Guilt flashed through her expression but was gone faster than I could comment. "You're faster than anyone here, though, and fight just as well as I do. Your demon has been cooperating when still given the chance to fight. I know you haven't merged yet, but Keyla and Tori will be safest with you protecting them."

"She's right," Alec said, finally making himself known in the conversation. "Alexandra will be more useful using fire to burn away the bloodsuckers. Tori will be with Keyla, and while she can hold herself in a fight with her ability, she's going to be at a disadvantage here. Blair's the fastest and best equipped to protect them both." I had a feeling he spoke up for Blair's sake more than anything.

"You protect her with your life," Amber said, ceding at that.

"Of course," came my cousin's cool reply.

"That doesn't answer where you want me, Johanna, or Oliver," Alec said.

"You and Oliver need to go on Victor. He's going to want to stay close to Lily, but I need to get her alone." Alec nodded, and while Oliver didn't say anything, I could tell he had mixed thoughts. Whether it was because I was giving him an order or because he didn't like the assignment, I wasn't sure. In the end, it didn't particularly matter.

"And me?" Jo asked.

"You're coming with me," I said.

"You just said—"

"If I fail, someone has to give them enough time to run."

I watched as the words sunk in. A shudder ran through her, but she didn't dispute it. A quiet hush settled over the room as the reality of our situation really set in. This plan was risky. Dangerous. Wrought with errors and too high a chance of failing. Amber was right about that, but I was also right. It was our only real plan, but in the end—it might not work.

I might still fail.

The darkness might still come.

The world may still fall.

"Is everyone clear on what our roles are tomorrow?" I asked. One by one I looked around the table as they nodded. "Alright, then. That's all I got. Get some rest." With that, the room began to filter out. First Alexandra, storming past me with Tori hot on her heels. Blair went next, squeezing my shoulder before she left. Alec followed after her at a distance, and I wondered if tonight was the night he'd approach her or if they'd both let things rest where they may. It wasn't my place to ask.

Amber and Keyla left next, speaking loudly. When it was only Jo and Oliver, I turned to leave. "Can I have a minute with you, Selena?" Johanna asked.

I paused and looked over my shoulder. "Okay."

Oliver looked at her, and she waved him off. "I'll catch up with you in a bit, Oli." He looked at me and then her. His lips quirked downward, and I could tell his opinion of me hadn't changed much over the months. Still, he stepped out, closing the door behind him. I walked back toward the table and cocked my hip, resting against its edge.

Johanna waited a few moments, her head tilted to the side as she listened to Oliver's retreat. When we were as alone as we could be in a residence full of Shifters, she took a step forward and mimicked my motion.

What she said was the last thing I expected to hear.

"You don't want to kill your sister, but you have no choice because the ancient's demanded it."

My lips parted, my jaw hanging ajar. "How-how do you know?" I spluttered.

"You hold the soul of the Mother, whose ordained duty is to kill the heirs of the monster that Livina created a thousand years ago. I can't imagine any world in which you want to deal the death blow to your own sister. Not with how you've tried to protect her. Your insistence that she needs to be dealt with and that you have to do it leads me to suspect that she is indeed one of the heirs." Her eyes flashed a shade brighter. "Which means you are too."

I floundered for a moment, unable to find any words. What could I even say to all of this? She'd managed to figure out the exact prophecy I'd been spending my days trying to prevent.

I opened and closed my mouth twice before saying, "You figured it out."

She came to the conclusion on her own, which allowed me to finally speak.

"You're part-demon. Something that's never been. A monster in itself. Your sisters are too, which leads me to think there's more to the tale than what I've been told. How high is the price they're asking of you?"

I tried to speak, but once again found myself unable to talk.

She knew of Lily, but not the rest of it and the damned curse prevented it.

Johanna pressed her lips together in a sad smile. "There's a block on you. That explains a lot."

"If you don't know already, I can't say." I could sense it was testing the boundaries, but as she'd already figured it out, the curse allowed it. I just confirmed it. Jo nodded.

"I have a feeling what it asks, knowing what I do now." She sighed and looked away. "I'm so sorry."

"It's okay," I said.

"No." She shook her head, blowing out a breath. "It's not. Not really. The legend says the mother is to hunt and kill all of the monster's descendants. I don't know if the exact wording I've been told is accurate, but I can glean enough from your behavior. Milla said a sacrifice is not payment without a choice. They're asking you to kill yourself."

"They are." I nodded. "I've known that for a while now, though. I hate it, but I can't change it either. I have the Mother's soul, and the ancients want me to choose to pay the price. I have to kill her."

"And if you fail?" Johanna asked. I twisted my lips around.

"Alexandra has to."

"But you haven't told her," Jo surmised. "This is a difficult situation, Selena."

I laughed bitterly. “You have no idea.” I paused. “Well, you have some. More than the others.”

“Do you want me to tell them?”

I weighed that. For long enough, I’d wanted them to know the truth. To give them their answers so that I was unburdened. The end was basically upon us, and in truth there wasn’t enough time.

“No,” I said. “If you tell them now, Alexandra will try to stop me. This is already a small enough window I don’t even know if I’ll succeed.” Johanna nodded.

“I suspected as much. That explains why you don’t want her near in the end.”

“Yeah . . .” The word trailed off as my thoughts turned down that winding path of despair. My end wouldn’t be a pretty one.

“Will you tell them when it’s all over? Tell them why I did it. Why I had to go?” My voice broke. Emotion clogged my throat, making it hard to talk. My eyes watered, but I refused to cry.

“I will,” Jo said earnestly. “I’ll tell them the truth, and I’ll make them understand.”

“Thank you,” I whispered. Johanna leaned forward and took my hand in hers, squeezing tightly.

“Anything you need me to do, I will do it. For all that you’re giving, you’ve earned that much.”

I nodded. “There is one more thing.”

“Name it.”

“You have to promise me you won’t tell them, and you won’t stop me,” I said solemnly. Her lips quirked up in a rueful if not tired smirk.

“Tell me. Whatever it is, I’ll do it.”

I nodded, taking a deep breath. "I'm going to need your help for some logistics when I'm gone."

THE MANSION WAS QUIET, but not silent. It was well past midnight, but the Shifters knew what was coming. The entire paranormal community did at this point. Tam had done his job and word spread like wildfire that any able-bodied paranormal that wished to prevent the Vampire invasion be in Central Park.

Tomorrow we would know if it was enough.

But today, I had one last thing to do.

One last person to speak to before it was time.

I knocked quietly.

The floorboards creaked as footsteps approached the door. The knob turned. A man peeked out through the crack and then did a double take when he saw it was me. The door opened completely.

"Alpha," he said and bowed his head respectfully. I nodded, not comfortable with the title because it reminded me of what I'd cost them. Still, I didn't correct him. For this task, it paid to be the Alpha.

"I'm taking over here. Take the night off to be with your family." He moved away, taken aback.

"Are you certain . . ."

"Yes," I nodded, stepping aside. He walked out of the room, murmuring a gruff thank you, and disappeared down the hall.

I stepped inside and closed the door behind me.

The chair was exactly as I'd left it, and he looked nearly as dejected as the last time I saw him.

"Come to spend your last night with me, Selena?" he asked. It was meant to be mocking, but the hint of desperation underneath was unmistakable.

"Hello, Lucas," I said quietly. I went behind him and pulled the knife from my side. His body didn't even tense at the zing as the metal blade scraped its sheath softly.

"Ah, so this is it. You really will be the end of me." He was scared, but there was also a faint note of relief. I shook my head. Before, I'd been so angry, and now there was only pity. I cut through the rope binding his hands behind his back.

It was only then that he tensed.

I walked around his side and took a seat in front of him.

"Let's have a chat."

CHAPTER 26

THE SUN WAS SHINING, AND THE WINTER AIR KISSED MY SKIN AS I sat on a balcony overlooking the city, my legs strung through the bars so they could dangle over the edge. For a day in New York this time of year, it was almost perfect. Bright blue without a cloud in the sky. I couldn't believe it.

Today was either the day the world ended, or the day it was saved.

You wouldn't know that by just looking.

I hummed my childhood bedtime lullaby under my breath, the haunting melody soothing me. Inside, Tam was on the phone, speaking as quietly as he could to give orders over the phone. In the span of three days he'd rented out rooms all around Central Park to set up as havens for paranormals coming to fight. We were in one of those rooms now as the sun steadily rose and started to fall. It was early afternoon, but this far north darkness fell well before six o'clock in the evening.

We had hours at most.

I swallowed, trying and failing not to think of it.

The sliding door opened behind me. Booted feet walked up to my side. I didn't look as Alexandra plopped down beside me. She stuck her long legs through the gaps in the metal poles and leaned back, putting her hands palm down behind her.

I stopped humming, waiting for her to speak.

"Do you ever wonder what happened to the people at Daizlei?" she asked. "How they died? The way it felt?"

"No."

"Why not?" she said, sounding surprised by that answer. I sighed.

"Because I'm too busy worrying about the people here," I answered. It was only a partial lie. I thought about it sometimes. The sins I'd committed had grown so great that the deaths of those that perished when the building collapsed were eclipsed by the earthquake, and now the residence. "What do you want, Alexandra?"

"To talk," she said without looking at me. "I've been hard on you."

"You're not wrong for it," I said. "Well, not completely."

She snorted. "No," she said. "I am. It's not like it was before. You're not like you were. I'm angry because of what happened to the Shifters. I'm avoiding what will happen if we fail. I've been displacing my anger on you, and that's not right."

I sighed. "I get it though. I knew what and why you were doing it. It's okay."

She let out a shaky breath. "While you haven't gotten to know them much since you came back, I lived with those people for two months. I made friends with them. I trained with them. I ate with them. I drank with them . . ." She took a stuttering breath. "And now some of them are just gone and that's hard. It's really hard. Especially when I know more of them will die tonight."

She stopped talking before her voice broke, but I understood what she was getting at. "Living is hard, I think. Harder than dying. When you die you go somewhere out there," I waved my hand at the empty air before us. "But it's the people you leave behind who suffer most."

"Was it quick?" she asked hesitantly. "When she killed them?"

"It was," I said. "Seconds at most."

She nodded and let out a puff of white as she exhaled. "I'm happy it was quick."

"Me too." I meant it. Every single death that happened as a result of my actions weighed on me. We lapsed into comfortable silence for a while until Alexandra asked, "What is dying like?"

I lifted both eyebrows and squinted over at her. "Are you asking me?"

"Well, yeah," she frowned a little. "You died at Daizlei, technically. That first time after the demon attack. It was only after the telekinesis exploded out of you that your heart started to beat again."

I nodded slowly. "Well, it was a bit . . . odd."

"Odd?" Alexandra asked, questioning my word choice.

"I'd been hearing voices long enough that I just assumed it was worse at first. Our parents were talking to me, calling me from the other side. I remember wanting to go and then . . ." My words trailed off as I recalled Lucas' face.

"And then?"

"Lucas called me back, or at least what I thought was Lucas at the time. It was actually Ash. He reminded me that I have something to live for."

"What was that?"

"You guys." We shared a look and she smiled, knocking her shoulder lightly against mine.

"You know, you can be a real sap sometimes." The retort was so off the cuff I was caught by surprise as I started to laugh.

"And you can be a real bitch on occasion." She let out a chuckle that seemed it never wanted to end, and she was soon doubled over with tears dotting her eyes. It wasn't even that funny. I found myself laughing again, mostly at her response. When it all died out she resumed leaning back, her palms against the concrete floor of the balcony.

"Will it be like this? After it's done?" she asked.

I swallowed hard, searching for an answer that wasn't a lie.

The screen door slid open again, saving me from having to respond. This time it was Blair that stepped out. She dropped to her butt beside us, opting to sit criss-cross with her elbows on her knees. She leaned forward, rubbing her hands together slowly.

"Are we out here to contemplate the end of the world and our possible demise?" she said lightly. I raised both eyebrows.

"I mean—" I paused.

"Yup," Alexandra inserted. "Totally what we're doing."

"Awesome," Blair said. "There room for a third in this shindig? I promise to be equally as depressing as this last month has been." I snorted, and Alexandra let out a sharp cackling laugh.

"You're ridiculous," my sister said.

"There's worse things in life," Blair shot back with a slight smile on her face. "Besides, my personality is probably the least ridiculous thing there is about me."

"I'll give you that," Alexandra muttered.

"So," Blair drawled. "This whole moping thing is hard to do with it this sunny outside. I'm thinking we need a change of scenery to be as dramatic as you two." Alexandra was right, she was being utterly outrageous for her. In the last month there had been a serious damp on Blair's personality ever since her demon came forward. They seemed to be making some progress. She pointed her index finger and whirled it around. Instantly clouds began to gather, thick and somber as the mood.

"You really had to ruin the only good thing about today," Alexandra said with a sour twist of her lips.

Blair chuckled. "Actually, it's going to help us. Once the sun sets, the bloodsuckers have better eyesight in the dark. The clouds are going to reflect the light pollution from the city so it'll actually be brighter than it would be with a clear sky. We'll be able to see better, but it will be a disadvantage for them."

Alexandra's mouth slipped ajar. "Oh."

"Yeah," Blair snorted. "I was smart once, before all of . . . this."

She motioned to the sky, like it was some small feat. I thanked my lucky stars now that she was on my side given the ease with which she did that. Her strength made me have faith that Keyla would make it out of this and Ash wouldn't hate me forever.

"Who's being a downer now," Alexandra muttered sarcastically.

"I told you I was coming to join the pity party of a century," Blair deadpanned.

"I didn't think it was possible for you to get more dramatic than when I met you, yet here we are," Alexandra shot back. They bickered because it was safe. It made it feel like things weren't as bad as they really were. Beneath our exteriors and playful facades, the unease was growing the lower the sun sank. Like an undertow, it tried to pull us all down, but we banded together, spending our last guaranteed moments with each other. They didn't know what was to come.

They didn't realize the gift they were giving, and the strength that it helped me find.

I loved them, just like I loved Ash, and Lily.

Despite it all, I loved her so damn much it hurt sometimes.

Their light teasing made it better because this was it.

A prophecy went into play a thousand years ago.

For a thousand years the ancients moved the pieces on the board.

Today was the end of it, and if I succeeded—the beginning as well.

The lip of the sun touched the horizon and our laughter fell quiet. The clouds turned a shade of violet. I wondered if it was a sign but didn't have long to think before the screen door opened again, the finality of it reverberating in the silence.

Johanna stuck her head out and said, "It's time."

CHAPTER 27

Dressed in black and armed to the teeth, I knelt in front of Keyla at the edge of the park.

"You told me once that you were 'damn good' with a mace," I said, extending the weapon between us, pointed spikes angled away from her. She reached out with a trembling hand and grasped the leather-wrapped hilt.

"I am." She nodded.

"Good." I released my hold. "You're staying back until we're ready for you. Once you start doing your thing, every Vampire in the park is going to want to get ahold of you." She shivered, and while I wasn't trying to scare her, she'd be an idiot to not be terrified right now.

"I have Blair and Tori," she said. Such confidence. Perhaps it was for the best she believed that.

"You do, but as great of fighters as Blair and Tori are, they aren't infallible. None of us are. I'm giving you this weapon because I expect you're going to need it tonight." She swallowed but kept nodding. "If you see red eyes, you swing. If you don't recognize them, you swing. If they're trying to lure you away from Blair—"

"I swing," Keyla repeated. "I know."

I smiled but it didn't reach my eyes as I leaned in and kissed her forehead.

"I will never forgive myself if you die because of this. We're going to get your brother back, but you need to make sure he has something to come back to."

"He has you too," she said almost playfully. I had to force myself not to grimace. She was going to hate me when she learned what I'd done. Young and obstinate, she wouldn't understand for a long time—if ever.

Perhaps that was for the best as well.

"It's alright, Selena," Blair said, stepping up beside her. "Keyla will be safe with me." I leaned back and regarded my cousin. We clasped forearms and then I brought her in for a tight, swift hug.

"I know," I said quietly. "When Lily goes down, you get her out of here. If you can't find Tori, take Keyla and run. All hell is going to break loose after that happens."

I pulled away and looked into my cousin's keen eyes. She nodded once in understanding and we released each other. I stepped away from her and the mass of paranormals behind me. They blocked the road and covered the sidewalks surrounding the entire park from every angle. Sirens were going off around the city left and right as the human police tried to figure out what was going on and why thousands of people had brought New York City traffic to a grinding halt.

That noise faded into little more than buzzing in my

ears as I approached the park. Dusk was upon us. Only moments away.

I reached out tentatively and sensed Ash.

"Are you okay?" I sent down the bond. A minute passed. As the second one approached and fear began to creep in, I got a response.

"Alive. No one's bit me yet." I let out a sigh of relief, but it was quickly brought to a halt. A sweet, soft crooning came from the park.

I lifted a hand to the crowd behind me, and silence fell with the night.

"Run, run, girl of fate. Your dark mistress is here to stay."

Alexandra and I shared a look, instantly knowing who is was. While I'd expected her, the lilt of madness in her voice was a punch to the chest. She'd never known the lullaby. I wondered if Cirian taught her.

"Run, run, and I pray. The madness won't take you away." My sister, my dead sister sang in a haunting melody.

"Run, run, child I made. The darkness wants to come and play," Lily continued. The wind blew through the trees and leaves scattered in a rustle of branches.

"Run, run, don't delay. She will take you far away," she sang louder. Stronger. I felt a trickle of something—not in the air, but in the world around us. My heart began to beat faster.

"Run, run, Mother of fate. They are here, you cannot stay." We were running out of lines. Lily, in all her time gone she found she loved to play games, and tonight was the biggest game of all. She wouldn't be singing that song if there wasn't a finale at the end.

"Ash—"

"Run, run, don't delay. They will burn you at the stake." Her voice changed, becoming deeper. Raspier. Harsher. She still sang, but there was an edge in those words.

"Don't," Ash answered.

"Don't what?"

"Run, run, daughter I made. So you can come back one day." Closer. I sensed her coming closer. Her and her alone.

"Don't enter the park," he said, struggling though I couldn't tell why.

"*Why?*" I asked, toeing the edge of the line.

"Run, run, soul in pain. So you can make them pay."

No answer. Nothing. Panic seized my chest and I stepped on the brown grass.

"Lily?" I called into the near void.

A pause.

"Run, run, they will say. You will take *revenge* one day."

My body shuddered. I realized then that she'd been confused. She thought it spoke of her. Of her pain. Of her loss. Of her rise.

A dark wave of power rose in the sky, but it wasn't coming from the park. Horror washed over as I realized what she intended.

She never actually wanted to meet in the park. She just wanted us to surround it so that we were all out in the open in one spot. Fish in a barrel.

Her and her legion of Made had planned to ambush us.

Screams echoed into the night as her dark power blotted out the night sky. Rising higher and higher above.

"Everybody! Get in the park! Spread out!" I shouted, using my power to project. A wave of people ran past me as they tried to do what I said. There were so many, though. Shifters, Supes, the odd Fae or Witch. Thousands had banded together for this, and while they tried to do as I said, they couldn't move fast enough.

Too many of them would react too late and be devoured by that cloud of death.

I acted without thinking and my own power rushed forth.

I'd always referred to my block on it as a dam. That wasn't quite true, though. A dam once broken eventually lost its strength and the water eventually slowed to a steady, even pace. While initially it was devastating, there was an end. A bottom to how much water could pour.

My power was not like that. It was as endless and never ending as the universe. It was the power of the ancients of old, and the only thing that held it back was me and my mortal body.

I was a vessel as much as Milla.

My demon stepped forward as the valve turned and magic thickened the air.

Her cloud of dark energy crested in the sky before surging downward as my own power came forward as purple and black tendrils.

Time slowed.

A second lasted an eternity.

Hers rained down and mine held as they collided in a boom that echoed through all of New York City. I pushed inward, forcing her back and away from the people fleeing behind me. I'd worried before this started that she'd wipe out everyone. That I would be all that was left to face her. But we had Keyla. I just had to buy us time.

I had to hold her back from killing our own long enough that her and I could come face-to-face and finally end this.

My neck strained as my hands came up, opening the valve further. More than ever before.

If I was to win this I needed my full strength, no matter the cost.

I walked forward with arms raised.

My fists clenched.

My power shot through her own, a stab in the darkness, and then drilled down through the earth toward the source of where that cloud of death had come from. The darkness receded, as if sensing my intent to find her.

Quiet fell once more.

Staring out from the edge of the park toward the skyscrapers around us, dark figures dropped by the hundreds. They descended into the last of the fleeing crowd as the tables turned. Instead of boxing them in to try to prevent their escape, we'd been the ones boxed.

"They're coming from the streets!" I yelled, using my power to let my voice carry over the park. But it was too late, screams filled the air as the feast began.

The stragglers who hadn't made it to the park were

ripped apart on sight. Blood splattered the concrete as a viciousness born of death descended onto us.

"*Ash*," I called as the Vampires rushed forward toward the park. "*Where are you?*"

"Behind you," he whispered before his connection went still. I didn't have time to think about his sudden silence. The only thing behind me was a park full of paranormals I now needed to protect as best I could.

I waved my hand and the first row of Vampires dissolved into nothing more than dust.

This happened twice more before I noticed a murmuring through the crowd. I turned and behind me on the other side of Central Park, the black cloud of death was eating through the paranormal army we'd managed to gather.

"You've got to be fucking shitting me right now," Johanna growled from beside me.

"You told us she was strong," Alexandra said, watching in horror as the mass rolled over the park. "Not this." They fell like flies and once more people tried to flee into the streets. They ran past me, willing to brave the Vampire horde still falling from skyscrapers instead of the instant and imminent death that was my sister's power.

I started to run.

Blood pumped through my veins. I dodge around people trying to flee as I mentally pushed the cloud back.

It resisted me, but not for long as shoved with enough force I could have cleaved the city in two. She was incredibly strong, and based on the piles of bones I had to run through to face her—she was growing stronger by the minute.

"Selena, wait up!" Alexandra called behind me. I sensed them chasing but I needed to get ahead. I needed to be there first to shut her down before she could kill anyone I loved.

Especially Ash.

"Selena . . ." His voice filtered through my mind. *"She's too strong,"* he warned me. I pushed harder, clearing the opposite edge of the park in record time.

There, at the border where landscape and cityscape met, was Lily, her back turned to me. Victor stood beside her, holding Ash by the cuff of his tattered shirt. He'd been beaten to a pulp and I wasn't sure how he was even conscious.

"Lily," I said quietly, ignoring them both.

She paused.

Her long black hair whipped around. She'd dressed in a light blue camisole and dark brown capris. Ballerina flats molded around her dainty feet and it occurred to me that while we'd armed ourselves, she didn't think she needed anything more. Judging by the show in her power, I almost agreed.

She looked back at me and smiled cruelly.

The most unsettling part of all was that her eyes were not red.

They weren't the black of a demon.

They weren't a shade short of black like a Vampire.

They were brown.

Warm brown. The same color they'd been before she was turned.

"Did you know they have speakers in the park?" my sister said softly. "Well, they do. Or did, I suppose. After the fighting they might have been destroyed." She smiled, but there was none of her in it.

None of the girl she had been. Only the monster she'd become.

"Se-lee-na," Ash murmured in broken syllables. I took a step forward and Lily tsked, turning to fully face me.

"None of that now," she murmured. Victor changed his grip to hold Ash by the back of the neck. He picked him up like a rag doll and revulsion filled me as he swung his other hand forward, like he meant to clap. Only Ash's head was between them.

"Stop," I growled through gritted teeth. A flick of my hand and Victor froze, unable to move. I started forward the moment Johanna finally caught up and fell in step behind me, just like we'd talked about. Keyla was further back, and given the ice storm starting up, I'd say Blair's demon was already out to kill.

"Oh," Lily drawled. "You poor, pathetic girl. You really think you can stop this, don't you?" She laughed. It was a peal of windchimes that haunted me.

Another surge of her power blossomed from her skin and drifted down the streets to wash over those closest to them. Vampires and Supernaturals and Shifters alike, all ceased to breath as she pulled the life from them and left only ashes behind.

We wouldn't be able to hold long like this. Not with her killing them scores at a time, her own people included.

"No," I whispered, striding forward. I knew she could hear it, though, because the laughter paused and she tilted her head, narrowing her eyes. "But I'm not trying to stop what's happening. I'm trying to end what will be." My hand was a blur and a dagger went flying. Victor dodged by only a hairsbreadth. The edge of the knife kissed his cheek, leaving a thin trail of black blood. He hissed and Lily grit her jaw.

I threw again and again and again, blowing through my throwing knives in quick succession. Once more Victor dodged, but in order to step out of the way of one, he went into the path of the other. The blade sank into his shoulder. He dropped Ash at his feet like trash to be taken out.

"You bitch," he snapped. "Flower."

It was a single word. A command given. I knew better than anyone how little his commands truly affected her.

I used that to my advantage.

"Are you his dog now?" I asked. "Obeying your master's every little whim?" I goaded her, using her insecurities regarding power and place. Her eyes narrowed, and while she tried to hide it, those barbs struck true.

Hatred, pure and evil, filled her face. She smiled, and I knew I wouldn't like whatever came next.

Then she lowered a hand and reached for Ash, that terrible energy swirling at her fingertips.

I fired a shot at her, knocking her back and through the air ten feet. A flashback hit me of the first time I'd killed her. When I'd sentenced her to this life. I tried to shake it off. The echo of a neck cracking following me into the present as Victor dove toward Ash and I repeated the motion, launching him into a metal street sign in the opposite direction.

"Alec! Oliver!" I shouted.

"They're already on it," Jo murmured just loud enough to be heard in this chaos.

"Alexandra, I need a perimeter," I called, closing in on Lily.

Black fire split the earth as a circle formed around us. The winds blew harder and the flames went higher, the swirling vortex locking us in it. Lily took one look and dove to the side, but the flames wouldn't let her through.

She stilled, a shudder running up her spine.

"I didn't want it to be this way," I said. "In the beginning I didn't know if you were dead or alive, and by the time I knew, it was too late." She turned, her eyes bleeding from brown to black.

"You left me," she said in a cold voice. "You abandoned *us.* You both did." I pressed my lips together. Was it her talking now? Or was it Cirian? It was clear they both blamed us. Perhaps my guilt was what made Valda and I most well-suited, just as he and Lily had betrayal.

"It wasn't intentional," I told her, though I didn't know why. I already knew there was only one way to end this. Maybe I hoped that when it was all over she would understand. I doubted it. Not this way. Not now.

"It doesn't matter," the apathetic voice of a demon answered. "You made *your choice* and I've made mine."

She lifted her hands and began walking toward me.

Ten yards. The circle of fire shrank. I wonder if she noticed it, or if her sole focus on killing me was all that existed now.

Five yards. I held onto my bond with Ash and my beating heart that gave me the strength to do what I needed to.

Four yards. I thought of Alexandra. I thought of Blair. I thought of Keyla.

Three yards. I thought of Lily. Of who she had been and who she was now.

Two yards. I tried not to think anymore, but my mind raced. There were only a handful of moments in my life where I could see them so clearly as they happened, almost as if I were outside of myself.

One yard. This was one of those moments.

I let her close the distance, all the while that circle of fire encroaching on us. She lifted her hands.

I stared into her eyes, searching for anything left to hold onto as she touched my skin.

Then I gave the signal.

CHAPTER 28

In between one second and the next the circle of fire dropped.

Black tendrils dove beneath my skin. Alexandra had asked me what it felt like to die. The truth was that once it set in that you were going to, the panic receded. Your brain can't cope with the implications of death and how painful it truly is. In many ways, it's like coming home.

Only in being saved from death do you realize that home is with the living.

Then the pain returns.

It's living that's truly hard, and that's what I did here. I held onto that, onto myself, as she tried to pull my life from me. A whirl sounded only a second later, followed by feet landing on the crumbled street.

Another second went by.

Then another.

Hope started to fail me. The bleakness began to close in.

Come on, Keyla . . .

Golden light burst from behind my eyelids. Lily's dark tendrils faded into nothing, and my body began to regenerate itself. The beautiful thing about Keyla's ability was that it stripped powers away, but not my being. I was still part demon and healed all the same. My power drained away into nothing and blissful silence filled me for a brief moment.

I opened my eyes.

"What is this?" Lily asked in confusion, not stepping away. I held my last dagger. The one I'd saved for this moment.

"Me ending it," I said. Johanna appeared behind her. Our eyes met. She gave me a nod.

I rammed the dagger through her ribs. Bones cracked under the impact, but I couldn't miss, as much as it pained me to strike true.

The first time I killed my sister it was an accident.

This time it was intentional.

There was no fracture of pain that she often saw on people's faces. No relief. No happiness. Only confusion and betrayal.

"I am . . ." She struggled for words. Coughing twice, golden blood splattered her lips.

"Mortal," I said, dislodging the dagger from her chest as I wrapped an arm around her waist. Her knees buckled first as she started to slump and then fall. I went to my knees with her. Holding her tight in her last minutes because that was all I could give her now.

A gamble. This entire thing was a massive fucking gamble, and I had to hope that I made the right choice.

That I'd finally come to understand what Milla and the Crone and Valda had all been telling me.

I sat with her as the fight raged around us. A roar unlike anything else sounded from not so far away. Like an animal in pain—or a signasti losing their other half.

Lily clung to life, though she saw herself as death, and in those final seconds she whispered, "Why?"

Why? Such a small word for a big question.

There were so many things I could say to it. But I gave her the only answer I could.

"Because I love you and this was the only way."

Her eyebrows twitched as she tried to frown.

Then she faded.

Her eyes closed.

"Tell them I love them," I said on a shaky breath. Johanna knelt across from me. Holding pressure on Lily's wound. I didn't see it, but I felt it—that ancient voice my sister spoke of. An essence of evil. Cirian's soul as it slithered from one Fortescue to the next.

Only once I sensed Keyla's retreat, her power ebbing and mine beginning to return, did I lift the dagger again. In truth, I didn't need for her to be gone for this to work. I just didn't want her to see. I didn't want any of them to see.

"*Selena . . .*" His voice whispered in my mind. Barely there. I ignored him. I had to.

"I promise," Johanna vowed. "Goodbye, my friend."

Her eyes were watering as I positioned the dagger at my own heart. I swallowed once. My breathing ragged.

"*What are you doing—*"

I stalled, waiting for something.

"Selena, stop. Stop!"

Seconds ticked by and my palms sweat.

Then I heard it.

"Don't do this," he begged.

The sound of a heartbeat starting again.

It was the single loophole in my curse and the only way I could leave and be at peace.

"I love you so much. I'm sorry." It was all I could say as I thrust my chest forward and pulled my hands inward.

The metal pierced true, and just like my sister I began to fade, taking the souls of Valda and Cirian with me.

I barely registered it as I fell backward. My head banging against the uneven gravel. The other end of the dagger met resistance and twisted painfully as it partially dislodged.

Unlike Lily, there would be no coming back from this. Whereas she could heal herself from even death, I would not let myself. Johanna knew to keep the dagger there until I was dead and truly gone.

A sacrifice is not payment without a choice.

Lily never made the choice to pay it. Her death wouldn't suffice.

But mine would.

I chose to go to the grave so that the curse ended.

So that Alexandra, and even Lily, could live another day.

This time when the other side appeared, I didn't fight it.

I felt the faint pull of my signasti bond being stretched too thin. Ash was reaching for me. Pleading.

Begging. Fighting. I wished I could have said a real good-bye. I wished I could have been able to tell him the truth.

This was the end. Our end.

Me and my demon walked to it hand in hand, ready for whatever came next.

Hoping our sacrifice was enough.

CHAPTER 29

I ASSUMED THAT THE OTHER SIDE OF DEATH WOULD BE LIKE before life.

I had no conscious memory. No sense of being. No anything.

I thought death would be like that. Like my demon and I would simply fade into nothingness. That we would cease to exist and that was that.

As it turns out, death was nothing like that.

I crossed over into the next plane of existence and my body instantly materialized. I blinked, staring at my own hands and the twin pentagrams that adorned them still. My skin had been cleaned but my clothes were the same as before. Tight black jeans and a long-sleeved black shirt. Leather jacket, tattered, but whole. I pulled at the collar and lowered my nose to it, taking a whiff.

It still smelled like *him*.

He was the smoke to my fire.

The ash to my flame.

I inhaled deeply, searching inside of me—wondering if somehow, someway—I'd survived. But the only presence inside was me and my demon. For once, not even Valda was present.

A pointed cough drew my attention.

I released the jacket from stiff fingers and looked up.

My breath halted in my chest as the muscle squeezed. I wasn't sure how I was breathing, but I knew in that I moment I certainly wasn't alive.

Not when I stood before a raised platform. The steps were made of black stone. Opaque in color. Reflective enough to show every contour. My gaze continued to rise to the four thrones that sat atop it.

The first was a chair ornately carved from a stone so brightly blue I wondered if it came from my world or another. In it sat a man with white linen robes. His skin was tan, his hair dark, the topknot cinched and adored with a golden circlet. A sheen of golden scales traveled up his neck and over the smooth planes of his face. Dark slanting eyes with a slit pupil stared down at me in silence.

I swallowed and turned to the next.

This chair was built almost crudely. Made of obsidian stone but forged into sharp points and jagged edges. In it sat a woman with her head held high. She wore a gown of black mulberry silk that clung to every curve, making her body blend with the shadowed corners of the chair. Her skin was pale as moonlight on a dark ocean. Her hair a wave of lush curls. It was her eyes that told me the most.

They glowed violet as she watched me in silent judgment.

My heart began to hammer as I followed the length of her arm to the hand she clasped in her own. The man beside her sat on a simple chair made of pure gold. He wore leather and steel across his form, but they were merely another skin for him. He was tan and had a face more beautiful than all the statues in Rome. His thick wild mane told me exactly who he was, as he too looked upon me as if measuring something I could not see.

The last chair was almost underwhelming compared to the greatness of the others. Its simple wood frame was modest. The woman on it even more so. She wore brightly colored fabrics with intricate beading. The sheer mass of cloth swaddled her stomach and breasts entirely, twining around her body in more layered methods than I wanted to count. The colors were a stark contrast to her dark skin, so black it was almost blue. Her hair was a mass of tiny braids that cascaded down her form. But her face . . . it was young and old. Wrinkled and not. She had laugh lines around her eyes and age spots. She glowed vibrantly from the inside out with youth. She was ageless.

Her pale milky eyes blinked, and she stood.

"Do you know where you are?" she asked me.

I licked my cracked lips and said in dry croak, "No."

"Do you know who we are?" she asked, lifting her right eyebrow a touch—as if daring me to lie.

"I have suspicions."

The other Goddess, the one dressed in night, pressed

her lips together as if amused. "And who are we, daughter of mine?"

"Nyx," I said, answering with her given name. She smiled, pleased that I knew her. I looked to her partner who'd yet to speak. "Consort." He nodded once. "Three-Faced Goddess," I continued. The one who had spoken first only blinked, watching me intently. I turned to the final of the four deities. The one the world had largely forgotten. Though it seemed that perhaps he hadn't forgotten the world. "The Dragon." He tapped one clawed finger against the bottomless blue stone arm of his throne. "You're the ancients."

"Very good, child," the Three-Faced Goddess said. "Do you know why you're here?"

"I died," I stated matter-of-factly. The Consort snorted once.

"That is one way of putting it," he said. I didn't know what he wanted me to respond with.

"What he's trying to say is can you be more specific?" the Three-Faced Goddess said.

I bit the inside of my cheek as I considered it.

Why was I here? That was a great question.

"I fulfilled the prophecy. I did what you asked."

"Did you?" the Consort asked. My blood chilled. I was too hot. I was too cold. There was no heat or lack thereof and yet my body still acted as if I were alive as a flare of anxiety and anger ran through me. *Did you?*

"Three deaths by the Mother's hand from Valda and Cirian's line," I said in a hard voice. "I completed the task you *demanded* of my family for the mistake *your* vessel made." I looked at the Three-Faced Goddess who seemed to be regarding me with no small amount of amusement.

"While she carried the soul of the Mother and her signasti is the Consort's heir, this one is most definitely yours, sister," the Goddess said, ignoring my prior statements entirely. Nyx let out a dark, lovely laugh. It was a sultry chuckle that whispered sweet nothings and terrible delights in the middle of the night when the moon was full. It was a laugh I'd heard before. When I declared myself a Fortescue. When I declared war.

"She is the daughter of my heart," Nyx said in a breathless sigh. "The bearer of my power."

"But did she truly sacrifice?" the Dragon asked.

"That remains to be seen," the Three-Faced Goddess remarked. My pulse sped up, and despite being dead, my heart hammered.

"A sacrifice is not payment without a choice," I argued. "That's what you told me."

"What my vessel told you," the Goddess corrected.

"Given none of you would tell me yourself, it's the same thing," I replied, clenching my fists tightly. "Your vessel is what originally brought this upon the world. Livina is who severed Valda and Cirian's signasti bond and then turned them into demons. Livina brought them back. Regardless of that, it was me and my family you asked to pay your price. Three deaths. You never said anything about whether they needed to stay dead."

"And your own death?" the Goddess asked. "Why not simply kill Lily a third time if you truly believed that?"

I swallowed hard. "Someone had to take Valda and

Cirian to the grave. One of us had to die, truly die, for the last part to be fulfilled."

"And you choose yourself?"

"Yes." Blood rushed in my ears, and my head pounded. "I waited for Lily to die long enough for Cirian's soul to truly pass. I cannot control that she returned. I suspected as much, given she came back from a true death, but either way, I completed the prophecy and broke the curse—no matter how you try to swing this."

"But how are you so certain when you did exactly as Livina did in trying to circumvent it?" the Goddess prompted. She strode forward and down the stairs with bare feet. The loose swaths of her colorful skirts skimming the steps behind her.

"Because I didn't do exactly as Livina did," I answered. "She was too scared to die or kill them. I made a choice. I chose to kill myself so that they could live. I followed the rules and I found another way, even if it wasn't what you originally intended."

The gods grew silent as the Three-Faced Goddess walked around me, examining me from every angle.

"You admit you knew it was not intended that way." It wasn't a question, so I didn't answer it like one. "Curious," she murmured after a few moments. She came to a stop in front of me.

"What is?"

"You." In her eyes was knowledge. Pure and powerful. "You did sacrifice, though you did it selfishly."

"How did I—"

"Do not interrupt me," she said. My jaw snapped shut, and I pressed my teeth together to keep from defending myself. "You did sacrifice. You chose to give your life. You also chose not to end your sister's instead —the one that *can* die. Lily is something that has never been. Something that never will be again. We had not predicted that when we set the terms."

"What is she?" I asked. The corner of her mouth curled ruefully as if she knew.

"That's not important for the moment. What is, is that you sacrificed yourself so that your sisters would live. It was a selfish sacrifice in itself. However . . ." Her voice trailed off, and I sensed that what she said next was going to decide something, though for the life—or should I say death—of me, I didn't know what. "In doing so, you did it with balance. You didn't swing the scales to the side of good—as we'd intended."

I lifted both eyebrows, not sure what she was getting at. "What's that mean for me? For the prophecy?"

A ghost of a smirk crossed her features and then she lifted her head indifferently and started back for her throne. "That remains to be seen."

I blinked, anger starting to build, though I let them keep talking. "She is a neutral entity," Nyx said. "The only true one, aside from ourselves. She is neither good nor evil. Perfect and imperfect."

"She holds honor but does not seek glory," the Dragon noted. "A curious combination."

"She has might," the Consort asserted. "Though she hides it, instead preferring to use cunning until the time is right." His savage eyes slid sideways to the dark beauty on his right. "Much like another I know."

"Somehow, a child of the two most destructive families that we've unleashed upon the world grew up to be a completely balanced entity," the Three-Faced Goddess mused. "She completed the prophecy, but the wrongs have not been righted. There is still work in the world to be done. Red to be wiped from the ledger. Death to bring so that the dawn may come—a match to the thousand years of darkness." She tapped her nails against the wooden arms of her chair, similar to the Dragon. "In allowing Valda to be your spirit guide and Livina to shape the events of your life, they somehow managed to mold you into something that has not been for a very long time."

"And perhaps will never be again," Nyx inserted, drawing a sly glance from the Three-Faced Goddess.

"Perhaps," she relented with a hard tone. Nyx's face betrayed nothing, but I got the sense they were debating something without saying it.

"There is the matter of the sister . . ." the Dragon started.

"She must be watched," the Consort added.

"Should she ever grow in strength again . . ." Nyx murmured, allowing her voice to trail off. "None other can face her."

"And then there is the matter of the world itself," the Dragon said, a weary note taking root in his tone. "My people have been punished for silence long enough."

"Mine have paid their debt in blood," Nyx added.

"Mine have lost too much in this war so that balance may be had," the Consort added, his voice booming with strength.

"Yes," the Three-Faced Goddess said after a moment

of tense silence. "We demanded payment and it has been given, but in doing so it left the world without a protector."

"Then we are in agreement?" Nyx asked.

"Yes," the three gods said in answer.

They stood then, the four of them in their beautiful and terrifying forms. While they wore human skins, it was their eyes that betrayed that there was more to each of them than what they seemed. Four beings so great the world worshipped them for millennia. I always wondered why the Witches put their Goddess above all. It was hard to look upon one and not see why.

"Selena Foster, Daughter of Nyx, you did what was asked of you, unlike your ancestors before you," the Three-Faced Goddess began. "You learned from your mistakes. You grew beyond the hard beginnings. You aren't perfect, but we don't need someone perfect."

My eyebrows drew together. That anger that had started was already fizzling out as confusion took its place. "What do you need?" I asked.

"Someone we can trust."

My lips parted. "I don't understand."

"We need a Vessel," the Goddess said. "One whom has honor, and power, and might, but above all —balance."

"But . . . don't you choose three among the Witches?" I asked her. The Goddess shook her head, her braids swaying as she did so.

"I do, but you would not be *my* vessel. You would be *ours.* A Vessel of the Gods. Someone to right the wrongs and usher in a new age. Someone that can maintain the balance."

"Wait a second," I started. "I'm dead."

"Perhaps," the Three-Faced Goddess said. "Or perhaps, there is another way."

"You're offering me the chance to go back," I said, not quite believing what I was hearing.

"If you want it," she answered. "With conditions."

I stilled, my heart already sinking. I should have known it was too good to be true. These were the same gods that demanded the price to begin with. "Conditions?"

"You are to hold true to our tenants. To be honorable and not seek glory. To be mighty, and not crush those beneath you simply because you can. To be powerful enough to stop any threats you may need to. To correct the balance, for which my vessel—as you've pointed out—broke."

"What do you mean by correct the balance?" I asked her suspiciously.

"In punishing the world we allowed evil to grow. Now that evil must be removed. Torn out by the roots if you must. You're not to replace it as evil, nor are you to decide what is good. You're not to choose sides because we have chosen for you. You would exist to maintain both good and evil so that neither grow more powerful than the other again."

"Will you ask me to kill my sisters again?" It was the question I actually had been trying to ask without saying it. The truth was that if they said yes, it still tempted me to go back, but ultimately I wouldn't. If they said no . . . maybe there was a deal to be had.

A balance to be struck.

"No," the Three-Faced Goddess said solemnly. "However, it will be your duty to ensure that she never grows to be as she was."

"And if she does?" I asked.

The gods looked between themselves. It was Nyx who spoke.

"It's a large world that we created. There's a lot of places to fix. As the darkness grows so must the light. A night without stars is simply darkness. A star without night is only day. You're to commit your life to finding the middle, in every way you can."

"That doesn't answer my question," I said. There was light in her eye. A glint of something that the other gods didn't have.

"Perhaps you're asking the wrong questions," Nyx replied.

"Your time to choose grows short, child," the Three-Faced Goddess added. "The aether calls to you, but your signasti holds the shreds of your soul tight. It's your decision whether you choose to return to them or remain here."

"Wait," I paused. "How will I know if something is good or evil? Most things exist in-between. You say I'm not to choose because you've chosen for me. How will I know if it's your will?"

"Use your judgement," the Goddess answered.

"And if I judge wrong?"

"Fix it."

I blinked. Was it truly that simple? I wasn't sure, but I knew with a certainty that I wanted to go back.

"I'll do it," I said, the words pouring out as the timer ticked down. "I'll be your Vessel. I'll right whatever wrongs I need to. Just . . . send me back to them."

The four gods nodded, and in the blink of an eye, three of them disappeared.

Only Nyx remained, standing in front of her throne. She looked on me with an emotion I hadn't seen from anyone in a long while.

"It is done," she told me quietly.

"Then why am I still here?" I asked. She smiled then; a real smile. A true one. It was so beautiful my knees went weak.

"I have a gift for you," she said.

"A gift?" She nodded, striding forward. Her silk gown trailed behind her, sliding down the steps with the fluidity of water. "What is it?" I asked.

"A chance to say goodbye." Her attention flicked to something over my shoulder, and I knew without looking who stood there. My heart swelled.

"Why?" I asked. She regarded me with a quiet sort of content.

"The way you look upon us is the way your world looks upon you. In all the years the earth has stood, none of my children have been as truly mine as you." She reached up and brushed the hair from my eyes. "I have loved you more than any before you, and any that will come to be." She kissed my forehead and then turned to leave.

"Wait." I reached for her. She paused, glancing back

over her shoulder. "I have to know. Why did the gods leave us? Why did you leave us?"

Nyx lifted an eyebrow.

"There are forces out there even more powerful than gods. Why do you think you're my chosen heir? The one I've been waiting for?" I tried to take it in, knowing that this was probably the only chance I would ever have to ask.

"Why does a god that can never die need an heir?" I asked.

Nyx smiled and it was mischievous and full of secrets.

"Fix the balance, Selena, and perhaps you will find out."

With that, her presence dissipated into a scattering of dust and my heart ached.

She wasn't really gone. I knew that now. I felt her in the air and through the floor. She existed in the very matter of the universe. She existed in me.

And maybe, just maybe, if I did the job they asked of me—I'd see her again.

But now was not the time for that. It was the time to say goodbye to my oldest and dearest friend.

I turned around, and she stood before me.

Black hair and violet eyes. We looked so alike we could have been twins. She was dressed in leathers and fur. I knew without asking that they were the clothes of her people a thousand years ago.

"The aether calls," Valda said.

"Are you ready for it?" I asked.

"I am." She nodded and then smiled. It wasn't manic or crazed. It was genuine.

My heart wanted to break with this goodbye. I was getting a second chance, but it was without her. She'd been with me so long I couldn't remember a time she wasn't there.

My eyes watered, and she threw her arms around me, pulling me to her. Tears ran down my cheeks as I hugged her fiercely. "It's okay," she whispered. "I've passed from generation to generation of my children and watched them die. It's my turn now. I can finally be with my baby and my true love. We never got to be together in life because of who I was and what I became. Now we will be. You gave that to me." She clung to me tight enough that as I fell apart, she still held me together.

"I don't know if I'm ready." I felt her lips curve up against my temple.

"You broke the curse. You did it, and you're getting to go back and live out the rest of your days with them. There's nothing to be ready for. You've already done it. You fought and you won the war. Whatever is left will be easy compared to the path you've already walked. It's your reward, and when your time comes—I'll be here. Waiting. We have eternity." Wet, messy tears poured from my eyes, smudging against her skin.

"I'm going to miss you, Valda."

"I'm going to miss you too." She kissed my temple. "But it's not forever," she insisted. "Just for now."

I opened my mouth, trying to find words to say something meaningful in the end. It came too soon. She broke apart in my arms, much like Nyx, disintegrating into dust.

I didn't even have time to fall to my knees in anguish. The darkness closed in again, and this time there was that nothingness. I don't know how long I was suspended in it.

One moment I closed my eyes.

The next I opened them, and the pale light of a new dawn greeted me.

CHAPTER 30

SUNLIGHT FILTERED THROUGH WISPY PALE BLUE DRAPES. THEY played in the breeze, lifting and twining with the air, dancing just for me. I lifted a hand for them, and the soft material slipped between my fingers.

"You're awake."

I turned my head, pulling my gaze from the gentle show to the man at my side. His hair was clean but messy and unkempt. His eyes tired. Those were the first hints that I'd been gone for a while, yet again. Then there was the clash of metal kissing metal from beyond the open window. The wild grunts. The boisterous yells. I knew those sounds. These people.

It was the Shifter training yard.

I was home.

"I wasn't sure you'd wake," Ash said. "But I was determined to be here this time if you did."

I smiled and reached for him. My joints popped with the movements, and my muscles ached to be stretched. I leaned up and wrapped my arms around him, holding him to me. His arms came around my form, pulling me from the cushy bed to where he sat in a chair, cradling me in his lap.

I leaned in, resting my forehead to his. Our noses brushed.

"Not even the afterlife could keep me from you," I whispered.

"Forgive me for not being so sure," Ash murmured, brushing a lock of dark hair from my face.

I allowed that as I curled into him, my head falling to his shoulder. We stayed that way for a little while, watching the drapes drift in the breeze and listening to sounds of Shifters training once more.

"A long time has passed, hasn't it?"

"Not as long as you might think," Ask said. "It's only been a week this time."

That was less time than I'd thought, and I was grateful for it. Grateful for the time I still had. For the gift I'd been given.

"What happened?"

"I should be asking you that given I spent most of the battle struggling to maintain consciousness until you died." He gripped me harder. Held me closer, as impossible as that was.

"Didn't Johanna—"

"She did," he said, his voice gruff. "But it didn't change the fact that you were gone. Our bond snapped and I was lost to the world until I felt it reappear almost a day later. We were preparing your body for a burial when suddenly your wounds healed, and your heart started to beat again." He let out a ragged breath. "I was scared at first you'd been turned."

"And if I had?" I asked.

He lifted his head to look me in the eye. "I would have loved you anyways, even if my people couldn't accept it. You're it for me. I'd appreciate it if you stopped bartering your life for everyone else so I could have it."

"Have it?" I repeated.

"You," he breathed. "Your moments. Your time. Your stolen kisses." His lips brushed over my cheek, and I shivered. "Your future. I want it all."

I sighed in contentment and leaned into him, whispering back, "You will. In due time."

"I'm holding you to that."

"I'd expect nothing less."

One of his hands skimmed over my bare thigh and down my leg to my calf, kneading the muscle. I hummed in delight, and he let out a growl. I placed a hand on his chest. "Tell me more. I want to know everything."

He sighed, his fingers slipping from my calf.

"The battle raged for a while longer after you and Lily went down. She alone killed over a quarter of our forces. If you hadn't gotten to her when you did, the estimates say it would have ended less than an hour later with everyone dead. But you did it, and afterwards Johanna used the time to get your sister out without being seen. Lily's still being kept sedated while Lucas tries to implement the rest of your plan. I'm not sure I agree with it after what she's become, but I don't want to argue. I thought I lost you again, and I'm done with fighting."

"And Victor?" I asked.

"Escaped. Turns out he's a slippery one, even for a Born. The bastard was able to overpower both Alec and Oliver. There's been no sightings of him since . . . but we think he might be trying to track Lily."

I sighed. "That's why you haven't woken her, isn't it?"

"Partially," he said. "We're also not certain your plan will work. Lucas is a skilled telepath, but to wipe all her memories. To erase her entire past, that's a challenge for any telepath, and if he doesn't get everything . . . we can't risk it."

"He will," I said with absolute certainty.

"How do you know?"

I smiled. "Because he owes me that much. Lucas would give his right arm if it could fix the things he's done. He's filled with self-loathing, and he needs something to focus on. That something will be Lily."

"And when he's done?" Ash asked.

"He never will be," I answered. "The way his power works is like draping a blanket over memories. It's not a full reset like a computer. With time she'll start to pull back the corners. He'll be there to smooth them back out."

"It's a good plan," Ash nodded. "But I worry that you have too high of hopes. After everything she's done, the world may not know her face, but thousands do. Every Vampire that exists will know. Every person that has met her and survived will know. If someone is able to find a picture of her and give that to the media . . . she's toast.

The battle in New York revealed magic to the world. There's no going back from that."

"Which is why"—I paused—"she'll be hidden. Forever."

"That's a long time to hide someone," Ash commented.

"It is, but we'll figure it out. Now tell me, how is everyone?" I specifically didn't give a name. Any name. The truth was I wasn't sure who or what to ask about. I didn't know if any of them lived. I didn't know if any of them died.

Ash raised both eyebrows, partly amused and partly annoyed.

"My sister is fine. She grieved when you died. We haven't told her you might be back, though she's been asking about why we haven't had a funeral at all. I didn't want to get her hopes up in case you didn't return this time." I nodded, understanding that reasoning. "Johanna and Oliver are acting as ambassadors between the different factions. No one has stepped forward to create or lead a new Council yet, but it's only a matter of time. The paranormal community has been revealed and the world is now asking questions. We have to find an answer."

"Alexandra?" I asked, noting how he pointedly skipped right over her. He lowered his eyes. There was hesitance there.

"She's alive," he said. "But she lost a hand in the battle. Blair was caught up in a five-way fight keeping the Vampires off Keyla, and Tori was left open. Alexandra stepped in to save her at the same time as one of the Fae. He accidentally cut her hand off. She healed well, all things considered, but it's been a rough week. She didn't know if you'd be back or not. She now has one hand on top of flaming hair. The world knows we exist and there's no way to hide from it all. Tori's been helping her . . . adjust," he said, searching for a diplomatic word. The breath left my body as I contemplated it.

"She must be crushed." I should have been there. I didn't say it, but I didn't need to.

"She's struggling, but I think you coming back will help." I nodded because it was all I could do. "She'll be okay, Selena. That girl's a fighter if there ever was one."

I snorted, but it didn't change my feelings on the matter.

"How's Blair?" I asked, changing the subject to one I hoped was easier.

"Better," he said. "She and her demon still haven't merged, but they seem to have come to a truce. She's here at the mansion helping Alexandra while we waited for you. Alec is fine. Helping where he can; staying close to Blair but far enough away that she doesn't explode. Amber has also been helping. She had to take over her mother's role as the Alpha Cat to help assist in leading the Shifters through this."

When I died, I didn't think I was coming back. I tried to lay plans so that they could move on. All of them.

A week had passed and still, they waited.

All of them.

It touched me in a way I couldn't completely understand. My heart didn't feel heavy, though. It felt happiness. Joy. The world was far from perfect. Our lives just as much so.

But we still had them, and that was what mattered.

"Johanna told us what she knew," he started. "But it wasn't the same. Will you tell me the truth of it now? Can you?" I'd been expecting this the last few minutes. It was only fair.

I searched inside myself, trying to see if the same block that prevented me before was still there. Only my demon and I were inside me now. With Valda's presence gone, the curse was lifted. I was free.

"It's a very long story," I warned him, a smile curling around my lips.

He stood from the chair and laid me on the bed, crawling into it beside me.

"I have time," he mused, resting on his side.

"It started a thousand years ago with a young Witch named Livina . . ." I began, telling him the story from the beginning. Ash didn't interrupt me as I told him of Valda and her lover. How her parent's killed him and then forced her to marry Cirian. Of their bond and the choices they'd made. Of the payment the gods demanded for those choices. I told him of the years that went by and how I came to be. I told him of that voice I heard in my mind and who she was and who she became to me. I told him of the Crone and the prophecy, of the silence exacted on me. Of the sacrifice the gods demanded. I told him about my struggle over these past months, unable to say anything but wanting to desperately.

I told him of the choice I'd made and why I made it.

And when the story came to part where I died there

was only silence between us.

Silence and truth.

"Where did you go?" he asked quietly. "Afterwards? Was there anything?"

Mortals were funny about death. I was only beginning to realize it. Strong or weak. Young or old. Everyone was cowed by death. By the unknown.

"There was," I admitted, testing the words to see if I was truly free to speak. "When I died I saw the ancients."

His eyes went wide. "The ancients?" I nodded. "What did they want?"

I thought about that.

"A Vessel," I answered eventually.

"For?"

"Them. It appears that in preparing me to complete the prophecy, the Crone and Valda did too good of job. I fulfilled the requirements but the balance wasn't corrected. They sent me back to fix it." It wasn't that I didn't trust him or didn't want to speak the truth. What I'd seen on the other side was beyond anything the living could understand. Nyx told me that they look to me as I looked onto her. There were some things that you simply kept to yourself after dying. Like how they weighed whether or not I truly sacrificed.

Ash didn't need to know that I was close to not coming back.

Only that I was here to stay.

"How do you go about fixing the balance?"

"I have some thoughts," I whispered, leaning in. My lips brushed his and all talk of life and death and even the gods ended.

CHAPTER 31

THE FOLLOWING WEEKS WERE DIFFICULT. NOT AS HARD AS THEY had been, but still wrought with complications. The unveiling of paranormals had shook the world to its core. Mass panic had spread, and with it the media fanned the flames higher. There was a new attack on the news every night and a new reported suspicion every morning.

It was a New Salem, and for that reason, we created a New Council.

One that was composed of leaders from every faction of paranormals, all the way from Fae to Pixies to Witches and Supes. It was an umbrella meant to represent everyone and be the outward face of the magical world for the times we faced, and the times to come.

Stationed in a conference room inside Tam's club, paranormals from all over crowded in to be a part of this one very important meeting. When you brought together this many species that weren't used to getting along, things got messy.

"A group of Pixies entered my border last night and

have yet to be dealt with," the infamous Fae queen who refused to fight argued. I still wasn't a fan of her. Nor she of me.

The Pixie head, an older woman with magenta eyes and turquoise wings scoffed. "You can't call them your lands when we share all land with the humans."

"Why you—" Right as the Fae queen started to drill into her, a growl ripped through the room. My head whipped toward Blair who stood with a Fae warrior against the wall. Or more accurately, she stood, pinning him to the wall by his throat.

"No touching," her demon snapped. The paranormals in close proximity stepped as far away as they could to escape the demon's wrath.

"Blair," Johanna said, saving me from interfering. The demon looked over her shoulder, weighing the golden-eyed one. Her nose wrinkled in dislike but the black faded and Blair released him. The warrior fell to his knees, gasping for a breath as Blair pushed through the crowd, coming to stand behind Ash and me.

He thumped his fist twice on the oak conference table, drawing their attention.

"We don't have time for this," he said. A pang of sadness went through me that his father wasn't here to see this. To see him, stepping into his rightful role. I accepted it as he called the meeting to attention.

"The humans are only a few steps short of trying to impose laws and sanctions on paranormals as a whole. No one has stepped forward to stop them. We've gathered here today because as the heads of our people it's *our* responsibility to ensure that they're spoken for." The squabbling bunch grew quiet, listening intently.

"Actually," I said. Ash paused and looked up at me in confusion. "I'd like to start this meeting if I can?" He nodded once, figuratively passing the mic to me. I stood from my chair and faced them as a whole. "Your people are under fire. Groups of human factions have banned together to hunt any and all with magic. Organizations in the government have been put together to find them for a different reason. We exist in a world where we are the predator and our prey have now realized it."

No one said a word; a hush had fallen over them.

"We've already waged one war. We are not ready for another. Which means we need to make peace with that prey. Find a way to coexist because we share the same domain as we always have. Even when they didn't know it."

"*You* are not ready for another war," the Fae queen interrupted. "Some of us might be more equipped and willing."

"That's not your call to make," I responded.

"Neither is it yours," the Fae queen answered. "The Supernatural hold has been broken, and yet I see multiple representatives for your faction. I can't help but wonder if this is a farce."

I swallowed hard. This was the moment. The one I'd prepared for these last weeks. "You're right," I said. There was a collective gasp. "That's why I'm abdicating my seat and it won't be filled again. The Fortescues ruled this world for too long. They unleashed unspeakable horrors on it. I won't continue that legacy. I refuse."

At this I looked to Ash, and while he didn't speak, I knew he understood.

This was one of those things the ancients had asked. I don't get to choose sides.

Frankly, I hadn't wanted to in this case. It made my decision quite easy.

"I have no intentions to rule. No ploys to overthrow anyone. I don't plan to spend my days on this council making decisions for the rest of the world. That's not my purpose. It never was." My gaze slid to Johanna who sat three seats down. A slight smile curved up her lips, and I wondered if she knew. Or perhaps, she simply guessed the reasoning.

"What are you saying?" the Pixie asked.

"I'm saying that I don't exist to make the rules, but I plan to enforce them. The world has spent too long fighting for scraps. We fight amongst ourselves. We fight each other. We fight with the humans now. For so long, all we've done is fight. It's time to make peace, whether you like it or not. We all live here. We all hold a claim and no one faction or species is greater than another." I looked at the Fae queen. Her honey blonde hair and golden skin so similar to that of Cade. Her son wasn't here now, and I thought it for the best. "Not even Supernaturals, Your Highness."

She pressed her lips together but nodded once.

"The old Court has fallen. The world has changed. It's now on you guys to change with it. To lead your people forward. I died at the battle in New York, though few of you likely realize that. I met the ancients, and they sent me back with a task. My job is simple. I'm to wipe the red from the ledger. To stop evil from further encroaching on the world. War is death. Should you choose to pursue it, Your Highness, it's not just the humans you will answer to. I am a Vessel of the Gods now, and if this council ever decides to lose its way again—I will be a Vessel of Destruction."

I bowed my head once, signaling my end as I turned from the table. You might have heard a pin drop as each person stepped out of the way to let me pass.

I'd done what the Gods asked.

I held my might but did not subjugate.

I did not seek glory.

I did not rule.

I turned over my family title and seat to people who could—and hopefully would—do better.

"Thank you," Johanna said. Before I left the room, a murmur spread through the crowd. They whispered their thanks, though I didn't need it.

"Make the world a better place than we found it," I told her. The door opened and beyond it was the booming of Tam's club. I stepped out, free of the shackles of my past for once.

As I started down the stairs a voice called out.

"Wait." I paused, looking back over my shoulder. My cousin stood there. Her faded blue jeans changing color beneath the red and blue lights. "Where are you going?"

I lifted my shoulder in a shrug. "I don't know yet."

Her expression didn't change. "What are you doing?"

I smiled. "Hunting."

She smiled too. "Have room for another on this god ordained journey you're taking?"

I snorted and tilted my head toward the door, motioning for us to get out of here. She took the steps two at a time, and we walked out together.

Two demons, hell-bent on making the world a better place by doing bad things for good reasons.

Fate was fickle, but then so was death. The only thing you could truly count on in life was change.

The world changed.

Now we were changing with it.

CHAPTER 32

THE PAVEMENT WAS FRESHLY LAID OVER THE DIRT ROAD. THE diner was tiny; dingy. It had six booths and a nine-car parking lot. The sign out front read "Darlene's" except the L flickered in and out. There wasn't a smaller town in the state, let alone the south.

With a sun hot as hellfire and a single road that led in and out, it was the place we chose to hide her.

The windows were dirty, but her black hair was unmistakable as she flitted from table to table, completely unaware of our presence.

"Do you think she'll be safe?" Alexandra asked. She wore sleek leather gloves despite the heat. One of them covered a mechanical hand a Shifter and a technopath created for her. It was supposed to link her physical reactions and brain transmitters, allowing her to use it almost as well as her real one.

"As safe as she can be," I replied. Sitting at one of the booths in the diner was a young man with dark hair. She asked him his order, and he looked up at her and smiled. Never the wiser to who he was. "Lucas will watch over her."

Alexandra made a disgruntled noise. "He betrayed you and got her killed to begin with. I still don't understand why we're trusting him with this."

"Because ultimately he's the only one who can. Besides," I lifted my eyes to hers. "Life is too short to hold grudges forever. He already hates himself more than either of us ever could. He'll watch her and check in with me every week."

Alexandra made a tsking sound but didn't comment on it further as we watched them interact. Her brown eyes were earnest and not a slither of power crawled beneath her skin.

"You gave him the potion, right?" she asked me.

"I did."

"With instructions?" she pressed.

I sighed. "Milla explained it to him herself, Alex. He knows the deal. One drop, every day, will keep her powers at bay. As long as he spikes her drinks with blood periodically and keeps the memories away she'll be safe —from everyone."

The Witches hadn't joined us on the battlefield, but as promised, Milla did indeed remember. She had already devised a potion that would hold Lily's powers back before I'd awoken. Her way of saying thank you. I wondered if perhaps it was her Goddess' way as well, but I never asked.

"What if she attacks someone? She's still got vampiric tendencies?" Alexandra asked.

"A couple of drops once a week and her eyes stay brown. You know this. We've ran through the trial to see how she really did." And we did. Repeatedly. Before we'd placed her in the human world, we tried it on a smaller scale. It took about a month to get it right, but not once did her memories slip. Lucas's hold was just that tight, and as much as I struggled to trust at times, this was her only chance at a real life.

Ash wasn't wrong that it would be difficult to hide her. Too many people had seen her face. We had to find the smallest, most inconspicuous town there was to let her live out her life, however immortal or mortal it may be. Much as the Fae queen was a pain in my ass, she relented when I reminded her that she didn't answer my call for help and was now out from under both Supernatural and Vampire thumbs, so to speak. It also didn't hurt that I now owed her a favor. Me, the matter manipulator, the Vessel of the Gods, the Alpha's signasti. In return for that favor, she kept her people out of town and watched the borders, since Alabama was technically her land.

The catch to all of it was that we could never see her again. Part of keeping her safe was staying away. If she ever saw our faces again, there's a good chance all this could be for nothing.

Anyone else besides Lucas risked triggering her memories. Just as too many people knowing her location risked word getting out.

It wasn't the greatest solution, but it was a solution.

The best we had. For now.

"Do you remember when we first showed up at Mariana's? Back when you hated everyone and didn't want to go to Daizlei?" Alexandra asked.

"Yeah," I said, only half paying attention.

"Would you do it differently?" she asked. "If you could?"

I watched the diner. The way my other sister, the one that I would never know again, flitted about. Despite the potion to cancel out her powers, despite the memories being gone, despite all of it—her reactions to things were still too quick. A tray toppled from the counter and she swiped it out of the air with reflexes she didn't understand. I could see it in her eyes, the way they glazed for a moment, contemplating it. Much like humans had for a thousand years, she wrote it off as being nothing. As being ordinary.

But for the first time in all our lives, she seemed genuinely happy.

Content.

"I don't know," I told Alexandra honestly. "We sacrificed a lot. Lost a lot of friends. Lost our family." She swallowed harder, and I ignored it when her eyes teared a little. "We also gained a lot too. I found my signasti. You found Tori. We fought and we won. The prophecy is over and we're finally free to live as we may." I hooked my thumbs into the pockets of my jeans as I watched the girl in the diner, oblivious to the family she lost. The life she lost. The person she lost as she became someone new. "I wish I could say that I would, but the truth is I don't know, and I don't have to know."

Alexandra nodded, like she suspected as much. "I

don't think I would," she told me. "I've thought about it, not that it even matters. She's finally getting exactly what she wanted our whole lives. She's normal, and she's happy for it. I'm going to miss her, but . . . she's changed so much she's not the girl she was. With or without her memories."

"She's alive, and she's not killing anyone," I said. "That's what matters in the end." Alexandra snorted but behind it there was a sadness. I knew it too, because this was goodbye.

"Do you think we'll ever get to see her again?" Alex asked.

"I think"—I glanced at the sky, remembering Valda's words— "this is only goodbye for now. One day, in this life or the next, we'll know her again."

I hoped I was right. That Valda was right. I couldn't imagine she was wrong after my time with the ancients.

Alexandra chuffed. "You're a bit out there ever since you came back, you know?"

I laughed. "As opposed to before?"

"Well, I mean, I knew what to expect before. Now you're 'the Vessel of the Gods'," she repeated with air quotes. "And you won't even tell any of us what *actually* went down."

I snorted. "In good time, sister."

"Speaking of time," Tori chimed in, strolling down the sidewalk. She came to a stop between us. "It's time for us to go. My brother can handle it from here."

She held out both of her hands. I grabbed one and Alexandra grabbed the other. It was the diner we looked at—the sister we left behind that we watched—as Tori tore a hole between dimensions.

Lily's smile was the last thing I saw before the black hole sucked us in, and as much it hurt, I was happy for her.

ONE YEAR LATER...

My alarm went off, pulling me from sleep. I jerked, toppling out of bed. My body hit the cheap carpet with a thud.

"You good in there?" Blair called, popping her head in. As usual, she was up earlier than me these days. She preferred to 'hunt' earlier in the morning. Whereas I'd finally learned to sleep through the night and I wasn't giving it up, not even to kill a couple of demons.

"Ugh," I groaned.

"I'll take that as a 'yes, I'm fine, Blair. Thank you for asking,'" she said, ducking out of the room. Keyla strolled past my door in sweatpants that read 'Booty Call' on the ass, and I made a mental note to burn them before Ash visited and Blair and I got in trouble for letting her run wild.

As I laid there, contemplating getting off the floor, Roar came bumbling into my room. His paws were giant compared to his lanky body. He peppered my face in kisses, and I jumped away when he turned to trying to nibble my ear.

"Keyla," I called.

"What?" she yelled from the bathroom the three of us shared in our tiny upstairs apartment.

"Your dog wants out."

"Can't you do it?" she whined. "It's early and Blair coming home woke him up." She sounded so pitiful my demon pushed me to relent.

"Fine," I groaned. "But he's your dog. Get him some food while I'm out, won't ya?"

"Okay dokay," she called back through the bathroom door as the shower started, her voice more chipper than it was a moment ago.

I dragged myself up and slid my feet into my flip flops. I grabbed his leash. Roar bounded after me as I took the stairs two at a time. I maneuvered around our desks toward the front door of the shop. Roar ran smack dab into it, making the bell that hung off the handle jingle.

"What was that?" Blair called.

"The damn dog just being dumb again," I said. She chuckled under her breath as I leaned over and clicked his leash. The door swung open with only a thought from me and we strolled out into the chilled morning air. Los Angeles was already up and moving this time of day as I walked the dog halfway down the street, unable to help myself from monitoring for threats.

Over a year had come and gone. Blair and I settled here, opening up a shop to hunt rogues and demons. To some it would be an exciting life, but after the one I'd lived, it was downright peaceful. Simple. After the Alpha's death, Keyla struggled too much with her own kind, and while she loved her brother, Ash wasn't truly equipped to help a young teenage girl dealing with grief. Just over nineteen, Blair and I took her on as an apprentice—training her to protect herself and teaching her to use her powers while simultaneously raising her as best we could.

It wasn't always easy. I'd learned a lot from raising my own sisters, though. Keyla was just as wild as Alexandra, but inquisitive like Lily. She swore like a sailor when Ash wasn't around, and Blair and I let it go—choosing to pick our battles with her. Battles like getting a damn dog.

I scowled at Roar as he tried to run into someone's legs. He curbed last second as an invisible barrier rebuffed him without anyone noticing. The dog turned and gave me a look, like he knew. I snorted, turning and heading back for the shop.

On the outside our windows were tinted black. The sign above read that we were a kickboxing school, though anytime someone came in to sign up for classes we were always 'full'. Most passersby didn't bother us, unless they were looking for it, and that suited our purposes well. I grabbed the handle and wrenched it open. Roar ran past me, and I let his leash drop as he bolted between the gap in the desks and up the stairs to our apartment loft. Sighing, I locked it behind me and followed after.

The puppy pawed at the bathroom door while the shower ran. Instead of unleashing him upon her, I turned and opened Blair's door next to it. The dog decided she was a decent consolation prize and launched himself onto her bed. Blair huffed, pulling her pillow over her head as she growled, "Whyyyyy would you do this to me?"

"You woke the dog up. You can deal with him," I said, closing her door with him in there.

She groaned, and I heard as she shifted, making room for him. I snorted, knowing that she secretly liked him. Even if it was Keyla's dog.

I walked back to my room, humming to myself and stepping past the door, I blinked. In the middle of my room stood Ash, my signasti, and the current ruling Alpha.

"What are you doing here?" I asked. "I was supposed to come to you this weekend—"

He closed the gap between us and pulled me in for a kiss, slamming the door shut behind me with one hand.

Both Blair and Keyla groaned loudly. Advanced hearing was a bitch sometimes.

"Our apartment is too small for you and your shenanigans," my cousin griped. "I can hear your damn heartbeats in sync. It's disgustingly sweet."

"They'll manage," Ash murmured against my lips. I smiled.

"What about that important meeting with the Council—"

"Amber is representing the Shifters. As my second, she can handle it."

"The residence—"

"Alexandra and Tori took a weekend off to come down from Montana and watch over it. They just finished the monuments honoring Liam and Scarlett's families for their service and their lives. Johanna is overseeing some of the final reconstructions at Daizlei while they do that."

"But—"

"Shhhh," he whispered, pressing his lips to mine. I groaned, opening up for him as my back touched the door. "It's all been sorted. Don't worry so much."

"Mmhmm," I muttered even though I really liked that he took Friday off early. "How'd you get in here anyways? That's a safety hazard."

Ash started laughing under his breath, resting his forehead to mine. "You're incorrigible."

"I'm a paid demon hunter. If my house isn't secure—"

"I climbed through the window. I was hoping to surprise you while you were still sleeping . . ." He trailed off. Blair loudly grumbled about people having to work around here.

"Well, I'm awake now," I said suggestively, twining my arms around his neck.

"That you are," he grinned. "What do you suggest we do now with all this free time you have?"

I opened my mouth to tell him exactly what we could do when the phone rang downstairs. I froze.

"Don't answer it," he said.

"But I gotta."

"No, you don't," he said. "As your Alpha, I command it."

My head hit the door as I laughed.

"She's a demon," Blair groaned, "and as her partner

who was up dealing with a band of Made in south Los Angeles, I say she's gotta answer it."

I leaned up and kissed his cheek. Ash sighed and stepped back.

"Sorry, babe," I said as I dressed in a hurry. The phone still rang but being demon fast had its perks. "Duty calls."

Ash flopped back on my bed. "I'll be here when you finish up. Happy hunting," he called after me as I threw the door open. Keyla walked by at that exact moment, and Ash lifted his head.

"Hey sis, how's it—" His words came up short, and I sensed it the second he saw her sweatpants. "What the hell are you wearing?"

"Nothin'," she called back, slamming the door of her room. My bed creaked as Ash got up, and I raced down the stairs. Two thumps sounded above me as Ash called out, "Why does your ass say booty call?"

I chuckled and blocked out her response. I was going to hear all about it later.

I grabbed the phone and the caller ID was unknown, but I answered anyways.

"Hello?" I said, not revealing anything past that.

"Street camera shows suspected demons. Took three hostages, appear to be human. Corner of Mason and 42nd," my contact within the police force said.

"On it." The phone clicked as I hung up and started for the door.

As I stepped out into the morning air all I could think was that it was going to be a good day, because it was.

Every day I was still breathing was a good day, and I was grateful for each and every one of them.

I'd yet to hear or see the ancients again since they'd unleashed me back upon the world. I had to think that meant I was doing a good job. I don't know how, but something told me they were watching. Waiting to see what I would do.

If I would succeed.

The way I saw it, I spent too long fighting for this life.

Nothing was going to stop me from living it now. Not failure. Not fear. Not even myself.

I was given a second chance.

And I was going to make the most of it.

Even if that meant hunting demons and other evil for the rest of my days.

I rounded the corner to the warehouse location, pulling a knife from my belt with each hand. I kicked down the front door in a single motion.

It fell back, hitting the cement floor. A plume of dust shot up.

Two demons jumped to their feet and behind them the hostages looked on with pleading eyes. I threw my daggers, and they landed true with a unified thud.

"Hello, boys..."

I winked as they burst into ash.

"Damn," I muttered. I didn't even get to finish the introductions.

The end.

Acknowledgments

This was one of the hardest books to write. Not because I didn't know what happened. For once Selena actually followed the plan. It was difficult because this is the end. The end of the story that started it all. The story that started me on my journey as an author.

I'm pretty sure I bawled like a baby the day I typed 'the end.' While Selena and co. rarely listened and were so unbelievably difficult to write most of the time, this goodbye has been the most difficult for me. I did it, though. And you, dear reader, walked with her to the finish line.

So first and foremost, thank you for sticking with me and Selena to this point. Thank you for being invested in Selena's journey and seeing it to the end. I didn't make it easy on you, but hopefully I made it worth it.

To Analisa, thank you for editing, but more importantly—thank you for being there. I dedicated this one to you because your support and encouragement as a friend not only helped shape the story, but made it so that I could finally finish it. I'm so grateful for that, and for you.

To Matt, I love you, babe. Thank you for handling my mood swings and hippo hunger rages when I forget lunch because I spent too much time writing. Your love and support has been the strength that's helped me get this far. Thank you for believing in me when no one else did.

To Courtney, you were one of the first advocates for me to drop everything and chase this wild dream of mine. Some might call that crazy, but the crazy part to me is how long ago that now seems. You're an amazingly supportive friend and I'm lucky to have you.

To my Aunt Raquel, Uncle Shon, Greg, and Carol: thank you for being the role models I needed. Thank you for holding on and not giving up as I learned to be better than what I knew. Thank you for everything, really. You four deserve way more thanks than I give you for putting up with my ass all this time.

And last but not least, to my author friends that have stuck with me: You guys are fucking amazing. There's a lot of you I have to thank for being supportive and kind and helping me through the hard days. Special thanks to Amanda, Graceley, and Meg. You ladies have helped me through so much these past months. Thank you for pushing me and supporting me and standing with me through the rough times. You're some of the best friends a girl could ask for.

Printed in the USA
CPSIA information can be obtained
at www.ICGtesting.com
CBHW020849220624
10493CB00023B/87

9 781951 738068